Before The Swallow Dares

by

Tony Whelpton

First published 2012

Text copyright © 2012 Tony Whelpton
All rights reserved

ISBN-13: 978-1480000322

Daffodils, that come before the swallow dares,
And take the winds of March with beauty.

A Winter's Tale

FOR JOAN

Chapter One

'Oh, I say!'

'Well bowled, sir! Bravo!'

Anywhere other than the pavilion at Lord's, filled largely – in more ways than one – by elderly gentlemen unused to expressing themselves with unrestrained enthusiasm, these comments would merely have indicated a routine reaction to a routine occurrence in a routine cricket match. But the rest of the ground was erupting with hysterical shouts and screams, a reaction which reflected more accurately the events which had just taken place on the field of play, for England had bowled out the West Indies for a paltry 54 runs, one of the lowest scores in the history of test cricket.

The shock of being awoken from their customary state of somnolence by a highly unusual display of competence on the part of the England bowlers led inexorably to a more frequently observed phenomenon: the mass exodus, sedate but still redolent of a sense of urgency, to the members' bar.

'Double gin and tonic, please.'

'Yes, sir.'

Once served with his drink, his fourth of the day – it was, after all, just after 6.30, and both lunch and tea intervals had needed to be adequately observed – Ted looked round for a seat, but the only one available was at a table already occupied by a man of roughly his own age, wearing the almost mandatory red and gold striped tie of the MCC (affectionately known as 'egg and bacon'), and a smart navy-blue jacket, rather than the gaudy blazer whose colours matched the tie, which was worn by some members – a damned sight too flashy in Ted's opinion, although he would never have dared to give voice to that point of view in the hallowed precincts of the headquarters of world cricket.

Ted too was wearing an MCC tie, but there the resemblance between the two men ended, for, physically at least, they could not have been much more different. Although, as he was seated, it was difficult to assess exactly how tall the stranger was, he must have been a good five or six inches taller than Ted. Nor was there any sign of a hair on his head. The hair he presumably once had, however, must have been jet black, for although he would undoubtedly have regarded himself as being clean-shaven, he was one of those men who are so dark that their five o'clock shadow begins to descend shortly after midday. Ted, on the other hand, still had a good head of hair despite his age, and, colour-wise, it was at the other end of the spectrum, being so fair that when, during his student days, he had tried to grow a beard, he had been obliged to abandon the attempt after two weeks, because all he had so far succeeded in doing was achieving a look which would today have been classed as 'designer-stubble'; at that time it was considered merely scruffy. These days, of course, it was on the greyish side of blond, but at least, Ted consoled himself, it was still there.

The two men were differently built too. Although by no means fat, Ted was quite solidly built – a little overweight, he had been told a week or so ago by a nurse at the 'Well-Man Clinic' when she calculated his Body Mass Index, a description which Ted rejected out of hand. As he told his wife later, it was merely a bit of 'pseudo-scientific gobbledy-gook, dreamed up by some boffin who had plucked a figure out of the air, in the hope of making a name for himself'. By contrast, the man before him was very slim, almost of bean-pole proportions, although he looked respectable enough, thought Ted, as he moved in the direction of the vacant chair.

Edward Bryant, known for as long as he could remember as 'Ted', a retired academic in his late sixties, had been enthusiastic about sport – virtually all sports – since his early childhood, except for a dozen or so years when his enthusiasm was voluntarily but, with hindsight, mistakenly suppressed out of deference to his then wife, who considered all sport to be not only a waste of time but a prostitution of the human mind and spirit. Being French, she had a particular loathing of cricket, displaying that total refusal to make even the slightest attempt to understand the mysteries of a cultural phenomenon originating beyond her shores which one finds in some, though thankfully not all, members of her race.

'Do you mind if I join you?'

'Not at all. Please do.'

The two men sat for a while speechless, and motionless except for the occasional raising of a glass – in the one case a glass of gin, in the other a goblet of red wine. In the Lord's pavilion conversations were normally slow to start; in fact very frequently they never started at all, but Ted, who by his nature was not a particularly taciturn man, made a tentative move to break the silence by referring, in an appropriately low-key way, to the extraordinary events they had just witnessed on the field of play.

'Quite a turn-up for the books, eh?'

'Yes. It's taken a quarter of a century to get the West Indians to grovel.'

Ted's companion spoke in a voice a little more gruff than he had anticipated and, he thought for a brief second, it seemed vaguely familiar. The allusion, not lost on Ted, nor likely to be lost on any Englishman with a modicum of knowledge of what had occurred on the international cricket field within living memory, was to an England captain in the seventies, who had promised, as the series of matches was about to get under way, to 'make the West Indies grovel'. The almost inevitable outcome was that England spent the entire summer being comprehensively thrashed by the West Indian tourists.

'Rather more than a quarter of a century, really,' said Ted. 'More like half a century. Do you remember 1950, with Ramadhin and Valentine, and with Weekes, Worrell and Walcott making runs seemingly at will?'

'I certainly do. I watched every run of Frank Worrell's 261 in the Trent Bridge test, and a month before that I saw Everton Weekes score 279 against Notts.'

'That's extraordinary! So did I! Do you come from Nottingham then?'

'Yes, originally. A long time ago, though, and I haven't lived there since schooldays.'

'I went to school in Nottingham too. Which school were you at?'

'I was at the Pavement.'

'Good God, so was I! We must have been there at the same time. What's your name?'

'Fletcher, James Fletcher.'

'Jim! My God! I thought your voice sounded familiar. I'm Ted, Ted Bryant.'

'Ted! Good gracious! Who would have thought it! I didn't recognise you – you've changed a bit since we were at school!'

'You too – not surprising, though, seeing how long it is!'

'We'd better have another drink!'

The last time Ted had seen Jim Fletcher had been over forty years earlier. That had also been an accidental meeting, and in London too, as they walked in opposite directions along Charing Cross Road. Ted had been in his final year at university, Jim was working for the Foreign Office. Both had been brilliant linguists. They had both, Ted recalled, taken the Civil Service Executive Grade examination while in their final year at Grammar School, and between them had occupied two of the three highest places in the French section of the exam, but in the end only Jim was selected, and Ted had pursued a fairly conventional route through National Service, university and teaching – first in Grammar Schools, and then in a university. Ted had been rather relieved at the time to have escaped the red tape associated with a Civil Service career, but after a life-time spent in the educational world, he came ultimately to realise that he had merely exchanged one potential straitjacket for another.

Ted still had a photograph of Jim somewhere, in the company of two or three other boys on the deck of the *Arromanches* as they returned via Dieppe and Newhaven at the end of a six-week visit to France in 1948, a visit which had left its mark on Ted in so many ways, not least of which was his first real encounter with death; little Miguette, the ten-year-old sister of his exchange partner Michel, had died of leukaemia during Ted's stay. It was one of many events in his youth which Ted looked back upon with some embarrassment, feeling in later life, a little unreasonably, that his reactions at the time had been inadequate, that he should have been more sensitive, more understanding – in other words more adult than his fifteen sheltered years enabled him in reality to be.

And the match at Trent Bridge which Jim had mentioned, when Everton Weekes had made all those runs: Ted had travelled home on the 43 trolley-bus with Jim, and then, on arriving home, discovered that his mother had been rushed to hospital that afternoon, having had a horrific accident and sustained injuries from which she never really recovered, although she survived for a number of years before she finally succumbed.

'What's it to be then?'

'Oh, another G and T, I think.'

They clinked their glasses, not for the last time that evening, the cricket forgotten, although play was continuing outside, as the occasional ripple of applause indicated, and they began the lengthy process of filling the information-gap engendered by forty years of lack of contact.

'Where do you live these days?' asked Jim.

'I live in Crowthorne, near Reading. But I often come up to London – I have a daughter called Sophie, who lives in Hampstead. She's a consultant at a teaching hospital, specialising in gynaecological oncology, and I stay at her place whenever I come up to town.'

'It's a pity her specialism isn't a bit more relevant to you, considering the stage in our lives that we've reached! I live in Kensington, so we could get together quite easily when you come up to town. Does your wife come up with you?'

'Sometimes, but not very often. She's not Sophie's mother, you see. My first wife is French

– her name's Arlette. We met when she was an *assistante* at a school where I was teaching, and we got married quite quickly – something I lived to regret, though. We split up when Sophie was about fourteen. After that I had a few years on my own before I met Valerie, and then we lived happily ever after... What about you?'

'I've been married to the same woman for nearly forty years – don't believe in divorce, anyway. We met at school, actually – you may even remember her. Her name was Dilys, Dilys Anderson.'

Ted paused a moment, in truth unsure as to what to say, but to Jim looking as if he were simply searching the depths of his memory. 'No, I can't say I do remember her, I'm sorry.'

'I'm not surprised. She left school and went to Scotland for a while when she was in the sixth form. It was only when she came back the following year that I got to know her properly, because they moved into a house near ours. Anyway, I must just pop to the loo. Excuse me a moment.'

During the few minutes that Jim was away, Ted's imagination ran riot. Dilys Anderson! My God, the beautiful Dilly! And did he remember her? Yes, you bet he remembered her!

Suddenly he was eighteen years old again, and standing in the doorway of a cavernous hall full of young people. Immediately one person in particular attracted his attention. 'Bloody 'ell!

Look at that!' he said to himself. "Oo the 'ell's that?'

The object of his admiration stood for a moment and looked round the room. For a brief moment their gaze met, she smiled in his direction, then turned away, with a gentle sway of the hips which engaged Ted's attention even more, and joined a group of girls who were sitting on the other side of the hall. Immediately absorbed in their excited conversation, she did not look in his direction again, to Ted's great disappointment; he nevertheless resolved to discover her identity as soon as he could – and perhaps even dance with her.

It was March 1951. The place: not a dance-hall, but the assembly hall of an old school building which doubled as the school gym. At one end climbing ropes hung from the ceiling, like huge tie-backs securing vast invisible swag curtains, and most of the walls were adorned with wooden climbing bars. At the other end of the hall stood a pommel-horse, a buck, wooden benches, and other gymnastic equipment, whilst in the middle of one long wall stood the rostrum on which the headmaster, Harry Davies – universally known, even to the staff, as 'Taffy' – stood each morning to conduct assembly. The only concessions to this unusual extra-curricular event were the installation of a small table on the rostrum, on which stood a record-player and amplifier, and the introduction of seventy or eighty chairs which had been taken from the adjacent classrooms and now lined the gymnasium walls. The building itself had seen better days; the commonly-held belief was that it was in such a bad state that it had been condemned before the war, although in the event it was to be many more years before the school was eventually re-housed, and, indeed, the building is still standing to this day, although it is no longer home to a boys' Grammar School.

The occasion: a sixth-form dance – officially described as 'the annual sixth-form dance', although the tradition had started only two years earlier. As the school in question was a single-sex school, girls were imported from the girls' Grammar School half-a-mile away. Such functions were undoubtedly arranged with the best of intentions, and pupils of both sexes looked forward to them with great enthusiasm, but, despite the fact that many of the boys and girls knew each other extremely well out of school, these were always very stilted occasions, with the boys sitting on one side of the hall and the girls on the other. There were a few boys who were bold enough to ask a girl to dance, but most were not, and it was usual for about 80% of the dancers to be girls, because the girls actively *wanted* to dance, and they preferred to dance with another girl, rather than not dance at all. They also wanted to be seen by the boys, and they had a better chance of being noticed if they were dancing than if they were not; for their part, the boys discussed the latest achievements of Nottingham Forest or Notts County – which did not prevent them from having the occasional surreptitious glance at the dancing girls.

Ted, however, stole more than the occasional glance at this girl; in fact he could hardly take his eyes off her for, he thought, he had never beheld such a beautiful creature in his life. She was quite tall, perhaps as tall as Ted was himself, although her high heels undoubtedly added two or three inches to her height, and her blonde hair fell over her shoulders in a sensuous wave which served to emphasise the shape of what was concealed beneath a calf-length, violet-coloured, taffeta dress. There was something about the way she carried herself too, which made her look a little older – no, not older, more mature – and certainly more sophisticated than her companions.

'A penneh for yer thoughts, serreh!' This abrupt invasion of his private fantasies emanated from one of Ted's friends, and seemed all the more unwelcome for being expressed in Nottingham dialect; moreover it made Ted realise that his glances had been rather less surreptitious than he had intended.

'I was just looking at that girl over there, the one with the long blonde hair. Do you know who she is?'

'Ooh ah, ah do that. She lives up in Sherwood, near our kid. 'Er name's Anderson.'

'What's her first name, do you know?'

'Ooh, ah'll 'ave ter think. It's a funny name – Dilys, or summat daft like that. Never 'eard that name before. Yeh, Dilys, that's it, Dilys Anderson.'

Ted murmured his thanks and moved away so that he was standing at the end of the hall, near the entrance, from which point he would be able to make a less obvious approach than if he had had to traverse the entire width of the dance-floor in order to reach her. He stood there self-consciously for several minutes, stock-still, like Patience on a monument, he thought to himself – Shakespeare being his current academic obsession – waiting for the music to stop before he made his move.

At last the music did stop, and he heard the voice of Mr Blackburn, the young English teacher who had been given the job of changing the records and announcing the dances: 'Please take your partners for a gentlemen's excuse-me quickstep.'

Ted strode purposefully in Dilys's direction, not simply because he wanted to make sure he asked her to dance before anybody else did, but also for fear that his courage might fail him altogether if he did not move quickly.

'May I have this dance please?' He took care to make sure that the 'h' of 'have' was properly aspirated, being conscious that Sherwood, or at least parts of it, was a slightly more up-market area than Hyson Green, which was where he lived. She looked at him, smiled her acceptance – what a smile! Ted thought – and stood up. A moment later they stepped out onto the dance-floor, and at last she was in his arms.

'What's your name?' she asked, as they moved off.

'Edward,' he replied. 'Well, Ted really ...'

'Nice to meet you, Ted,' and once more she gave him the same smile with which she had accepted his invitation to dance. 'I'm Dilys, Dilys Anderson.'

'Pleased to meet you too, Dilys.'

Just at that moment, Ted felt a tap on the shoulder. 'Excuse me.'

Ted turned round, and saw one of his class-mates standing there. 'Yes?' he said inquiringly.

'I said excuse me. It's a gentlemen's excuse-me, Ted. That means you have to give way to me.'

Ted reluctantly released Dilys, who gave him yet another smile as she danced off with her new partner; he was relieved to note that she did not bestow the same smile on the intruder.

After what seemed like a life-time the music stopped again; Dilys's partner escorted her back to her seat, she murmured a quiet 'Thank you', and, Ted was pleased to see, he then moved away. Dilys was alone again.

'Take your partners for a fox-trot,' said Mr Blackburn. Ted had absolutely no idea how to dance the fox-trot, but that did not prevent him from making a bee-line for Dilys, and asking her once more to dance. Again he saw that smile.

'Yes please, Ted, I'd love to.'

'There's only one thing – I don't know how to do the fox-trot.'

'Don't worry,' Dilys reassured him with that engaging smile on her lips again. 'We can do a slow quick-step instead. That's what a lot of the others will be doing anyway.'

So for the second time they took to the floor, but this time no one had the right to intervene. Ted was not a great dancer, and normally, especially when tackling a dance with which he was not very familiar, he would be so conscious of the need to put his feet in the right place that he would inevitably fall over them; but then he had never been so absorbed by a dance partner to the extent where he forgot all about the dance and simply enjoyed the feeling of two beings happy in each other's company, and moving as one.

For her part Dilys felt happy too. She had noticed Ted the moment she had entered the hall, and had immediately formed a silent wish that he would ask her to dance; in those days it would simply not have been acceptable for a girl to issue the invitation, except on the two or three occasions during the evening when the MC announced that the next dance would be a 'Ladies' Invitation'. The resolve had already established itself in Dilys's mind that she would avail herself of that privilege if Ted did not ask her first. He was, in her opinion, by far the most presentable of the boys: his shock of blond hair, perhaps even more blond than her own, was his most striking feature. What is more, he had not attempted to force it into the over-greased style known as the 'DA', which was rapidly becoming fashionable – as was the wearing of yellow socks, which Dilys also deplored; they made her think of Malvolio in *Twelfth Night* – for she too, as Ted would shortly discover, was a Shakespeare devotee – even if they didn't appear to be wearing cross garters with them. He was not short, but he was not tall in the gangly way that many boys of that age were – 'lanky' was the local word; and when she finally heard him speak she found his voice attractive too, with none of the roughness of tone and expression which she associated with most of the local boys. Even better, she found that he was happy to talk about literature and music, as well as sport; in truth few boys of his background could be termed 'cultured', but he was at least showing signs that he would become so one day, once he had been exposed to influences which were lacking in his milieu in the years following the war.

'Dilys,' he said as they danced. 'Dilys. That's a nice name. I've never come across it before.'

'Oh, that's my mother's doing,' Dilys replied. 'She's fiercely Welsh, and she married a Scot. She couldn't do anything about being saddled with a Scottish surname, but she insisted on a Welsh Christian name for me.'

From that moment on they had every dance together, with no further intrusion, for it was now clear to all that they had 'clicked', as the local expression had it. All too soon, Mr Blackburn announced the Last Waltz. Immediately, with no word necessary, Ted and

Dilys stood up, melted into each other's arms, and began the dance. Whereas most of the other couples kept a slightly-embarrassed, comfortable distance away from each other, for the first time in his life Ted felt the warmth of a young woman's body close to his. He held her more tightly; she responded by putting her cheek next to his, and they danced on, oblivious to all else.

'Dilys,' whispered Ted. 'Dilys ... Dilly ... Daffy-down-dilly ... who comes before the swallow dares, and takes the winds of March with beauty ...'

'Yes, Florizel,' Dilys responded. 'Your Perdita is found.'

'Ted...' said a deep voice suddenly, and Ted looked up to see Jim standing by him. 'Ted, you looked miles away! Did you drop off?'

Ted shook himself and tried to drag his thoughts back to the 21st century. 'No,' he answered. 'Just day-dreaming. It was the talk of schooldays, I suppose. I seem to think about those days more now I'm older than I ever used to.'

'Yes, I know what you mean,' Jim replied. 'Sorry I was so long. I stopped off to get us another couple of drinks.'

So the two old friends reunited had another drink, and then another one, and continued reminiscing about schooldays in general; eventually they returned to the subject of cricket, with which their conversation had begun, as they recalled pitching stumps on the Forest one frosty day in February, because they couldn't bear the thought that the cricket season was so far away; and how, in 1948, they had played a game of cricket in a street in the Parisian suburb of Sceaux, as the local residents looked on in a state of total bewilderment.

'Are you coming to the match tomorrow?' asked Ted.

'No. Can't make it tomorrow. Dilys has got a concert in Oxford, and I said I'd go along too.'

'A concert? What sort of concert?'

'Oh, she sings with the Bach Choir – the London Bach Choir, as they insist on calling it in the provinces. Unusually, it's an all-Bach programme. They're doing the *Magnificat,* and a couple of motets, I think – *Jesu, meine Freude* is certainly one of them.'

'Sounds wonderful. I do a lot of singing myself – with the Reading Bach Choir, in fact. Bach is my favourite composer after Mozart.'

'Well, everyone comes second to Mozart, don't they? You'll have to come to one of her concerts some time.'

'Love to.'

With that, the two friends exchanged phone numbers and parted.

As he walked towards St John's Wood underground station, where he would catch the bus to take him to where his daughter lived, Ted found himself thinking: 'Why did I tell Jim I didn't remember Dilly? I wouldn't have had to go into details and tell him what we did – it was fifty years ago, for God's sake! Why couldn't I just say yes, I do remember her, and God, how lucky a guy he was?'

When Ted was about a hundred yards away from the bus stop, to his initial annoyance he saw a bus arrive, stop momentarily to pick up two or three passengers, and then leave again. 'When I was eighteen I would have run for that bus and caught it,' he thought. 'But I'm not still eighteen, so I'd better come back to earth again. At least I have my bus pass – if I was still eighteen I'd have to pay!' Fortunately the buses on route 46 run every ten minutes at that time of day, so Ted did not have long to wait.

Once he was seated on the bus, his memories of 1951 took over his imagination again. The school dance was over, and he and Dilys were leaving the school premises together. When they reached the corner of Stanley Road and Berridge Road, Ted stopped. 'Can I walk you home?' he asked tentatively.

'If it's not out of your way,' she replied, 'I would love you to.'

The way Ted was feeling about her, he would have walked her home even if she had lived on the other side of the city, but felt that he ought at least to go through the motions. 'Where do you live then?' he asked.

'Sherwood. Caledon Road.'

'Oh, that's not far out of my way at all,' he answered untruthfully. 'That's this way, isn't it?' He made as if to turn left up Berridge Road.

'Yes, that's one way,' said Dilys. 'But this way is a nicer walk...'

Although Ted knew that the road Dilys was indicating was in totally the wrong direction, he acquiesced readily enough. As they crossed Berridge Road and continued to walk down Stanley Road, their fingers touched accidentally for a second, then at once, as if sensible of the pain of separation, eagerly sought each other again, and on they walked, joined in body as well as in mind.

'I love those lines from *A Winter's Tale*,' said Dilys.

'So do I,' replied Ted, 'but when I first read them I never expected to find myself needing to quote them like that ...'

The young couple stopped, looked into each other's eyes, drew slowly closer. Finally their lips met; when they resumed their journey they held each other round the waist, not by the hand, and adjusted their step so that their bodies were in constant contact too, as they had been in the dance-hall. Every few yards, however, their lips made them stop, aching with the desire to maintain their own contact. From Stanley Road they turned into Austen Avenue, from Austen Avenue into Leslie Road – they did not even notice. But at the end of Leslie Road they needed to turn left, along Gregory Boulevard. The alternative was to go straight on and enter the vast recreation ground known to everybody in Nottingham as 'The Forest'. They stopped once more for the briefest moment, looked at each other, then, without a word, moved as one onto the Forest. Alongside the cricket pavilion stood a large brick shelter, which was open on one side, and looked out – at least when it wasn't dark – across the cricket square, and was furnished with wooden benches. They sat down on one of these benches, oblivious to their hardness, kissed once more, and then surrendered fully to their mutual passion.

Afterwards, as they walked together in the direction of Caledon Road, Ted said 'Can I see you after school tomorrow?'

'Yes, but only for a short time, I'm afraid, because we're going away tomorrow night, and I shall have a lot to do when I get home, you know, packing and things.'

'Well, I'll see you outside school – your school, I mean – at half past three. I mean, you've got to walk home anyway, so I'll come and walk with you.'

'That would be nice,' she smiled. 'But we'll have to walk a bit quicker than we did tonight or I'll be in trouble. But just a minute – you don't finish till quarter to four, do you?'

'Not usually, no, but I've got a free period last thing tomorrow, so I'll sneak out early'.

The difference in time-tabling between the two schools was legendary. For many years the boys had finished lessons a little earlier than the girls, but, because this invariably led to a crowd of boys waiting in the street for the girls to come out at the end of the day, the Headmistress had altered the timing of afternoon school – partly in response to neighbours' complaints, partly because she wanted to discourage the practice herself. The principal effect of the change was that most of the girls – apart from the very junior ones – decided to walk home up the street where the Boys' school was situated, regardless of whether they lived in that direction or not; as a result, they would just happen to be passing at the very moment when the boys came out. The girls were generally under the impression that their Headmistress had no idea of what was happening; the more mature among them realised that it was really little more than shifting the problem onto somebody else. The Headmaster, perhaps a little more in tune with adolescent thinking, did nothing – probably, if truth be known, considering that his boys were jolly lucky!

Ted and Dilys walked in silence for ten minutes, their arms still around each other's waist. When they arrived in Caledon Road Ted could not help noticing how different the houses were from his own; it was not just that they were bigger, but they were so much more stylish, with half-timbered gables above the front door, and a small garden at the front, protected by a sandstone wall – and a gate! Thus, protected from neighbours' prying eyes, they were able to stand entwined outside Dilys's house for a further ten minutes. There was only one final kiss, but it lasted as long as they stood together.

At length Dilys said: 'I must go, Ted. Good night, and thank you. I'll see you tomorrow.'

Before he could even respond, she broke away from him and ran into the house.

'I can't wait,' Ted said to himself, as he went back down Caledon Road, and began to walk the two miles which separated his house from hers, unsure whether the moistness he felt on his cheeks had come from her tears or from his.

In the normal course of events Ted would probably have run most of the way home, but tonight he was still too fully immersed in the unexpected and delightful adventure that the evening had presented, so he walked home fairly slowly, going over in his mind every word that they had exchanged, every glance, every gesture.

He unlocked the front door and went into the living-room. 'What time do you call this, Ted?' said the voice of his mother.

Ted glanced up at the clock on the wall above the door. 'Oh, I didn't realise it was that time.'

'Never you mind about you didn't realise it was that time! It's nearly midnight! Your dad's gone to bed already because he's on earlies this week, else he'd have something to say! What time did this dance finish anyway?'

'Ten o'clock,' Ted replied, realising that it would be pointless to lie, because he was aware that she already knew the answer anyway.

'It doesn't normally take you two hours to get home from school. Where've you been?'

'Oh, just chatting with some of the boys, that's all. We were having a lot of fun, so we didn't really notice how late it was getting. Anyway, I'd better get off to bed, because I've got to serve seven o'clock mass in the morning.'

'No, you haven't. Father Kerrigan came round earlier to let you know that there wouldn't be a mass in the morning because his mother's very ill, and he's had to rush over to Ireland tonight. Poor Father Kerrigan! He's such a nice man, isn't he, and he was so upset about his old mam ...'

Ted deliberately refrained from endorsing his mother's opinion of their parish priest: uppermost in his mind was the thought that until tonight, Father Kerrigan had been the initiator of the only sexual experience of his life. Thank God he would not have to see the odious man the next morning, with the sweet fragrance of Dilly's presence still enveloping his whole body and his whole soul.

'Excuse me,' said a woman sitting next to Ted on the bus. 'I get off here.'

Once more Ted awoke from his reveries with a start, looked out of the window, and realised that they were already in Pilgrim's Lane, Hampstead, only five minutes' walk away from Sophie's place in Downshire Hill. 'Oh gosh,' he exclaimed, 'so do I!'

Downshire Hill, in the heart of Hampstead, is one of the most attractive tree-lined streets in the capital – and one of the most sought-after addresses too, with many of the houses dating back to Georgian times, and displaying the elegant features of that age. It looked particularly charming on this still, sun-drenched evening on the last day of what had been a beautiful English June. Just around the corner was the house where Keats lived – now a museum to his memory – and where he wrote *Ode to a Nightingale*, whilst John Constable also lived nearby, only a few years later than Keats. Sophie and Peter, however, lived in a modern development of serviced apartments which displayed a twentieth-century version of opulent elegance, and which suited their busy life-style and the fact that they had no children.

When Ted arrived there he rang their bell but, as there was no answer, he entered the code – which he had written down on the cover of his cheque-book in case his memory failed him, as it did with increasing frequency these days – opened the gate, and made his way across the garden with its well-trimmed lawn and beautifully maintained shrubberies, and past the communal tennis-courts, before letting himself in, by virtue of yet another code, to Sophie and Peter's apartment.

Ted was not in the least surprised to find that there was no one at home. His son-in-law, Peter, was a corporate lawyer, a partner in a big City law firm, specialising in an area of banking law of which even the basic elements were totally beyond Ted's comprehension, and he often had to work late – sometimes all night. His daughter's hours at the hospital were a little more predictable, but depended on her current case-load and on whether an individual patient was causing particular concern. Although she did not make the mistake of becoming emotionally involved with her patients to an excessive degree, she did take her job very seriously, and was reluctant to leave a serious case to her juniors when spending an extra twenty minutes with the patient seemed the right thing to do, and Ted admired her greatly for this.

Ted poured himself a gin and tonic, picked up the newspaper, and sat down. He knew that either Peter or Sophie would be home soon, or they would have left a message for him. But instead of reading the paper, he started to think about the events of the day; not so much about the cricket, despite the dramatic turn the match had taken, but more his chance meeting with his old school-friend Jim Fletcher.

It had been nice to meet Jim again, he mused. They had always got on well together at school, and there had been many occasions during the forty years which had elapsed since their last meeting when he had found himself thinking about Jim, and wondering what had become of him. They shared a common background; the area in which they lived had not been really deprived, but life there was by no means easy, and it was a real struggle for parents like Ted's and Jim's to keep their children at school beyond the statutory leaving-age of 14. But they did appreciate the value of education, and made sure that their children did so too. As a result, a good number of them went to university; in his street alone, Ted reflected, he could think of at least eight boys from a row of sixteen houses who went to university, including three who went to either Oxford or Cambridge, one with an Open Scholarship in Classics. It was the sort of thing which could happen to that generation but, unhappily, would now be considered a freakish outcome to a state education in a working-class district.

Ted and Jim also had a connection outside school: they were both raised as Roman Catholics, and although they did not go to the same church, there was a bond established between them arising from the feeling of being different from the rest in a non-Catholic school, at a time when Catholics were not permitted to take part in school assemblies, or even practise singing hymns with the others. Ted had ceased to be a practising Catholic during his time at university, in part at least because of the indignation he felt when he came to realise that the Catholicism preached in his church in a poor area of Nottingham was very different from the much less rigid dogma which had been presented to his wealthier fellow-students in, say, suburban Surrey. The fact of having abandoned the religious practices of his youth, however, did not prevent him from marrying a Catholic, although Arlette, accustomed to a more free-thinking attitude to religion, as is often the case in France, never made any attempt to convert him back. Curious, really, thought Ted, because during the years they were together, she had tried to change him in most other respects.

From Arlette, he rapidly switched his thoughts to Dilys. The day after the school dance Ted had had no problem whatever getting away from school early, for it was the last day of term, and term traditionally ended with a school assembly, held in the very same hall in which he and Dilys had been dancing only a few hours earlier. But Ted, being a Roman Catholic, was excused assembly. True, he should have been in one of the adjacent classrooms with the other Catholics and the handful of Jewish boys in the school, and joined in the assembly towards the end, once the hymns and the prayers had finished, but they were usually unsupervised, except by a prefect, and it had not been difficult for him to avoid joining the others by staying in the toilets for a few minutes, until everyone had stopped milling around and assembly was under way.

Even so, he left the school premises from a side-door, rather than go through the main entrance, and he duly made his way down to the Girls' School, timing his arrival to coincide with the exit of the first girls to leave, so as not to excite the wrath of the Headmistress. He did not have to wait long, although he was a little surprised by what he saw when Dilys finally emerged: naturally he had not expected her to be still wearing her high heels and taffeta dress, but the white blouse, grey blazer, grey pleated skirt and red and white striped tie – to say nothing of the bright red beret – made such a contrast with the image that had remained in his mind from the previous night that he was startled for a moment. Still, he thought, she would have turned the head of any boy with a modicum of taste.

'Hello, Ted,' she said, coming straight up to him so eagerly that he was tempted to take her in his arms again and kiss her; discretion won the day, however, for both of them were aware that the price to be paid would be immediate expulsion, followed by exclusion from that summer's A Level exams. The route they followed to reach Caledon Road was also rather more direct than the one they had taken the night before, and, of course, the decorum required of wearers of school uniform meant also that they needed to keep a decent distance away from each other, for even holding hands would have merited the same punishment as a kiss.

But although an outside observer would not have been aware of the existence of the kind of intimacy which had been born the previous evening, neither Ted nor Dilys made any secret of the fact that they in no way regretted what had happened, and could not wait for it to happen again. They were none the less aware that they needed to talk about the future, at least about the immediate future, in practical, rather than idealistic terms.

'Were you in trouble for getting home late last night?' Dilys asked.

'Yes, I was a bit,' said Ted, 'but fortunately my Dad was already in bed, and Mum's bark is worse than her bite. What about you?'

'It wasn't too bad,' replied Dilys, with a laugh. 'It's a good job they didn't see us kissing outside the front door though! I told them I'd been seen home by three boys, so that was all right. Safety in numbers, you know!'

'You said you're going away tonight. Where are you going?'

'We're going to Scotland. One of my cousins in Edinburgh is getting married, and I'm going to be one of the bridesmaids. Then we're going to stay in Scotland for the whole Easter holiday.'

'The whole Easter holiday? So I won't be able to see you at all in the holidays?'

'No, I'm afraid you won't. But we'll be able to make up for it later in the summer when the exams are over and done with.'

'Yes, I suppose so – except that at the end of the summer holidays I'll be going off to do my National Service.'

'Aren't you trying for university then?'

'Yes, I am, but you can choose whether to do National Service before or after, and I'd rather like to get it over with. And I shall have to join up in September to make sure of getting out before the start of term in two years' time.'

'Why would you rather do it before university?'

'Mostly because I think I might get more out of university when I'm a bit older.'

'So you'll be spending the next two years in the army then. I hope they don't send you to Korea.'

'No, I don't think that's likely, because I'm going into the R.A.F., and I don't think the R.A.F. are involved in Korea – not yet, anyway. What are you planning to do?'

'It depends on my A Level results, but I've got a place to do English in London.'

'Which college?'

'King's.'

'Wow, you've done well!'

Dilys laughed. 'So far, maybe, but I'm not counting my chickens – we'll see! Are you planning to do English as well?'

'No, I don't think so. I think I'm going to do French, but I've got a couple of years to think about it. Anyway, look, we're nearly at your place – what date are you coming back home from Scotland?'

'April the thirteenth.'

'What day of the week is that?'

'Friday, I'm afraid. Friday the thirteenth – let's hope nothing goes wrong!'

'What could go wrong? You're not superstitious, are you?'

'No,' Dilys replied. 'Not at all. And at the moment everything seems just right.' She gave him the same smile that had captivated him the evening before. 'Give me your phone number and I'll try and call you from Edinburgh.'

'We don't have a phone. I'll have to write to you. Where are you staying?'

'Oh, that's difficult too, because we'll be touring about, not stopping in one place. I'll write to you though. And then we'll be able to see each other again at the beginning of term.'

'All right.' Ted sounded disappointed.

'If you want to, that is ...'

'Of course I want to. But it's not going to be easy next term, is it? I mean, we've got A Levels at the beginning of June, so we're not going to be able to see much of each other, are we?'

'We'll manage. Oh God, there's my Dad – we'd better say goodbye now before he sees us! But give me your address first, and I'll write to you.'

Ted scribbled his address quickly on a page in his pocket diary, tore it out and handed it to her. She glanced at it, folded it carefully, and put it in her blazer pocket. Then she fell into Ted's open arms and they kissed, more chastely than the previous night, but still in a way that promised commitment.

'Oh Ted,' said Dilys. 'You make me feel so happy. But I must go. It won't be too long!'

With that she turned away, and ran the remaining twenty yards or so, opened the front gate, and was gone.

The weekend seemed lonely and empty for Ted. He tried to bury himself in his work, but to no avail: he was unable to concentrate for more than a few minutes at a time. It was only when he opened *A Winter's Tale* and submerged himself in its poetry that he found a little peace, for while he was reading that, he felt that Dilys was beside him, breathing in the imagery at the same time.

When Monday came, he was not at all surprised that there was no letter, for he realised that it would have been virtually impossible for a letter to have reached Nottingham from Edinburgh so quickly, even if Dilys had written during her journey north – which in itself was unlikely, for she was catching the night train.

On Tuesday, however, he got up early, and stood in the bay-window of the front-room, which was normally only used on Sundays and at Christmas, and from which he could see the main road, for in this way he would eventually see the postman coming round the corner from Radford Road; but for half an hour or so all he saw were the drays loaded with casks from Shipstone's brewery less than a mile away, each drawn by a magnificent pair of shire horses with powerful, shaggy legs, and the green and cream trolley-buses which passed every few minutes on their way from Bulwell to the City Centre, and from there onwards to Trent Bridge. At last the postman came into view. Ted went to stand by the front door in order to catch the letter as it dropped, but ... nothing. He rushed back to the window, and saw the postman again... but this time he was further up the street, and it was clear that this particular delivery held nothing for Ted.

This became a ritual which occurred three times a day; in those days there were two postal deliveries in the morning and a third in the afternoon. But for the next two weeks there was nothing.

Finally, a day or two before the end of the Easter holidays, a small, pale blue envelope appeared in the post, addressed to Mr Edward Bryant, and bearing an Edinburgh postmark. Feverishly he tore it open, and read the letter it contained. This is what it said:

Dear Ted,

> *I don't want to hurt you at all, but I think a little hurt now is better than a big hurt later on. We both have exams to do, and then you'll be going away to the R.A.F., so I think we should stop now. It's for the best.*
> *But I'll always be your Perdita.*
>
> > *Dilly x*

Ted turned the page over. The other side was blank. His eyes filled with tears, and his mind filled with one thought: Perdita is lost again...

What could he do? He read the letter again, again, and then again. It made no sense. What was it she had said to him just before they said goodbye? 'Oh, Ted, you make me feel so happy. But it won't be too long!' So what had happened to make her change her mind? Had she changed her mind? He looked at the letter again: 'I'll always be your Perdita', she had written. 'Dilly', she had signed herself, not Dilys. And at the end, one solitary kiss, which made him think of the one kiss they had exchanged a few seconds before she disappeared to Scotland for the Easter holidays. At the time he had thought 'for the Easter holidays' meant for ever; now it seemed as if it really was for ever, because, despite the undoubted indications of affection, her letter appeared to signify a final, irrevocable farewell.

Ted's mother came in from the shops. He hurriedly hid Dilly's letter. 'What's the matter, Ted?' she asked, seeing him sitting at the table looking, she thought, rather agitated.

'Oh nothing, mum, I'm fine,' he answered.

'You don't look fine, you look worried to death,' she retorted. 'What is it?'

'Oh, it's all right, it's only work. I'm thinking about a French essay I've got to do, and it's not working out right …'

'Oh, okay.' Ted's mother didn't know what to say, for she was already out of her depth: essays in French, or any essays come to that, were literally foreign to her; but like many parents of her generation, although she had not been able to benefit from the educational advantages now being offered to children in the years immediately following the Second World War, she did appreciate the benefit that would accrue from the hard work it obviously demanded. 'Would it disturb you if I put the wireless on?'

'No, of course not, mum', Ted answered.

She switched on the radio, and the unmistakeable, relaxed voice of Perry Como invaded the room, singing the latest hit from *South Pacific* – a great success in the United States, and eagerly awaited in London, but not likely to be staged in Nottingham in the foreseeable future:

'Some enchanted evening... You may see a stranger...
You may see a stranger, across a crowded room...'

'Yes,' thought Ted. 'I know about enchanted evenings', and his mind was suddenly transported back to the school hall and the sixth-form dance.

'Once you have found her, never let her go...
Once you have found her...'

Ted stood up, and left the room quickly, for how would he have been able to explain to his mother the tears that were beginning to flow?

Even in his room he could still hear the music, and when it stopped the words pounded in his brain:

'Once you have found her, never let her go...'

'Okay,' he said to himself. 'I won't let her go!' And he took out a writing-pad, and began to write the first love-letter of his life.

Friday, April the thirteenth arrived, the day Dilys had said she would be travelling back to Nottingham. On that day, or at the latest on the Saturday, she would read his letter. On Monday morning he was back at the window, watching out for the postman. Three deliveries, thrice nothing. The next day, the same.

'Once you have found her, never let her go...' He wrote another letter. Another two days passed; still no answer.

By the time the new term started Ted had written five letters, and still had apparently been unable to persuade her to put pen to paper once more. At the end of the first day back at school he managed to leave school early, and arrived outside the gates of Dilys's school just as the girls were starting to come out. He waited, waited, waited. Every single one of the girls, and most of the teachers too, walked past him, but there was no sign of Dilys.

On the way home he noticed a telephone kiosk, went in, leafed through the directory, and found the number. Feverishly he dialled; he heard the tone indicating that the phone in Dilys's house was ringing ... but no one answered. In the next two or three days he tried again, several times, but still with no success.

Two further weeks passed; each day he stood outside her school and then telephoned her home. Then one day, after yet another fruitless wait, the tone he heard through the earpiece was different: it was the tone indicating 'number unobtainable'. He immediately started walking not in the direction of his own home, but towards Sherwood.

He saw it as soon as he turned into Caledon Road, but could not at first be sure whether it was outside her house or not. A few seconds later, however, his worst fears were confirmed:

outside Dilys's house a board had been erected, giving the name of a local estate agent and bearing, in large letters, the words 'For Sale'.

It was not really until that moment that Ted began to lose hope. The following day he made enquiries through one of his friends who had a sister at the Girls' school; after what seemed an eternity, the message came back that Dilys appeared to have left.

He was devastated, but threw himself into his work, and – largely because of the work he had done earlier in the year, for he had done very little since meeting Dilys – he achieved the results he needed; when they appeared in the local newspaper he could not help looking at the girls' results too, but Dilys's name was not in the list, and from that time on it was as if she had vanished from the face of the earth.

In due course he went into the Royal Air Force, served his statutory two years of National Service, then went to University College, London, to read French. After achieving a first, he became a teacher. For four years he taught French in a Grammar School in south-east London, where he met and married a young French woman who was working there for one year as an *assistante*; the following year they had a baby, a little girl whom they called Sophie. Not very long after that he was appointed to a lectureship at Reading, and stayed in that post until his retirement.

During the whole of that period, the name Dilys Anderson never crossed his lips; indeed the thought of that enchanted evening only rarely crossed his mind, and now, all these years later, all these memories were flooding back. Even more than forty years had elapsed since he had last seen her – nearly fifty, in fact, and it amazed Ted to think that whereas he had frequently thought about Jim and wondered what had become of him, he had only rarely thought of Dilys. Certainly he never dreamt that they might one day meet again, especially since she never answered the many letters he had sent her. And yet the moment Jim had mentioned her name, Ted had experienced an unmistakeable frisson of excitement, as if he were just about to hold her once more in a teen-age embrace.

Ah yes, a teen-age embrace, that's what it was, and Ted realised that he was, of course, thinking about the girl to whom he had made love fifty years ago, when she was seventeen. Now she would be 67, and it was highly unlikely, he reflected, that she would still have the svelte figure and the beautiful face exuding adolescent charm which had so attracted him when he was only a few months older than she was. There were women of his acquaintance, of course, who had maintained their good looks well beyond the age of sixty – his own wife among them - but a good many more who had not. The chances were that the beautiful, lithe girl of the fifties had, by the Millennium, metamorphosed into a dumpy, maybe even fat and ugly creature. He would, no doubt, have the opportunity to find out, because he did intend to maintain contact with Jim, and that meant he was likely to meet Dilys again one day, but that meeting could be left to look after itself, and any fantasies that might arise within him should remain just that, and nothing more.

Or could it? It had actually been a bit more than an embrace, hadn't it? He thought once more about how he had been unable to sleep that night, and how frustrated he had been during the Easter holidays knowing that she was in Scotland and he wouldn't see her again until next term; about the five letters he had written, none of which had evoked any reply.

And then that letter had arrived, ending it all; a brief, enigmatic note, peremptory – tinged with regret, perhaps, or was that only in his imagination? – but ultimately saying thank you and goodbye, and giving no reason at all that made sense. He thought again about all the hours he had spent waiting outside her school; all the phone-calls he had made – or tried to make – and the desolation he had felt when he heard the 'number unobtainable' tone, a desolation made even worse when he saw the 'For Sale' board which had been erected outside her house in Caledon Road. All the memories of that lovelorn summer which had followed the golden spring jostled for space in his crowded mind ...

At that moment, Peter came in. 'Hello, Ted. Good day at the cricket?'

'Yes, thanks – a really good day.'

'Extraordinary happenings, I understand. What were England at the close?'

'Do you know, I haven't the remotest idea!'

'Too many celebratory drinks at the end of the West Indian innings, I suppose!'

'Well, that was how it started, but...'

Before Ted could elaborate, the door opened, and in walked Sophie, looking drained. 'I'm sorry, I couldn't face cooking tonight,' she said, 'so I've brought a take-away, I'm afraid.'

'You've had a hard day then, darling?' inquired Peter.

'Yes, I lost one of my patients this afternoon – breast cancer, at least it was to begin with – and it really upset me. I mean, obviously, it's never an easy thing to cope with, however hardened most people seem to think we doctors are, but this lady, well... To be honest, I thought she was going to die about a year ago, and then a most remarkable improvement took place. She was so courageous, she really fought hard, and I suppose I fooled myself into believing that she was going to pull through, but really the cancer was too far advanced... She ignored the early signs, as many women do, and that's always a big mistake. Anyway, come on, we'd better eat, you must be starving, both of you...'

They ate their meal in relative silence, which was most unusual, for none of them was known for being short of something to say, but on this occasion Sophie was clearly preoccupied with her lost patient, and Peter and Ted were sufficiently sensitive to realise that they would only be intruding if they were to return to their original, comparatively trivial, conversation.

Just as they finished their meal, the telephone rang.

'I expect that's Valerie,' said Ted. 'I'll get it.' He was right. She usually did ring about that time when he was away from home. 'Hello, darling. How are things at home?'

'Okay. Nothing much to report, really – except that when I came back from the shops this afternoon the old bat next door collared me, and kept me talking about absolutely nothing for the best part of half an hour. What sort of day did you have?'

'Oh, pretty good. The cricket was good – you probably saw that on the news. But I ran into an old school-friend called Jim Fletcher, and we had a drink or three...'

'As you do...'

'But of course! We had a lot to catch up on – we haven't seen each other for forty years, and there was a lot to talk about.'

'I suppose there'll be some more boozy reminiscences tomorrow...'

'No, there won't, actually, because he's got something else on tomorrow and can't go to the test match. But we've agreed to get together next time I'm in town.'

'He lives in London, does he?'

'Yes, Kensington, I think he said.'

'I wish we could afford to live in Kensington!'

'Dream on, darling! Crowthorne's expensive enough! I should never have stayed in education, then I might have been able to keep you in the style to which you'd like to become accustomed...'

'You still could if you eased back on the gin a bit...'

'Oh, come off it! You should see the way Jim knocks back the red wine – he'd soon drink me under the table. He must have hollow legs! Anyway, you wouldn't deny an old man one of his few remaining pleasures, would you?'

'What old man? You'll outlive us all!'

'That's what you always say, darling!'

'When are you coming home, do you know?'

'Probably tomorrow evening, I think. I can't see the match lasting beyond teatime, whatever happens. Unless, of course, it rains... I'll give you a ring and let you know.'

'Okay, Ted. Till tomorrow, then.'

'Okay, my love. Sleep well.'

'Thank you – you too. Bye.'

'Bye.'

As Ted replaced the receiver a thought suddenly crossed his mind: he had told Valerie all about Jim, but had uttered not a word about Dilys...

'Coffee, Dad?'

'No thanks, Sophie. I'll take myself off to bed, I think – which is what you should do too...'

'Yes, doctor!' Sophie replied, with a laugh. 'Okay, Dad, sleep well.'

'Goodnight, darling. See you in the morning.'

With that, Ted withdrew to his bedroom, and in a few moments was fast asleep. He dreamed of being eighteen again, and of dancing intimately with... a French girl named Arlette.

At about the same time as Ted was sitting down to eat with Sophie and Peter, Jim arrived home. Home was an elegant apartment in Kensington, just off Gloucester Road. When he arrived, his wife was just putting the finishing touches to the meal she had spent the last two hours preparing.

'Hello, Jim,' said Dilys, without looking up. 'You're just in time. Supper will be ready in about ten minutes.'

'Do I have time for a shower? It's been such a hot day. I'm dying to get this collar and tie off.'

'Yes, if you're quick. But I don't understand why you have to dress so formally for a cricket match.'

'Because it's the done thing.'

'Not with everybody, it's not. I've seen cricket matches on television, even test matches, with men virtually wearing beachwear in hot weather – even some wearing no shirts at all.'

'And there was once a man who got arrested at Lord's for running onto the pitch absolutely starkers, but that doesn't mean I'm going to do it!'

'I'm not suggesting that. I'm just wondering why you can't wear something a bit more comfortable.'

'Because I'm a member of the MCC.'

'Ah.'

Jim disappeared into the bedroom, choosing to ignore his wife's laconic but telling comment.

Dilys returned to the kitchen, took the rack of lamb out of the oven, and wrapped it in foil to let it rest for a while before she carved it, then set about arranging the vegetables that would accompany the lamb. Cooking was one of her passions, and she took as much care over the presentation of the dishes she prepared, even when they were dining on their own, as she did over her own appearance. For her, elegance was everything.

A few minutes later Jim emerged looking much refreshed, and a degree more casual, although with Jim, even when casually dressed, there was still a hint of formality about him. He took his place at the dining-table. Dilys went back into the kitchen to bring in Jim's plate, and then returned to fetch her own, before making a final trip to the kitchen to fetch the glass of wine she had been drinking while cooking.

'What have you been up to today, then?' asked Jim, when Dilys eventually took up her place facing him.

'I had a singing lesson this morning...'

'Why do you still need singing lessons? I thought you already knew how to sing.'

'Of course I know how to sing, but if you sing with a choir like ours you have to work hard to make sure you keep up to the mark. And we've got re-auditions in a couple of weeks' time.'

'Again? It's not long since you had a re-audition.'

'It's three years.'

Jim grunted, ate in silence for a minute or two, and then resumed: 'And what did you do this afternoon?'

'I met Jemima, and we went to do a bit of shopping together.'

'Were the kids with her?'

'No, of course not. They were at school.'

'Oh God, yes. I'd forgotten it was Friday. I keep thinking it's Saturday. I suppose you spent the afternoon in Harvey Nicholls...'

'We did go to Harvey Nick's, yes.'

'Spending money again, I suppose. How many dresses did you buy today?'

'Only one – and why not? It's my money – it's not as if you have to pay for it.'

'But you have stacks of dresses! You buy a new one every week!'

'No, I don't! Don't exaggerate! And even if I did, so what? You like me to look nice when we go out to visit your Whitehall mandarins and their wives...'

'The Foreign Office isn't in Whitehall.'

'All right. You know what I mean.'

It was a full five minutes before Jim responded. 'Frankly I don't give a toss about my old Foreign Office colleagues. I got on much better with the chaps I used to work with at GCHQ. I wouldn't mind going back to live in Cheltenham.'

'Just chaps you worked with there, was it? I see.'

'What do you mean by that?'

'You know perfectly well what I mean...'

'And you know perfectly well that that was just a malicious rumour put about by an unscrupulous little bitch that I refused to recommend for promotion. What's the matter with you this evening?'

'With me? There's nothing the matter with me! You've been in a niggly mood ever since you came in – did you have a few too many in the members' bar?'

'What if I did?'

Dilys judged it best not to reply. She was by no means averse to a drink or two herself – she had started when she was in the Sixth Form at school, which was unusual for those times, but she always had been a bit precocious and unconventional – but she did worry about the extent of her husband's drinking. As with the matter of the carrying of dishes, however, she thought it best on the whole to avoid making a great issue of it.

A few more minutes' silence ensued. Then Jim spoke again: 'Yes, I did have a few, I must admit. I'm sorry, I didn't mean to be niggly... Didn't realise I was being really...'

Dilys waited until she had finished chewing, then replied: 'Okay, don't worry. Let's start again. Would you really like to go back to Cheltenham?'

'Well yes, I would. I mean, it's a lovely place to live, and we've got lots of friends there. And it would be a damn sight cheaper than living here.'

'You mean I wouldn't be able to buy a new dress from Harvey Nicholls every week.'

'I thought you said we were starting again?'

'Oh, all right, sorry. But if we did move back to Cheltenham we'd still have to have a place up here, or we'd hardly see anything of the grandchildren, and I'd have to give up the Bach Choir too.'

'Oh, I suppose you're right...'

'Anyway, you've told me nothing about your day.'

'But you're not interested in cricket...'

'I suppose you had all those drinks sitting alone in a corner drowning your sorrows.'

'No, of course I didn't. Actually I ran into an old school pal from Nottingham – well, he was from Nottingham, but he lives somewhere near Reading now.'

'Somebody I would remember?'

'Don't think so, though he and I were as thick as thieves at one time. We're planning to get together some time.'

'That's nice. What's his name?'

'Ted – Ted Bryant.'

'Ted Bryant? Well I never! I remember him.'

'Do you really? Did you know him very well?'

Dilys took a long sip from her wine-glass before replying. 'No... I just seem to remember having a dance with him once at a Sixth Form do, that's all...'

'That's funny – he said he doesn't remember you.'

'Women have better memories than men for things like that, and it was a long time ago,' Dilys responded, back-pedalling frantically, having another drink, and hoping that Jim would not notice that she was blushing. When she returned to the kitchen with their empty dinner-plates a few minutes later, her eyes filled with tears.

By the following day, the first of July, the balmy sunshine had given way to the kind of grey, drizzly English weather which always looks as if it will last for ever and which, Dilys felt, matched the mood which Jim appeared to be in as they sat in the car en route for Oxford. Jim was driving, as he always did, whilst Dilys was looking through the vocal scores of the music they would be performing that evening, and humming quietly to herself. She and Jim had exchanged scarcely a word that morning. The silence had been involuntary on Jim's part, but deliberate on hers, for she knew exactly the nature of the conversation which would take place once he did start speaking.

At last, a minute or two after they had reached the M40, the silence broke: 'I'm sorry. I really don't know why I was in such a foul mood last night.'

'Don't worry about it, Jim. It's forgotten.'

'I haven't forgotten it. I don't have the right to interrogate you like that and make things so unpleasant for you.'

'It's all right. Don't feel so bad about it.'

'But I do. You haven't done anything to deserve that sort of treatment. I'm just a bad-tempered old sod.'

'No, you're not.'

'Yes, I am. I feel so guilty about the way I treat you sometimes.'

'You always feel guilty about everything.'

'Bloody fool!'

'I beg your pardon?'

'No, not you! Did you see that idiot? It might have knocked five seconds off his journey-time from London to Oxford, I suppose – or fifty years off his life-time. Sorry, what were you saying?'

'Oh, it doesn't matter.'

'Yes, it does. What did you say?'

'You said you felt so guilty about the way you treat me sometimes, and I said you always feel guilty about everything.'

'No, I don't. But I really am sorry. I don't know how you can forgive me when I go on like that.'

'But I have done.'

'I don't see how you can.'

'It's a hell of a lot easier to forgive you for going on like that, than it is to forgive you for going on like this. What exactly do you want me to say? Do you want me to say, "Yes, Jim, you are a bad-tempered old sod, so leave me alone"? Would that make you feel better? Or would it make it easier if I said, "Bless you, you're forgiven, now say three Hail Marys"?'

'What do you mean by that?'

'Well, it's all tied up with religion, isn't it? Anything you do which isn't a hundred per cent virtuous you regard as a sin, so you feel bad about it, and then you have to go to confession to make it all right again.'

'It's not like that.'

'What's it like then?'

'Oh, it's no good trying to explain to you. You don't understand.'

Dilys did not understand, but she bit her tongue, feeling that it would be counter-productive to voice her lack of understanding. They had been down this route before a good many times, and always without any outcome that was satisfactory to either party. Jim, she felt, was a victim of the excessively rigid version of Catholicism which (although Dilys did not realise) Ted had come to reject, in which the two great sins against the Holy Ghost were that of Presumption and that of Despair. You committed the sin of Despair if you felt so guilty that you believed you were beyond God's forgiveness; you committed the sin of Presumption if, instead of being in despair, you told yourself that all you needed to do was go to confession and all would be forgiven, and you could make a fresh start. 'They've got you both ways!' she reflected, especially when the teaching was reinforced by the belief that, even if you thought you were free of sin, this was only because you had forgotten some of the awful things you had done. What a terrible state to get into!

Over the years, Dilys had tried to avoid discussing religion with Jim; it invariably led to conflict, particularly since he had retired. In the early days, before they were married, he had tried to persuade her to convert to Catholicism, saying that, although the Church did not go so far as to ban mixed marriages outright, it did not regard them with any degree of approval. When she resisted his suggestions, by arguing that her hypocrisy in converting to a faith in which she did not believe would constitute a greater sin than he would be committing if he married a non-believer, he changed tack, and concentrated on trying to persuade her to have their children brought up as Catholics. This too she resisted, and in the end his sexual desire proved stronger than his determination to propagate the faith. She was, after all, as Ted had recalled the previous day, an absolute stunner.

Not that Dilys herself had had any qualms at all about marrying Jim. She had been as attracted to him as he was to her, he was an interesting and amusing companion, and, although she did not entirely share his moral convictions, she did admire him for having them; many of the other young men who pursued her seemed to have no motivation whatever other than that of trying to get her into bed. So she married him, and they were content for a good many years. Their two children had arrived quite early in their marriage, which pleased Dilys as much as it did Jim. But, Dilys thought, two was enough, and, rather than risk confrontation by raising an issue on which she knew they would inevitably disagree, she kept quiet, and took matters into her own hands. For Jim's part, he never questioned her on the subject, never appeared to wonder why no more children arrived – which is not to say that he was unaware of the reality of the situation, for he was not stupid either. But at least in those days he had the sense to avoid conflict, whereas these days he sometimes appeared actively to court it.

As things turned out, their younger child, Michael, had eventually decided to embrace Catholicism himself, whereas his sister Jemima, when she went to church at all – mainly for christenings (including those of her own children), weddings, funerals and Christmas – followed the Anglican route. Strangely, it was usually Michael who engaged in doctrinal conflict with his father; combining his undoubtedly genuine faith with the liberalism of his age, he rejected much of the Church's traditional teaching. Truth to tell, he sometimes deliberately took up more extreme positions than his true convictions warranted, largely in order to bait his father: his advocacy of women priests on one occasion nearly brought Jim to a state of apoplexy, and probably would have done so if Dilys had not intervened and told Michael to stop teasing. What was certain, though, was that after Michael grew up, and especially after he got married, Jim had become more and more entrenched in his traditional – as Michael would say, his antediluvian – outlook.

The drive continued in silence until Jim, suddenly remembering that there was a test match still in progress at Lord's, switched on the radio, only to switch it off again with a snort a moment later, having discovered that the start of the day's play had been delayed by rain. After that, the silence resumed, and Dilys found herself thinking about Ted, and what had happened all those years ago. Jim had said that he and Ted were planning to get together, hadn't he? Did that mean she would get to meet Ted herself? If she did, she reflected, she would at last have an opportunity to explain to him about that awful letter which her parents had forced her to write, and which broke her heart. But how much should she tell him? There was, after all, a great deal that she had never told Jim ...

Before Dilys was able to begin answering that question, they arrived in Oxford, where they went their separate ways, Dilys to her pre-concert rehearsal, Jim to Blackwell's to begin a few hours of browsing through bookshops; they would not meet again until after the concert, by which time Jim's mood had lightened considerably, partly because of the music and partly because England – despite their best endeavours, he said sardonically to Dilys later – had eventually managed to win their match. As a result, the return journey was a much less gloomy affair than the one they had endured earlier in the day. Moreover the rain had disappeared and the sun was shining once more.

Contrary to Ted's expectations, Saturday's play in the test match did continue beyond tea-time, largely because play was disrupted by periods of rain, but partly at least because the England batsmen created their own heavy weather before eventually emerging triumphant. Nevertheless Ted was able to return home to Crowthorne that evening, and telephoned Valerie from the train to tell her so.

'Have you already started preparing something for dinner, or would you like to eat out when I get home?'

'I've just started, but I haven't got so far that I can't put what I've done into the fridge and save it till tomorrow. Okay then, yes, that would be nice – where shall we go?'

'Indian?'

'Yes, fine. Shall I ring up and book a table?'

'No, I'll do it from the train.'

Two hours later Valerie and Ted were sitting in their favourite Indian restaurant.

'Not many people here tonight,' Valerie commented.

'We're a bit early. The place will be heaving later on, when the pubs shut. What are you having?'

'Oh, the usual, I think, Chicken Madras. Anyway, how were things with Sophie and Peter?'

'Okay – didn't actually see that much of them. You know what it's like with them, always run off their feet...'

'But you spent the whole of yesterday evening with them, didn't you?'

'Yes, but Sophie was very preoccupied. She'd lost a patient earlier in the day, so conversation at dinner wasn't exactly scintillating...'

'She does get involved, doesn't she?'

'Well, yes, but not normally as much as this. Anyway, I had an early night...'

'Well, you did sound a bit sloshed...'

'Sloshed, me? Never! Anyway, I bet you had a glass or two here on your own...'

'I might have done,' laughed Valerie. 'So, tell me about your drinking partner.'

'Jim? Oh, he was one of my best friends at school. We did everything together – football, cricket – and we even went to France together. He was a fantastic linguist.'

'Better than you?'

'Yes, he was, actually. He did A Level French with me, but whereas I did Latin and English, he did German and Russian – started Russian from scratch in the Sixth Form and got it up to A Level standard in two years.'

'That's not bad going...'

'I'll say, especially when you think of the literature involved – I mean, Gogol and Pushkin, I seem to remember him doing. That really is a tall order when you've only been doing the language for two years.'

At that point the waiter arrived with their order. Once he had left them, Valerie resumed the conversation. 'So this friend of yours, Jim, was it?'

'Yes, Jim.'

'You seem to have had so much in common, so why didn't you keep in touch?'

'I don't know really. Well, I suppose the fact that I went into the R.A.F. and he went to work in London had a lot to do with it. And then when we did go home, we didn't live in the same part of Nottingham, and we didn't go to the same church, so there wasn't too much chance of our bumping into each other either.'

'Funny, really – that seems to happen with boys. Girls seem to make much more effort to keep in touch with their old friends.'

Ted immediately thought of one exception to that rule, but answered: 'Do they? I don't know – maybe that's so, but I don't know why it should be...'

'Oh, the waiter's forgotten to give us any lime pickle – there's some on that table, though. Can you reach it?'

Ted obliged, and Valerie continued: 'So why wasn't Jim going to the match today?'

'Oh, his wife sings with the London Bach Choir, and she has a concert in Oxford this evening, so he was going to Oxford with her.'

'Oh, that's funny – I was reading in the paper today that the Bach Choir are doing *The Dream of Gerontius* at Winchester Cathedral next month, and I was going to ask you if you'd like to go as a birthday treat.'

'That would be really nice. I should like that,' replied Ted. For a few brief seconds it failed to dawn on him that this would inevitably lead to his seeing Dilys again: perhaps it was just as well that their reunion would take place in the company of their respective spouses.

'We could perhaps meet up with your friends afterwards and have a drink, or a meal, or something,' said Valerie.

'Oh yes, I suppose we could. We'll have to find out what their arrangements are.'

'You don't seem terribly enthusiastic!'

'Sorry,' replied Jim, who had actually been thinking about what it would be like to meet Dilys again, and whether he would ever get an explanation for the way things had turned out when they were younger. 'No, on the contrary, I think it's a really nice idea.'

'Well, why don't you give them a ring tomorrow, and then, all being well, I'll ring to book the tickets on Monday.'

'Okay, fine. I love *Gerontius* – I haven't been to a performance of it for ages.'

'I have. I went to one last year.'

'Did you? Where was that?'

'In Reading, you fool – you were singing in it!'

'So I was, I'd forgotten. How silly is that!'

Just after eleven o'clock the following morning Ted went into his study and dialled the number that Jim had given him a couple of days earlier. He heard it ring a dozen or so times, and was just about to replace the receiver when the phone was answered. To his surprise, it was a female voice he heard: 'Hello,' said the voice.

'Hello, er, um... hello, er, is that Dilys?'

It had somehow not occurred to Ted that Dilys, not Jim, might pick up the phone, and now he was somewhat thrown. Naturally, he had anticipated the likelihood of speaking to Dilys at some point – in fact there were times, it seemed, when he thought of little else – but now here he was, suddenly thrust, quite unprepared, into a conversation with her. Or so he thought.

'No, it's her daughter Jemima. Would you like to speak to her?'

'Well, I really wanted to speak to Jim, er, to your father. Is he around at the moment?'

'No, I'm afraid not. Daddy's at church. He'll be back later – about 12.30, I expect, but we're all going out to lunch after that. Mummy's here, though – I'll pass you over. She's better at taking messages than I am. Here she is...'

Ted took a deep breath.

'Hello, Dilys here. Who's calling?'

'Hello, Dilys. I was calling Jim actually, but I understand he's out. I'm an old school friend of his, and we ran into each other at Lord's the other day. My name's Ted, Ted Bryant...'

'Ted! How wonderful to hear you. Jim said he'd met you. It sounds as if you had quite a boozy reunion too – he certainly came home the worse for wear!'

Ted immediately felt a sense of relief that Dilys's tone appeared so casual and relaxed.

'Well, so did I actually. We did have one or two, I suppose...'

'And the rest! But it really is nice to make contact again. Jim said you're planning to get together again some time...'

'Yes, we are. And before too long, I hope. How did the concert go last night?'

'Oh... Pretty well, I think, though it's always difficult to judge when you're actually part of it... But yes, I think it was okay.'

'I believe you're doing *The Dream of Gerontius* in Winchester next month. Will you be singing in it?'

'You bet! I wouldn't miss that for the world – it's one of my favourite works.'

'And mine...'

'Really?'

'Absolutely. Will Jim be going?'

'I'm not sure, but I expect so.'

'Who's singing the Angel?'

'Sarah Walker – it's her farewell performance before she retires from the concert platform. I used to know her quite well – we used to live in Cheltenham before we came up to London, and I sang with the Cheltenham Bach Choir. Sarah Walker was our President...'

'She has a fabulous voice. But listen... This is what we were thinking. Valerie – Valerie's my wife – Valerie and I were thinking that if we went to the performance, we might all be able to meet up afterwards, for a drink, or a meal or something? Is that feasible?'

'Feasible? I think it sounds a great idea.'

'Okay, so we'll phone to make a booking tomorrow, and then I'll get back in touch – we'll take it from there. Does Jim have a ticket already?'

'No, he doesn't, actually. I was going to organise that on Monday, at rehearsal.'

'Well, leave it to me. I'll get one for him, and then we can all sit together.'

'Okay then, that's fine. Er, just one thing, Ted, before you go...'

'Yes?'

'Jim said that when he mentioned my name to you, you said you didn't recall me... Is that true?'

'Er... yes and no.'

'Yes and no?'

'Yes, it's true I said that, and no, what I said wasn't true...'

'You have no idea how relieved I am to hear you say that, Ted. Do you know, your voice hasn't changed a bit... Talk soon... Bye.'

'Neither has yours, Dilly,' Ted whispered to himself, as he replaced the receiver.

Ted sat for a moment. He had just spoken to Dilys for the first time since March 1951. He had been very apprehensive whenever he thought about what this conversation might be like, and now it was suddenly over. It had been functional, friendly, a little tense maybe, though much less so than he had feared, but the ice had at least been broken; he felt that he would be able to manage their next conversation much more easily, and would perhaps get some sort of explanation for the break-up which he had found so devastating. He got up, went into the kitchen, made two cups of coffee, and took them into the sitting-room, where Valerie was going through the mail that had just arrived.

'Is that the mail? That's a bit earlier than usual...'

'Yes, it does make a change to get it before lunch.'

'You know, when they said last year they were going to cut out the second delivery of the day, I actually believed them.'

'What do you mean? They have cut out the second delivery, haven't they?'

'Not really – when you think that up to last year we always got the post before breakfast, I reckon it's the first delivery that's been dropped, not the second.'

'Oh, I see – playing with words again. You never change!'

'Why should I? I'm a linguist, aren't I? And playing with words is what linguists do. Anyway, I just rang Jim about that concert in Winchester.'

'And?'

'Jim wasn't there. I spoke to his wife.'

'What does she sound like?'

'Oh, she sounds very pleasant. Anyway, they are both going to Winchester, so I've said we'll get tickets for Jim and for us – Dilys doesn't need one, of course, because she's singing...'

'Dilys? Is she Welsh?'

Ted hesitated. 'I don't know,' he said at last. 'Why?'

'Well, it's a Welsh name. I used to have a friend at work that was called Dilys. She said that it meant 'perfect, reliable.'

'And was she?'

'No, she wasn't! Far from it, in fact! She had an affair with her boss and they were both caught with their hands in the till!'

'Oh dear! Well, I doubt very much whether this one's like that. Anyway, we'll get the tickets, and then we'll meet afterwards and go for a drink or a meal or something.'

'Sounds a bit vague. Is that as far as you got?'

'Well, it's what you suggested.'

'Yes, but I assumed you'd make more specific arrangements than that. I mean, where do we meet up with Jim? And if we go for a drink or a meal afterwards, who's driving? Or should we stay overnight in Winchester?'

'I don't know. We didn't talk about that. But we've got plenty of time – the concert's over a month away, and we're not even sure that we can get tickets yet. I'll have a word with Jim about it. I shall have to ring him to confirm that we've got tickets anyway.'

'If he's as useless as you are at sorting out the logistics of social events, you'd better let me sort it out with his wife.'

'What do you mean, useless?'

'I don't mean you're totally useless, it's just that you're useless when it comes to important details... I mean, you're actually quite good at making coffee – could I have another one?'

'Yes, dear. Of course, dear. Anything you say, dear. And I'll try not to overlook anything important like putting coffee in the machine...'

Acquiring tickets for the Bach Choir's Winchester Cathedral concert proved no problem, and Ted lost no time in calling Jim. Valerie was out, at the hairdresser's, but her playfully caustic comments from the previous evening were still ringing in Ted's ears. This time it was Jim who answered.

'Hello, Jim. It's Ted.'

'Hello, Ted. How nice to hear you. I'm sorry I missed you yesterday – Dilys told me you'd called. I was at mass – thought you would've been as well...'

'No, I...'

'Don't tell me you're one of those Catholics that's opted out of going to mass on Sunday by pretending that Saturday evening is just as good...'

'Well, no, I...'

'Never mind. I'm sorry I missed you anyway. Funny thing – you know you told me you didn't remember Dilys?'

'Yes...'

'Well, she remembered you.'

'Actually I remembered her once I'd been talking to her on the phone for a few minutes. Anyway, listen... I've got tickets for the *Gerontius* concert in Winchester – one for you as well as two for us, and we were wondering about where to meet, what to do after the concert, and so on. How are you getting there?'

'Oh, we shall go by car. We usually drive to Dilys's out-of-town concerts.'

'Well, we were thinking of having a drink or a meal together afterwards, but if you're driving all the way back to London...'

'Oh no, we won't be... We'll be staying with our son Michael – he lives in Winchester, and his house is within walking distance of the cathedral, so there's no problem with drinking and driving. I suppose that's what was on your mind?'

'Yes, it was.'

'Well, why don't you and – sorry, what's your wife's name?'

'Valerie.'

'Why don't you and Valerie stay over as well, and then we can have a meal together when the concert's over. There's no shortage of hotels and restaurants near the cathedral.'

'Okay, that sounds like a good idea.'

'I'll tell you what – are you coming up to Lord's for the one-dayer against Zimbabwe next week?'

'I haven't decided yet – I'm not as keen on the one-day game as I am on test cricket.'

'Neither am I really – not proper cricket, is it? But I generally go along anyway. I just thought that if you were going we could finalise arrangements for Winchester over a drink.'

'Sounds like a good idea. Why don't we do that? I'll just have to check with my daughter to make sure it's okay to stay with her, but I'm sure it will be. She and her husband aren't often away at the same time, but even if they are they don't mind my staying there on my own, so there shouldn't be a problem. Let's do that then.'

'Okay, but I'll tell you what. Why not stay at our place for the night? Dilys will be pleased to see you, and she's a fantastic cook, I can tell you that for nothing. What do you say?'

'Well, if you're sure that would be okay with Dilys.'

'Yes, absolutely certain. No problems at all.'

'Then that would be splendid. I should really enjoy that.'

'That's settled then. I'll see you in the pavilion at Lord's next Wednesday. One thing I can promise you is that a dinner cooked by Dilys is likely to be more enjoyable than a one-day match between England and Zimbabwe! See you next week, then – goodbye, Ted!'

'Bye, Jim.'

Immediately after speaking to Jim, Ted went to his only recently acquired computer, and searched for hotels and restaurants in the centre of Winchester. By the time Valerie arrived home from having her hair done, Ted had already not only booked a hotel room, but also a table at a restaurant just around the corner from the cathedral, an achievement which he announced to his wife without delay, not without a certain degree of self-satisfaction.

'Ted! I'm impressed! How did you know where to book?'

'I did a search on the internet.'

'I'm even more impressed, Ted – you're a reformed character, I take it all back!'

'There's another thing too – I'm seeing Jim at Lord's again next Wednesday, and I've been invited to stay over at their place on Wednesday night. Is that okay?'

'Yes, that's fine, we haven't got anything on that night. Anyway, what about making me one of your lovely cups of coffee – the coffee they give you at the hairdresser's is disgusting...'

That evening, in their apartment in Downshire Hill, Ted's daughter Sophie and her husband Peter were enjoying a quiet evening together, something which, given their busy professional lives, happened much too rarely. Today, however, both of them had arrived home early, and Sophie was able, for once, to use her not inconsiderable cooking skills, rather than retrieving something from the freezer and putting it in the microwave or – which was worse but which seemed to happen with depressing frequency – getting a take-away on her way home from the hospital.

Sophie was an excellent cook, and derived much pleasure from presenting high-quality dishes at her table; whether it was for a dinner-party with half-a-dozen guests, or just for herself and Peter, she made the same effort and achieved the same degree of success. She found it relaxing, a way of shedding the burden which her job as a doctor placed upon her – not that she didn't enjoy her job. The influence of her maternal heritage was clear; her mother, Arlette, had not been the most brilliant of cooks herself, but she did pass on the basics of French cuisine to her daughter. And then, of course, Sophie had spent a lot of time in France, staying first of all at her grand-parents' house just outside Béziers and, after they died, with various cousins, aunts and uncles, most of them living on or within easy reach of the Mediterranean coast between Narbonne and Cannes.

Once Sophie had completed her work in the kitchen, and she and Peter were settled at the dining-table, Peter suddenly said: 'How would living in Montpellier grab you?'

'Living in Montpellier? How could we? What do you mean?'

'Well, not *in* Montpellier, just outside Montpellier actually.'

'Talk sense, Peter. We both work here in London, and we're years away from retirement yet. We can't possibly go to live in France.'

'Not permanently, no, of course we can't. But that's not what I mean. You know we've often talked about the possibility of buying a place in France, a place where we can retreat to and, of course, since you mention it, ultimately retire to.'

'Yes, I know, but that's always seemed a pipe-dream, or at least a long way into the future. Why the sudden upsurge of interest now?'

'For two reasons. First of all I've heard today that our profits are up 35% on last year, and that means that my income will be considerably higher this year too, and secondly, because I was browsing on the internet and came across a property which might fill the bill. Oh, and there's a third reason – the pound is particularly strong against the euro at the moment, and that might not be the case for ever. So the conjunction of those three factors seems especially propitious.'

'You're beginning to sound more like an astrologer than a lawyer. But tell me about this property. You say it's in Montpellier?'

'It's actually in a village just outside Montpellier.'

'Well, you know how much I adore Montpellier, it's one of my favourite places, so that's a good start.'

'That's why I started looking there.'

'What's the house like then?'

'I'll show it you on the internet after dinner. There are quite a few photos on there. It's big – it has five bedrooms...'

'Five bedrooms! Are you mad?'

'No, I'm not. Just think. We wouldn't want to live in a place where we couldn't entertain people, would we? And when you have a place with a pool in the south of France there will never be a shortage of friends and relatives who want to come and stay. More to the point, although some people would regard that as a definite disadvantage, you'd positively revel in it!'

'All right, maybe... It depends. So... Five bedrooms... How many bathrooms and loos?'

'One bathroom...'

'Only one bathroom, for goodness' sake!'

'No, wait a minute. One bathroom, three shower-rooms and three loos. And it's got a big kitchen, a big sitting-room, a big dining-room, a big study...'

'Okay, it's big, I get the picture. What about the outside?'

'It has quite a large garden, with terraces front and back, a pool 10 metres by 5 metres, and...'

'Is it in a built-up area?'

'No, it doesn't appear to be. It's on the outskirts of a village called Saint-Gély, and it's on the edge of the *garrigue*.'

'Well, it does sound nice – I do know Saint-Gély, Saint-Gély-du-Fesc to give it its full name. Hey, hang on a moment – there's a golf course there, I seem to remember – are you sure that's not what attracted your interest?'

'I did notice that, I have to admit, but not until after I'd been quite impressed by the other aspects of it.'

'Okay, we'll have a look at it after dinner. Are you sure we can afford it?'

'Yes, I think we can. I'd need to do a few sums to make sure, but the figures seem to work out okay from what I can see so far.'

As soon as dinner was finished, Peter and Sophie took their coffee into the study, sat down in front of the computer, and looked at the details of the property in Saint-Gély.

'I can see why you were impressed,' said Sophie at length. 'It really does look very nice.'

'That's what I thought.'

'The only thing is, photographs are all very well, but a clever photographer can make anywhere look good. We'd need to have a good look at it ourselves, and I just don't see how we could find time to get away just at the moment, even for a couple of days. I couldn't anyway, that's for sure.'

'Neither could I. At least I probably could if we were in a position to make an offer for it or something like that, but for a preliminary visit just to see if it's worth thinking about, that's a different matter. There is one thing that occurred to me, though...'

'What's that?'

'Isn't your mother over there at the moment? She could perhaps go and give it the once-over for us...'

'Well, yes, she is over there, you're right, she's staying with Tante Émilie near Nîmes. I know she'd love the idea, and I'm sure she'd love to go and look at it too, but I wouldn't really trust her judgement – she does tend to have her own agenda.'

'Yes, I know what you mean. But what's the alternative?'

'Well, if we're going to ask anybody to have a look at it on our behalf, I'd rather trust Dad than anybody else. He'd probably jump at the opportunity too – he's always looking for excuses to pop across the Channel, and he might really enjoy doing that for us.'

'I'd go along with that. Sounds a good idea to me. Why don't you ask him?'

'Yes, all right, I will. I'll give him a ring now.'

As Sophie had predicted, Ted jumped at the idea, especially when she assured him that she and Peter would be paying his air fare. His only caveat was that, because of his visit to Lord's and to Jim and Dilys's house the following week, his trip to Montpellier could not take place until the week after that. That did not present a problem to Sophie and Peter, and so it was agreed that Ted would visit the villa on their behalf.

After his conversation with Sophie, Ted told Valerie about the errand his daughter was entrusting him with, and asked her if she would like to go along with him.

'No, I've got a lot on that week, and I'll only get in the way anyway. You'll have much more fun on your own. You know how much you love being in France.'

'So do you.'

'Yes, but not the way you do. I mean, France has been half of your life, if not more. You feel at home there.'

Ted did not try too hard to persuade Valerie to change her mind; he knew that fundamentally she was right, and he really fancied doing this trip on his own.

Tony Whelpton

Chapter Two

The following Wednesday, Ted caught the 8.44 train from Crowthorne to Reading, where he needed to change for Paddington. From Paddington, he travelled by underground to St. John's Wood, then walked the short distance from the underground station to Lord's cricket ground. As he entered the ground, a thought occurred to him: he and Jim had not arranged a specific place for their meeting. He need not have worried. For a start, there were comparatively few members there so early in the day for a one-day match against Zimbabwe. And then a quick glance inside the members' bar was sufficient: there was Jim, sitting at the table where he had first seen him a couple of weeks earlier, with a glass of red wine already in place before him.

'Ted! There you are! Good to see you – let me get you a drink!'

'Hello, Jim. No thanks, no – it's a bit early in the day for me, I'm afraid. If I drink anything during the day it's most likely to be gin, and if I start drinking gin at this time of the morning, I'll be flat out by lunch-time. I'll have a coffee if that's all right with you.'

'Yes, of course. Whatever you say – that's fine.'

Ted's coffee arrived quickly – at least there was something to be gained from being at Lord's for one of the less popular matches of the season – and the two old friends resumed the conversation they had started at their previous meeting: a mish-mash of reminiscences and information updates. After a while, a ripple of applause told them that play was about to start, so they made their way out of the bar and took their seats. Truth to tell, the match was not sufficiently riveting to stop their conversation; nor, however, was their conversation so significant as to warrant being recorded. In essence, they just chatted.

When the match finally ended, Ted and Jim were still relatively sober, despite having paid their customary respects to the barman during the interval. Probably the fact that there is only one interval in a one-day match, rather than the normal breaks for lunch and tea was the main reason for their sobriety – although Jim did say that, just as he was leaving home that morning, Dilys had given him a stern warning to the effect that, if they did come home very much the worse for wear, she would not let either of them in.

The journey by underground from St. John's Wood to Gloucester Road, Kensington, was quite quick; they only had to make one change, at Green Park. When they emerged from the station, Ted stopped off at a florist's to buy some flowers for his hostess, and then Jim led Ted into

what seemed a labyrinth of streets, with near-
identical Victorian villas; all Ted could have told
you was that they appeared to be somewhere in
the area bordered by Gloucester Road, Cromwell
Road and Earls Court. After a short while the
street down which they were walking opened
out into what was effectively a large square, in
the centre of which was a beautifully laid-out and
exceptionally well-groomed garden, enclosed by
railings and surrounded on all sides by more tall
Victorian villas, each with a stylish portico and a
flight of steps leading up to the front door.

'This is it,' said Jim. 'This is our humble
abode.'

'Hardly humble,' thought Ted, 'this must have
cost a bomb!' – although what he actually said
was: 'What lovely gardens you look out onto.'

'Yes,' replied Jim. 'The gardeners who look
after them regularly get awards for the best
garden square in London.'

He led Ted through the front door, then into
the lift. At the third floor they got out, and Jim
opened the door facing them.

'Dilys, we're here,' he called, closing the door
behind him.

'I'll be with you in two minutes,' came a reply
from a disembodied voice. 'You can be showing
Ted his room.'

'It's through here,' said Jim, opening a door on
their right, revealing a fairly large and very
elegantly furnished bedroom. 'This is your room.
You have your own bathroom through there.
Why don't you just drop your bag there for a

moment, and come and meet Dilys – she'll be out in a minute.'

Ted obediently put his bag on the floor at the side of the bed, and followed Jim back into the drawing-room, furnished with a carefully chosen mixture of the antique and the modern, with high ceilings, an ornate frieze, and enormous French windows leading onto a balcony which overlooked the gardens which Ted had admired when they arrived.

'Scotch?' enquired Jim. 'Gin?'

'Gin, thanks, Jim.'

'Scotch for me now, I think. And gin for you and Dilys. That's her usual tipple.'

No sooner had Jim poured the drinks than a door at the other end of the drawing-room opened.

'Hello, Ted. How nice to meet you again after all these years,' said Dilys. And she kissed him on the cheek.

If ever Ted Bryant had seriously entertained the notion that Dilly Anderson had grown, at the age of sixty-seven, into a dumpy, maybe fat and ugly creature, the evidence now before his eyes was enough to persuade him otherwise. Sixty-seven she may have been – actually, of course, he knew for a fact that she *was* sixty-seven – but, thought Ted, he knew fifty-year-olds who carried their age less well than Dilys did. She may not have been as slim as she had been at seventeen, but she was well-proportioned and elegant, her long, blonde hair, with a fringe that parted in the middle, framing a beautiful face whose wrinkles only added to its charm. She was wearing a Dolce & Gabbana fit-and-flare dress, made from a printed fabric quite appropriate for a Cordon Bleu cook, with images of vegetables typical of southern Italy; even Ted could recognise it as being a designer dress, although he had probably never even heard of Dolce & Gabbana. In other words, she was still an absolute stunner; simply a few years older than she had been when he last saw her.

'It's lovely to see you too,' said Ted, offering the flowers which he now felt were totally inadequate, being surpassed in beauty by the woman who stood before him.

'How sweet,' said Dilys. 'Thank you, Ted, I'll just put them in some water.'

When she returned, they spent ten minutes making small talk until Dilys announced that she needed to return to the kitchen, and that Ted and Jim had better go and change, because dinner would be ready in fifteen minutes.

When Ted returned to the drawing-room, Jim was already there; Dilys was carrying dishes through from the kitchen to the dining-room.

'You may as well come straight into the dining-room, Ted,' said Jim. 'We're virtually ready to start.'

'I hope you like fish, Ted,' Dilys interjected. 'Because we're having fish followed by fish, I'm afraid.'

'That's all right with me,' Ted reassured her. 'I love fish.'

'Jim said he was sure you would do, seeing you've spent so much time in France. Look – you sit there, opposite Jim, and I'll sit on the end, so I can get out to the kitchen easily. Jim, would you pour out some wine?'

Jim duly poured out three glasses of white Burgundy as Dilys brought out the first course.

'Mmm, scallops, I adore scallops,' said Ted.

'Me too,' said Jim. Dilys does them with Puy lentils. It's a superb combination. We came across it in Provence a few years ago, and then we started seeing it in TV cookery programmes over here.'

'Well, Provençal cooking takes some beating,' said Ted.

'Do you go to France very often, Ted?' inquired Dilys.

'Not as often as I did at one time,' replied Ted. 'But then I was married to a Frenchwoman at the time, so we often went over to stay with various members of her family.'

'You say you *were* married to her?' asked Dilys. 'You're not still married then?'

'Not to her, I'm not,' replied Ted. 'We got divorced years ago.'

'Divorced? I thought you were a Catholic!' exclaimed Jim, looking shocked.

'I was...'

Before Jim could react, Dilys jumped in with great alacrity, because she knew from previous experience where this conversation was now heading: 'Which part of France did she come from, Ted?'

'She came from the Languedoc. Between Béziers and Montpellier.'

'Montpellier, that's a gorgeous place,' said Jim. 'Or at least it used to be. I haven't been to Montpellier for years.'

'Funnily enough,' said Ted, 'I'm going there next week. Why don't you come with me?'

He went on to explain to Jim and Dilys the mission that was being entrusted to him by his daughter, and by the time they had finished eating their first course all but the most minute details of what was now to be their joint venture had been agreed. What's more, Jim was so enthusiastic about the project that he appeared to have completely forgotten the exchange in which Dilys had perceived such potential danger.

The main course was a perfectly cooked and equally well-presented sea bass, which was greeted by the two men with even greater enthusiasm than the seared scallops. Dilys accepted graciously their fulsome compliments, to which she was by no means unaccustomed, such was her culinary reputation among their circle of friends.

'Right,' said Dilys at length, 'that's your French trip sorted out. Now we need to talk about Winchester, don't we? I'm so glad you and Valerie are coming to our concert, Ted.'

'We're delighted too,' replied Ted. 'We're really looking forward to it.'

'Have you heard the Bach Choir sing before – live, I mean?'

'Yes, I have actually. I was in Birmingham at Easter, three or four years ago, and I went to their performance of the *St. Matthew Passion* in Symphony Hall. Funnily enough, Sarah Walker was one of the soloists then too. Good Friday, I think it was.'

'Yes, it would have been. We often do the *Matthew Passion* in Symphony Hall on Good Friday. What's more, I was singing in that concert.'

'Well, I never!'

'And I was in the audience,' added Jim. 'What a shame we didn't know – we could have got together a few years earlier!'

'How long have you been singing with the Bach Choir, Dilys?' asked Ted.

'Oh, it must be thirteen or fourteen years now, I suppose. It was a year or two after we moved from Cheltenham to London that I joined. I'd been singing with the Cheltenham Bach Choir for a few years before that, and they were pretty good – I understand they're even better now – but I was a bit hesitant at putting myself forward for such a prestigious choir. But I came through the audition okay, and I've really enjoyed it ever since.'

'What voice part do you sing?'

'Soprano 2. I used to be a first soprano, but at the last re-audition I was asked to move down a notch because my top notes were getting a bit dodgy – sign of age, I'm afraid! I wasn't very pleased, but it was a choice between that and giving up altogether. But tell me, didn't Jim say that you sing too?'

'Yes, I sing with the Reading Bach Choir.'

'What voice?'

'Second bass – the lowest of the low.'

'Ha, ha – we had a conductor in Cheltenham who used to call the second basses the Dyno-Rod section...'

'Yes, that's about right,' laughed Ted.

'How big is the choir?'

'Oh, it's about fifty or sixty strong. Frankly, I'd prefer to sing in a rather bigger choir, but it's the best one in the area.'

'You should come and join us – we have quite a few out-of-town members.'

'I'm not sure I'd be good enough to pass the audition.'

'That's what I thought too – but you don't find out if you don't try.'

From there the conversation moved on to the practical side of their forthcoming meeting in Winchester, before passing on to more frivolous, not to say hilarious, topics as the wine continued to flow.

By the time they went to bed they were all in the advanced state of inebriation which a few hours earlier would have guaranteed Ted and Jim's exclusion from the house. Ted slept very heavily, and in the morning, by the time he had dressed, showered and made his way to the drawing-room it was already half-past nine. Jim was sitting reading the newspaper.

'Ah, good morning, Ted. Did you sleep well?'

'I did indeed,' replied Ted. 'Like the proverbial log. I can't remember when I last slept as late as this.'

'Ah, the perils of alcohol,' laughed Jim. 'Dilys was up with the lark though, and she kept up with us pretty well, I thought. I'm afraid she's gone out already, so she asked me to say goodbye for her. Anyway, come into the kitchen, I've got coffee going.'

'The perils of alcohol indeed,' thought Ted, who suddenly realised that he would have happily sacrificed a couple of hours in bed for the pleasure of saying goodbye to Dilys properly. Considering the nature of their previous acquaintance, and what had happened during the subsequent few weeks, Ted was agreeably surprised to find that meeting Dilys again had turned out to be such a relaxed affair: they were, of course, a good deal older, and they had spent the best part of a life-time apart since then. In addition, Dilys was on home ground, she was clearly a consummate hostess anyway, and, Ted reflected, she was brimming with self-confidence and well able to guide things in the direction she desired – as he had discovered, to his undoubted and intense delight, all those years before, when she had chosen their route from the school dance back to her house. The only regret he felt was that they had not been alone together at any point during the evening, and consequently he was no nearer to getting an explanation for her having written such a curt letter.

Chapter Three

The following Tuesday Jim and Ted met at Heathrow, and checked in for their flight to Montpellier. Once they were on board, Jim immediately said, 'Okay, Jim, what's it to be? Gin and tonic?'

'Good God!' said Ted. 'Steady on! Don't forget I've got to drive when we get off at the other end.'

'That's a couple of hours away,' countered Jim. 'The effects will have worn off by then.'

'No, Jim. I'll stick to coffee till this evening. Then I'll start with a *pastis* and take it from there.'

'That's more like it,' said Jim. 'But listen, I'm happy to do the driving if you like. I'm used to driving in France.'

'Would that mean you wouldn't have a drink now then?' asked Ted.

'No fear! But I'd be okay.'

'Then no. I'll do the driving, Jim. You do the drinking. And I'm used to driving in France too, remember.'

'Of course you are, Ted. Sorry!'

So Jim had a glass of red wine and Ted had a coffee.

When they landed in Montpellier they picked up their hire car, a little silver Renault Clio, and Ted drove onto the A9 motorway, by-passing the southern suburbs of Montpellier before turning off and entering the hilly region to the north-west of the city.

'Look at that!' said Ted, indicating the line of white and pink oleanders which filled the central reservation of the motorway as far as the eye could see. 'You'd never see anything like that in England, would you?'

'You certainly wouldn't,' Jim agreed. 'The authorities might agree in principle, but the plan would soon be strangled at birth either on grounds of cost or else, because oleander's poisonous, some silly child might snuff it after leaning out of the car window, grabbing a handful and stuffing it into its mouth...'

'Not that the French authorities aren't equally capable of making crass decisions. But I have to say, I really do feel at home whenever I come to France.'

'Oh, so do I. I've often thought I'd like to live here.'

'Why didn't you?'

'Well, apart from the obvious point that GCHQ doesn't employ anybody in France – not officially, anyway! – there's the not entirely insignificant fact that they don't play cricket, and it takes far too long to get to Lord's, even by Eurostar. Watch out! You need to turn right here for Saint-Gély-du-Fesc.'

'Okay, seen it,' said Ted as he turned. 'Just one kilometre to go, then we turn left into the *rue des Cigales*. Then 150 metres up the hill and we turn left into a little private drive.'

'What time are we meeting the agent?' asked Jim.

'Not till four o'clock, but I thought I'd like to get up there a bit earlier and have a nose round the place before we get taken on a carefully-planned promotional tour.'

'Good idea,' agreed Jim. 'Oh look, there's the *rue des Cigales*.'

A couple of minutes later the little Clio drew to a halt alongside a thick conifer hedge which was, sadly, too tall for one to be able to see what lay on the other side, although, Ted reflected, the advantages of such a tall hedge would be greater for those who found themselves on the other side of it.

Ted switched off the engine, and the two men got out. A few metres along from where they had parked, they came across a big wrought-iron gate, the main entrance to the property. But almost before they had a chance to see what was beyond the gate, their nostrils were regaled with the perfume, first of lavender, then of wild thyme, and finally of rosemary, all of which seemed to grow in abundance in this idyllic garden in which also grew conifers of different species, copper beeches, olive trees and oleanders, and right in front of the house, providing shade for one of what they would shortly discover were four or five different terraces, a palm tree so well-established that it resembled an enormous pineapple.

'Wow!' said Ted, looking around and soaking in the atmosphere, so typical of that part of France. 'What about that then, Jim?'

'Wow indeed,' replied Jim. 'It makes me feel I can't possibly wait until this evening for that first *pastis*!'

'I know what you mean,' said Ted. 'There's only one place on earth where this could be. No wonder the French believe that France was God's first and most successful creation. Let's hope the house lives up to its setting!'

They walked round the outside of the house.

'God, this place is enormous!' said Jim. 'Surely it's too big for them – I mean, they've got no kids, have they?'

'No, they haven't, but they're looking for a big place anyway, because, as they said, when you have a house in this part of the world you'll never be short of friends who want to come and stay.'

'To say nothing of ageing parents!'

'Exactly!' Ted grinned. 'I think I could cope with the job of permanent caretaker in a place like this – as long as I didn't have too much work to do!'

The original house was obviously quite old, but had been extended greatly, especially, it would appear, over the last thirty years or so. The new sections, however, fitted in so well with the basic design that only a close examination would reveal exactly which bits were old and which were new. The whole roof was covered with traditional curved terracotta tiles, the walls rendered and painted beige, and those windows which were not used for ingress or egress were protected by elegantly bowed wrought-iron bars. The whole property was in splendid condition, and Ted's first impressions were distinctly favourable.

After their initial inspection, about an hour or so remained before they were due to meet the agent, so Ted and Jim drove down into the centre of the village to see what amenities were on offer there.

Everything necessary seemed to be there: *boucherie, boulangerie, charcuterie,* restaurant, bar, etc. The village seemed to pass all the tests, especially the bar, where Jim had his customary red wine and Ted a small beer. As they drank, Jim perused the local paper, which he had just bought at the little shop next door to the bar. After two or three minutes he grunted with disgust.

'Do you know, Ted, whenever I come to France I buy the local rag, and every time I look at it I feel as if I've seen it all before. The photos of teams of *boules* players, old people on outings, all the details of the local yoga and judo classes – even the news, fatal car accidents, neighbours' squabbles, vicious murders – it's always the same. Total waste of money!'

'Lucky it only cost you one euro then, Jim,' Ted chuckled.

With that they got up, got into the car, and made their way back to the villa, where they saw the agent, a woman in her thirties, standing waiting for them.

'I hope you're going to talk to her in French, Ted,' said Jim. 'You know what these people tend to be like. They always assume the English don't speak French, and they think their own pathetic attempts to speak English are in some way comprehensible.'

'I know what you mean,' replied Ted. 'We'll see how it goes. Of course she doesn't actually know we're not French, she just knows that we're visiting on behalf of a prospective purchaser from England, and that my name is Bryant.'

The agent duly approached Jim, holding out her hand. "Ow do you do, monsieur Bryant? I am ze agent for zis property.'

She pronounced 'Bryant' as if it were a French name, and 'agent' and 'property' as if they were French words. That was enough for Jim. *'Non, mademoiselle, vous vous trompez. Je suis Monsieur Durand, Jacques Durand. Voici Monsieur Bryant – il a un nom de famille anglais parce que son père était anglais.'*[1]

---

[1] 'No, you're mistaken. I am Monsieur Durand, Jacques Durand. This is Monsieur Bryant – he has an English surname because his father was English.'

'Well, at least that bit of it's true,' thought Ted to himself as he shook the agent by the hand and began to speak to her in French.

The agent seemed not a little relieved that she did not have to persevere with maintaining an English conversation well beyond her capabilities, and which would have been extremely painful for all concerned, for the fluency with which both Jim and Ted spoke French – hardly surprising after a life-time spent using the language professionally – easily convinced her that she was dealing with two fellow-countrymen, rather than the two Anglo-Saxons she had been led to expect.

When the tour of the house was completed, Ted thanked the agent for showing them round, and said what an impressive property it was, whilst stressing that they were not the actual purchasers and did not have the authority even to express an opinion on whether the people they were representing would be willing to meet the asking-price, or anything like it. The agent did not seem in the least perturbed by this, and simply shook them by the hand and left.

As soon as Ted and Jim were back in the car, Ted said: 'Well, Monsieur Durand – Jacques Durand – you're a cheeky old bugger, aren't you!'

'I know,' replied Jim. 'Good fun, wasn't it! Let's go back to the hotel and have a proper drink.'

'What a good idea,' said Ted. 'Perhaps Monsieur Durand will buy the first round!'

Jim laughed. *'Ce n'est pas impossible!'*[2].

They returned to Montpellier and checked in at their hotel: a very smart establishment, far removed from the type of budget hotel which Ted would have booked for himself. But then, of course, it was Ted's daughter Sophie who had made the booking and who would be picking up the bill. Jim's first move was towards the bar, but Ted hesitated: 'Look, Jim, I know we said we'd have a drink as soon as we got here, but I feel so hot and sticky I'd prefer to shower and change first, if that's okay with you.'

'Yes, of course, Ted. I'll just have a quick one and then I'll go and get showered too. But I feel so parched...'

'Okay, Jim, that's fine with me. Shall we meet here in, say, forty minutes?'

'Yes,' Jim agreed. 'I'll see you here in forty minutes.'

Ted returned to his room, whilst his friend made his way into the bar, at that time unoccupied except for the barman, and a lady sitting alone at the bar. Jim greeted them both and ordered a *pastis,* but noticing the lady's glass was almost empty, he asked her if she would like a drink too. She smiled and accepted his invitation, saying that she would like a *kir framboise.* The barman served them, and then

---

[2] 'That's not beyond the bounds of possibility.'

busied himself with arranging some glasses at the far end of the bar.

Jim's new drinking-companion was by no means young, but was a few years younger than Jim; she had dark hair, dark eyes, and a complexion which suggested that her origins were in that part of France, but, judging by her fashionable and figure-hugging scarlet dress as well as by the way she spoke, Jim would not have been surprised to find that she was a Parisienne.

They exchanged pleasantries to begin with, but it was not long before Jim learned that, like him, she actually lived in London, and was in Montpellier on a flying visit to see an elderly aunt whose health was giving cause for concern. Jim undoubtedly found the French lady attractive and agreeable to talk to, and was just about to ask her name before telling her that they would shortly be joined by his travelling-companion, when the door of the bar opened, and in walked Ted.

'Christ almighty!' Ted exploded. 'Bloody hell, Arlette, what the hell are you doing here?'

'I might ask you the same question, Ted,' replied the former Mrs Bryant, who at once drained her glass and flounced out of the bar, leaving the two men standing open-mouthed, with Jim in particular wondering what on earth had just happened to disrupt a perfectly innocent, and until that moment perfectly enjoyable, social encounter.

After what seemed an eternity, it was Jim who broke the rather embarrassed silence: 'Come on, Ted, let me get you a drink and you can tell me what on earth's going on.'

Ted simply nodded, then sat down, while Jim ordered another two glasses of *pastis* from the still bemused barman.

'Okay then, Ted, explain.'

'There's not much to explain really,' said Ted. 'It's just that... that was my first wife, Arlette.'

'Sophie's mother?'

'Yes. I had no idea we were likely to run into her, or I wouldn't have come.'

'She seemed perfectly civilised and house-trained to me. You've never said a great deal about her, but I had assumed that she must have been a harridan of the first water.'

'You can say that again! On first acquaintance you'd think butter wouldn't melt in her mouth, but she'd eat you for breakfast!'

'You seem to have emerged relatively unscathed...'

'With the emphasis on *relatively*.'

'But what would she be doing here? Would she have known you were going to be here?'

'No, I don't think so, but I think I can see how it came about. In the first place, she has a lot of relatives in this area, so it's not particularly surprising that she should be in this part of the world. And then this hotel was chosen for us by Sophie, who obviously knew of it herself. And – the final piece of the jig-saw – Sophie has probably been here with her mother, because it's one of the smartest places in town.'

'You don't think Sophie knew all along her mother would be here?'

'I doubt it. She's usually fairly careful about even making references to her when we're together. No, I think it was just an unlucky chance.'

'Maybe,' replied Jim, 'but when you've been working for GCHQ for a few years you tend to be fairly sceptical about unlucky chances! Anyway, what about another *pastis*?'

'Okay, but let's go somewhere else. I don't want to risk bumping into Arlette again.'

'Don't be daft, Ted. Think about it. You'd have a better chance of bumping into her again somewhere else than you would here. The way she waltzed out, she's not going to come back in here while we're about. Come on, let's have another one.'

Ted acquiesced, but when Jim returned with their drinks, he found that Ted had moved to a different table – one from which they could easily see, and be seen from, the doorway of the bar.

'How long is it since you and Arlette got divorced?'

'About twenty-five years,' replied Ted.

'Twenty-five years!' Jim repeated in a tone of disbelief. 'How on earth can such rancour last for a quarter of a century? What happened to make it all so bitter?'

'It's a long story,' said Ted, 'and I'm not going even to try to go through the whole lot, because an atmosphere built up over a long period of time, and there were scores of incidents which seem trivial in themselves now, but had a cumulative effect over a period of time.'

'Like straws on a camel's back.'

'Exactly. But I'll just give you one example. Arlette was always convinced I was having an affair with someone else, and nothing I could do or say would make her think otherwise.'

'And were you?'

'Was I what?'

'Having an affair.'

'No, I wasn't, and I never did while I was married to Arlette. But it did put a colossal damper on our social life, which eventually almost ceased to exist.'

'I can see that would cause problems, but that's all well in the past, isn't it?'

'Yes, it is, but there were a lot of other things as well, both during our marriage and since. Anyway, I didn't come to Montpellier to rake over the embers of my first marriage. What are we going to do about dinner?'

'I suppose it's basically a choice between eating in and eating out, isn't it?'

'Yes, I suppose it is. I don't want to meet Arlette in the restaurant as well as in the bar, but I know that Sophie said the hotel restaurant is particularly good.'

They agreed to have a surreptitious look inside the restaurant, but, just as they left the bar, they saw Arlette emerge from the restaurant and walk off in the other direction. Jim and Ted exchanged a glance, then, without saying another word, went into the hotel restaurant.

They enjoyed an excellent meal, and passed a pleasant, convivial evening. But although they covered all manner of topics – trivial, serious, even deep – throughout the rest of the evening not a word was spoken concerning Arlette. But by the time he returned to his room, Ted felt as if a cloud had come over this trip which had been intended to be a happy, relaxed old-boys' outing; not a thunderous, black storm-cloud perhaps, but enough to pose something of a threat, and he could not help thinking that something had changed in his relationship with his old school-pal.

It was some time before Ted fell asleep that night; instead, he lay awake reflecting on what had happened, and in particular Jim's observations on such bitterness lasting for a quarter of a century. Of course Jim was right; it was ridiculous to allow such emotions to persist year after year, especially if the people concerned rarely or never saw each other. But was it in Ted's power to make peace, or even sign a non-aggression pact? Nothing would please him more, he thought, especially since it would make Sophie's life a good deal easier if her biological parents ceased to be engaged in a permanent state of virtually open hostility. It takes two to start a quarrel, or at least, that is the commonly held belief. Ted's experience, however, tended to suggest otherwise: it only needs one seriously determined person to create a row out of nothing. All it takes is a series of abusive remarks, each one slightly more barbed than the last, which keep coming until the target of the remarks feels obliged to offer at least a token defence. That is the ultimate mistake, because at that point the battle is joined.

Such were the thoughts passing through Ted's mind until, at last, he fell asleep, still seeing no way forward. When he awoke, the warmth of the Mediterranean sun was already making its presence felt, and all the ideas which had been preoccupying him to such an extent a few hours before were now dissipated. He looked at his watch; to his surprise it was already eight o'clock; at home he was usually up before 6.30. Suddenly the phone rang.

'Hello.'

'Good morning, Ted, it's Jim. Are you conscious yet?'

'More or less,' replied Ted. 'How about you?'

'Just had a shave and a shower. Should be ready in ten minutes.'

'It'll take me a little longer. Shall I see you in the breakfast-room at, say, 8.30?'

'Yes, sure, see you then.'

Ted quickly showered and dressed, then made his way to the restaurant, where he found Jim already waiting for him. They located a vacant table, ordered coffee, and proceeded to have breakfast. Suddenly, Ted heard a voice behind him: '*Bonjour, monsieur*. Good morning, Ted. Do you mind if I join you?'

Jim turned and looked at Ted, but said nothing, feeling that it was Ted's place to respond rather than his. Ted, visibly embarrassed, heard himself say none the less: 'Not at all, Arlette. Sit down and I'll order some more coffee. I believe you two have already met, but you may not realise, Arlette, that Jim here is a very old friend indeed. We went through school together. Jim, this is Arlette.'

'Very pleased to meet you properly, madame,' said Jim. 'Ted has told me a lot about you.'

'That doesn't sound a very propitious start,' said Arlette. 'But listen, Ted, I wanted to apologise for the way I behaved last night.'

Ted felt slightly uncomfortable, not to say wary, being suspicious of any apology coming from Arlette, but he mumbled: 'That's all right. Don't worry about it.'

'It took me completely by surprise, you understand, seeing you here, and then your reaction to finding me here was so aggressive...'

'Here we go,' thought Ted, 'the sword is always two-edged.'

'...and Jim and I had been having such an enjoyable conversation, hadn't we, Jim?'

'Well yes, indeed we had,' said Jim.

'What has brought you two down here then?'

Ted had to think quickly. He realised that telling Arlette the truth could lead to trouble, for she was sure to feel offended if she realised Sophie had preferred his opinion to Arlette's, especially given the fact that she was already on the spot.

'Somebody asked us to come and check out a property he's thinking of buying, that's all,' said Ted. 'And he thought sending out two French-speakers who have a lot of time on their hands would be a sensible way of going about it, given that he would have to be off work for three or four days if he came himself.'

'I see,' said Arlette. 'Tell me, Ted, do you remember my aunt Julie, who lives at Juvignac?'

'Yes, I remember her well,' replied Ted. 'She was always very nice to me.' (Even when you weren't, he thought.)

'Well, I don't think she's going to last much longer. She is ninety-five after all, and she's been very ill for the last five years, but she took a turn for the worse last week, so I came over to be with her.'

'Oh, I'm sorry to hear that.' (Vultures gathering, he thought: Aunt Julie was very wealthy.)

'How long are you two staying in Montpellier?'

'Just until this afternoon,' replied Jim. 'We have to be at the airport by one o'clock, which means we shall have to have lunch there rather than in town.'

'That's a shame,' said Arlette. 'I was wondering if we might perhaps all have lunch together.' She smiled at Jim. 'Anyway, I have to go now. I need to be at Aunt Julie's before ten. It was nice to see you, both of you.'

She stood up, shook hands with Jim, still smiling, and kissed Ted on both cheeks, before leaving the restaurant almost as suddenly as she had the night before, but less dramatically.

'Well,' said Jim, after she had left. 'I thought you said she'd eat me for breakfast. She was affability personified.'

'Yes,' replied Ted. 'I wonder what the devil she's up to.'

'She seemed perfectly friendly to me – to both of us. You shouldn't be so suspicious, Ted.'

'What happened to that scepticism you said came from working at GCHQ? I know she's up to something. I'd just like to know what it is.'

Tony Whelpton

Chapter Four

Several hours later, Ted found himself at the dinner-table of his daughter Sophie in Hampstead. The return journey from Montpellier had passed without incident, Ted and Jim had said their farewells at Victoria, and now Ted was at Sophie and Peter's apartment in Downshire Hill, ready to give his report on the mission which had been entrusted to him. As he sat down at the dinner-table, however, something else was at the fore-front of his mind. 'You'll never guess what happened when Jim and I were in the hotel bar last night...' he began.

'My mother turned up,' Sophie interjected.

'How the devil did you know that?'

'She rang up yesterday evening and told us about it.'

'Oh God! Does that mean she knows I was doing an errand for you?'

'No, she doesn't – at least not via one of us. It was Peter who took the call, and he said he hadn't the faintest idea what you were doing there.'

'Good thinking, Peter!'

'Well, of course, I didn't know what you'd told her,' said Peter, 'but by the time she asked me the question it was clear that the conversation that you and she had had was fairly minimal...'

'You can say that again!'

'I'm afraid I told her that you and she were a pair of fools and that after such a lapse of time anyone with any pretensions to being civilised ought to be able to bury the hatchet and get on with things. I'm sorry, Ted.'

'How did she react to that?'

'With a stony silence at first, and then she said that perhaps I was right, and she'd try to see you again in the morning.'

'You were very brave, Peter,' said Ted.

'That's what I said. I'd never have got away with saying that sort of thing to her myself!' laughed Sophie.

'And did she come and see you this morning?' asked Peter.

'Yes, she did. She came and apologized. What's more, she seemed to be offering a more or less permanent olive-branch.'

'Well I never,' said Peter. 'I have to say I didn't expect that! I was just trying to get out of telling her that you were there on our behalf!'

'Well, your instincts were right, Peter. I couldn't believe my ears. I just wondered what she was up to, I'm afraid. I was even more suspicious when we were saying goodbye and she came over and kissed me!'

They all laughed, and then moved on to the main purpose of Ted's visit, his report on the house in Saint-Gély-du-Fesc that he and Jim had been to see. He tried to give a matter-of-fact, objective assessment of its features, although the reality was that he had quite fallen in love with it, and desperately wanted Sophie and Peter to buy it. They listened carefully and quietly to what he had to say, merely interrupting him once or twice in order to clarify certain details.

'How long has it been empty, Dad?' asked Sophie.

'I'm not sure, but I suspect not all that long. It certainly looks in good order – the pool is still full of water, for instance, and it clearly hasn't been neglected. There's still some furniture in the house too.'

'What about price, Ted?' asked Peter. 'Do you think it's worth the price they're asking?'

'That's difficult to say,' replied Ted. 'They're asking nearly 700,000 euros, which seems a lot to me, but you would be getting a lot for your money, and it doesn't seem to differ greatly from what people are asking for other properties in that area. But there is one thing I found out, namely that the French think the English are much too ready to pay over the odds...'

'And they set their asking-price accordingly?'

'Exactly. With a view to getting a price from an English buyer that no French person would even contemplate paying. An Englishman might very well offer a little bit below the asking-price, and be delighted if he got it down by 10,000 euros, but a Frenchman would be quite prepared to say 'it's not worth that money – I'd only be interested if it were 30,000 less', and then walk away – making sure that he'd left his phone number with them so that they would be able to contact him with a revised asking-price.'

'Did you find any snags in it at all?' asked Sophie.

'No, I can't say I did, to be absolutely honest.'

'Then I think we're going to have to go over and have a look for ourselves, Peter,' said Sophie. 'We can't make an offer without seeing it, and if Dad is as impressed as he seems to be, it would be silly to turn it down just like that.'

Peter agreed, and the conversation moved on to other things before they all retired for the night.

In the meantime, in another part of London, Jim and Dilys were also sitting down to dinner. Dilys too was anxious to hear all about the Montpellier trip, although she was naturally less concerned with the details of the property Jim and Ted had been inspecting than with the other aspects of the visit, such as the food, the hotel, what Montpellier was like, etc.

She showed an especial interest when Jim told her of their chance encounter with Arlette, wanting to know every detail of what she was like, what she was wearing, what she said, what Ted's reaction had been, what Ted had said about her afterwards, and, it seemed to Jim, a million other trivial things, until he ultimately reached breaking-point.

'Look, Dilys, give it a rest, can't you? It wasn't all about Ted's ex-wife, you know. I can hardly remember what she was wearing, and I probably wouldn't recognise her if I saw her in the street tomorrow.'

'All right, Jim, there's no need to be so tetchy. I'm only interested. I mean, she *was* married to your oldest friend...'

'That doesn't mean I have to be obsessed with her. If it hadn't been for Ted, I probably wouldn't have noticed her.'

To anyone who had witnessed Jim's initial encounter with Arlette, and seen the way they chatted together up to the time when Ted arrived on the scene, this would have appeared as an absolute lie, but then Jim had not told Dilys that he had been drinking with Arlette in the first place. The fact that Dilys was unaware of this did not prevent her from feeling extremely annoyed. More often than not she bit her tongue and said nothing rather than engage in a full-scale row with Jim, but something in the way Jim had been reacting led her, for some reason she could not have begun to explain, to feel that there was more to this than met the eye.

'So you didn't notice what she looked like! As you never notice what I look like! As you never notice what any woman looks like!'

'I don't know what you mean!'

'Don't give me that! We never pass a woman in the street without your head turning.'

'What are you getting at?'

'You know exactly what I mean. You've always had an eye for a pretty woman – sometimes more than an eye – and if you expect me to believe that you didn't even look at Arlette and you can't remember what she looks like, you're stretching credulity too far. For some reason, you seem to be hiding something, and I can't understand why.'

'All right, I'll tell you why. Because I found her absolutely ravishing, and after she waltzed out of the bar I rushed after her, took her in my arms, and we spent the whole night making passionate love in her room.'

'Ha, ha! That's a good one! That beggars belief even more than the first version, especially the last bit!'

'What exactly do you mean by that?'

'You know exactly what I mean. As if you were capable of making passionate love to anybody!'

And Dilys rushed from the room in floods of tears, slamming the door behind her.

Jim sat still for a moment or two, completely stunned, unable to comprehend what had happened in the last few minutes; unable to comprehend, indeed, exactly why he had not narrated everything just as it had happened. He refilled his wine-glass, then retired to his study, carrying both glass and bottle, and closing the door behind him.

Once in the study he sank into his favourite armchair and began to think. Why did he feel guilty? He had nothing to feel guilty about, at least with regard to Arlette. So why act as if he had? He drained and refilled his glass. Because Dilys always made him feel guilty. She was always half-suggesting things, with the result that he automatically went on the defensive at the start of any conversation in which relationships were being discussed. Once more, he drained and refilled his glass. What was it Ted had been saying when he was talking about Arlette? It only takes one seriously determined person to create a row out of nothing. Yes, exactly, that's just what Dilys was doing now. For some reason best known to herself she just felt like starting a row, and that's what she had done. It had nothing to do with him at all.

His glass once more empty, Jim reached out for the wine-bottle, only to find that it, too, had been drained of its contents. He got up, retrieved a bottle of whisky from a cupboard, and poured himself a large measure. And what else had Dilys said that had upset him so much? Oh yes, she'd made that nasty little remark implying that he was impotent. What a cheap thing to do! He'd never been impotent in his life until after he'd had that damned prostate operation, and everyone knew what happened to men after that. It was a reason for sympathy, not for scorn. He reached once more for the whisky-bottle. What was wrong with this wife of his? He did everything he could for her, and always had done.

His musings continued, becoming ever more out of touch with truth and reality as the level of whisky in the bottle diminished. At last, the bottle empty, and his brain wallowing in a morass of self-justification, he closed his eyes and slept until morning.

When Jim awoke, he was surprised to find that the curtains were closed and the light was on. He looked around him, failing to understand at first either where he was or what had happened. Then, his eyes lighting on the empty whisky-bottle, he began to remember. Ah yes, that would explain why he wasn't feeling so good this morning. What had made him drink so much? Of course, that was it, he had fallen out with Dilys. Gradually memories of their conversation and his reactions seeped into his mind, but he was unable to recollect exactly what he had said, and what he had merely thought and not expressed aloud. No matter: thinking these things was essentially the same as saying them, and little by little, the guilt to which he was habitually a prey, as Dilys had pointed out a few weeks previously in the course of their drive to Oxford, began to consume him.

He got up, pulled back the curtains, opened the study door and went into the dining-room. The table had been cleared, and everything was in its place. He went into the kitchen, and everything there was as it should be too; even the dish-washer had been emptied. For the first time he noticed the time: it was eleven o'clock.

He went into the bedroom. The bed had been made, all was tidy, and there was no sign of

Dilys. Where could she be? Probably she'd popped out to the shops. He went into the kitchen again, and this time noticed a card propped up against the coffee-machine. It read: 'Gone to stay with Jemima for a few days. D.'

At about the same time that Jim was reading Dilys's note, Ted was boarding a train at Waterloo, en route for Crowthorne. As usual he phoned Valerie from the train, and when he arrived at his destination he found her waiting for him in the car. 'I've missed you, Ted,' she said, as she greeted him with a kiss.

'I've missed you too, darling,' Ted replied. 'And things might have been easier if you'd been with us.'

'Why? What happened? Didn't you and Jim get on together after all?'

'No, it wasn't that. I'll tell you over lunch.'

As they sat having lunch, Ted narrated the whole story from beginning to end – or, at least, as much as he knew about the beginning, and what he imagined to have been the end. Valerie listened in silence until Ted told her of Arlette's change of attitude.

'No! I don't believe it! It sounds like St. Paul on the road to Damascus!'

'I know. I thought it was a pretty dramatic conversion too, but then I learned that Peter had had a hand in it.' And he went on to recount the conversation he had had with Sophie and Peter.

'So... Jim appears to have made friends with Arlette before you even knew she was in the hotel?'

'It would appear so, yes.'

'Do you think he was trying to chat her up?'

'No, I wouldn't have thought so. Not with Jim's strict Catholic attitudes.'

'I doubt whether that would be enough to stop him. I mean, Arlette's a very attractive woman, isn't she? And from what you've told me, Jim is very much a Francophile.'

Ted was about to say 'Not as attractive as Dilly, she isn't', but decided at the last minute to say: 'I suppose so. She doesn't attract me.'

'She must have done once.'

'That was when I was young and impressionable.'

'And now Jim's old and impressionable.'

'Me too,' said Ted.

They both laughed, and carried on talking about the house in Saint-Gély until they had finished lunch. Shortly afterwards, Valerie went out to the hairdresser's, whilst Ted settled into an armchair to read the newspaper. Almost inevitably he felt his eyes closing, and in a matter of seconds he was asleep.

Suddenly the telephone rang, and Ted awoke with a start. At first he couldn't think where he was, but he eventually regained a state of sufficient composure to be able to make his way into the hall and pick up the phone. To his surprise, he heard Dilys's voice.

'Hello, Dilly, what a nice surprise.'

'Ted – you called me Dilly! It's the first time I've been called Dilly in years. That's what you used to call me when we were at school, remember?'

'Of course I remember,' replied Ted. 'How could I forget? Anyway, how are you?'

'I'm fine, thanks. How did you enjoy your trip?'

'Very much indeed, thanks.'

'Except for bumping into Arlette, I suppose?'

'Ah, Jim told you about that, did he?'

'Yes, but he didn't tell me exactly how it came about. Did she just come up to you and Jim in the bar?'

'No – when I arrived in the bar she was already there talking to Jim.'

'Was she indeed? Jim didn't tell me that.'

Dilys's tone had suddenly changed. 'Oh dear,' thought Ted. 'What have I said!' But he replied: 'I think they just arrived at the bar at the same time and just started talking as they were waiting for the barman. Of course she didn't know who Jim was, and he didn't know who she was.'

'I see. So, quite innocent then?'

'Oh God, yes, I'm sure. Why do you say that?'

'Oh Ted, I'm sorry, I'm just being silly. It's just that Jim and I had a bit of a tiff when he got home, and I'm afraid I've walked out on him.'

'You've done what?'

'Well, not exactly walked out. I've just gone to stay with our daughter Jemima for a few days. I was ringing really to check whether Jim had been in touch with you.'

'No, not at all. If he does, is there anything you'd like me to say?'

'Yes, there is. There is indeed, Ted, but I'm not going to ask you to say it.' And she burst into tears.

'What's wrong, Dilly?' asked Ted anxiously. 'Is there anything I can do?'

'No, Ted.' She suddenly seemed more in control. 'Everything's fine. Don't worry about it. I'm just being silly. I shouldn't have said anything. Must go. Talk soon. Bye.' And she rang off.

'What was all that about?' Ted asked himself when she had gone. Clearly everything was not all right, and yet the impression he always got from Jim was that all was sweetness and light between him and his wife, but this outburst seemed to suggest otherwise. Presumably, he thought, there must be some reason for her to be suspicious, jealous even. Perhaps Valerie had been right, and his own conviction that Jim's Catholic faith was sufficient to keep him on the straight and narrow was misguided; after all, he had himself had experience as a boy of a supposedly devout priest's being susceptible to sexual temptation. Who could possibly say what was going on in another person's mind, even that of a person you know very well? And, of course, although he had known Jim well enough when they were boys, a gap of forty-plus years was more than enough to make his understanding of his friend relatively superficial. And if that were true with regard to Jim, it was even more true with regard to Dilys.

His musings were interrupted by the sound of Valerie's key in the latch. Ted made an instant decision: he would say nothing to Valerie about Dilys's phone-call. 'I have no idea what's going on really, so there's nothing to say,' he told himself. 'And if I can't understand fully what's going on, Valerie won't have a clue either, so it's best to say nothing.'

Three days later, Jim was still on his own; Dilys had not been in touch since leaving what he considered an unduly peremptory note saying she was going to stay with her daughter for a few days. During her absence Jim had fended for himself as best he could, which meant he had relied rather heavily on what had been a well-stocked freezer, and had been drinking rather more than was good for him.

It being Sunday, his first thought on rising was that he must go to church. That also meant going without breakfast, because he adhered strictly to the way he had been brought up over sixty years before, and would not have even contemplated taking Holy Communion without having fasted since midnight, although that prescription had long since been abolished, and most modern Catholics barely knew that it had once been the rule. It also meant that he had to be in a State of Grace; to his own mind he certainly was, although Dilys might have other ideas on that, but his conscience was clear.

Normally he would have gone to Brompton Oratory, which was just around the corner, but this morning he decided to go, as he sometimes did, to the little French church of Notre-Dame-de-France in Leicester Square, mainly because his recent visit to the country whose language and culture he loved – despite their abysmal failure to appreciate cricket – was still uppermost in his mind.

As usual the congregation was quite a large one, composed mainly of members of the London French community whose number seemed to be steadily growing, and supplemented by French visitors and a sprinkling of English Francophiles. As he was going out of church at the end of mass, he suddenly heard a smart-looking French woman just in front of him exclaim: '*Merde alors!*'[3]

Jim, shocked, reacted at once: '*Madame! On ne devrait pas dire des choses pareilles en sortant de l'église!*'[4]

The French woman spun round, and glared at him, but in a split second her glare was transformed into a smile: 'Jim! What a nice surprise! Fancy seeing you here! I'm sorry I shocked you – I'd just realised I left my handbag in church. I must go back and get it. Will you come with me?'

---

[3] 'Oh, shit!'

[4] 'You shouldn't say things like that when you're just coming out of church!'

So Jim found himself, willy-nilly, accompanying Arlette – for it was she – back into church. Fortunately the handbag was still where she had left it. As they came out of church once more, Arlette turned to Jim and said: 'Jim, are you in a hurry to get home, or would you like to finish that drink we were having in Montpellier when Ted came in?'

'No, I'm not in a hurry,' replied Jim. 'In fact my wife is away at the moment, so I was thinking about having lunch out.' He hesitated for a moment, then continued: 'Why don't you join me for lunch?'

An observer would have noticed that Arlette's acceptance was a little less hesitant than Jim's invitation, but it did not strike Jim in this way.

'There's a little French restaurant I know just around the corner from here in St. Martin's Lane,' he said. 'How would you like to go there?'

'That sounds delightful.'

Arlette and Jim duly made their way to St. Martin's Lane and were soon seated at a table in a quiet corner of the restaurant; one could easily have imagined oneself being in a typical Parisian *bistro*, although they chose to sit at one of the small tables, rather than one of the two long tables at which they would have found themselves elbow-to-elbow with other diners, which seems acceptable in Paris, where the conversation is always animated, or even noisy, but less so in London, where the customers are generally more self-conscious, especially if they are intent on having a more intimate discussion. A waiter, himself French, as were all his colleagues, came to take their order; in such surroundings it seemed natural to both of them to converse in French rather than in English, and this is what they did, although the switch was unconscious rather than deliberate, at least on Jim's part.

As he had found the first time they had met, Jim found Arlette easy to talk to, and he was particularly pleased to have the opportunity to use his mastery of the French language to proper, and indeed enjoyable, use. Both of them carefully avoided the topic of Ted, except that, fairly early in the conversation, Arlette had made a tentative inquiry as to the identity of the person who was contemplating buying the house in Saint-Gély. At that stage, however, Jim was still sufficiently sober to realise that it would be imprudent and inconsiderate for him to divulge any such information, and the matter was not raised again. Arlette did, however, quiz him about his wife: 'You say your wife is away, Jim... Is she away for long?'

'No, just for a day or two. She's gone to visit our son Michael in Winchester.'

The lie was deliberate; if Jim had told the truth and said that Dilys had gone to stay with their daughter Jemima in Wimbledon, he would then have had to invent a reason for her staying over there, when Wimbledon was not exactly a million miles from Kensington. In the course of his many years in the Civil Service, Jim had come to realise that being economical with the truth was often the easiest – and sometimes the wisest – option.

'How long have you been married?'

'Nearly forty years.'

'My goodness! I don't think there's anybody else I know who's been married as long as that. One or both of you must be remarkably patient.'

Jim decided that on the whole it was best to make no comment on that matter, especially considering the current situation which had arisen between himself and Dilys, which he was still at a loss to understand. Instead, he asked: 'Have you never re-married, Arlette?'

'No, I haven't,' she replied.

'That's surprising.'

'Why do you say that?'

'Well, an attractive woman like you...'

'You mean, what a waste of an attractive woman!'

'Well, er...,' Jim stammered, visibly embarrassed.

'I can assure you, Jim, that this particular woman has not been wasted. Not in the sense I think you mean, anyway. I have had a number of opportunities to get married again, but I've never really felt either the need or the inclination.'

Jim looked directly at Arlette, who smiled at him. He looked away again quickly, once more feeling embarrassed, for he sensed that he was beginning to feel both an inclination and a need. What was happening to him? He was too old for that sort of thing, wasn't he? Not that, in the unlikely event that anything should happen, it would be the first such occurrence during his married life; but that was a long time ago, in Cheltenham. It must have been the effect of the wine he had been drinking; and yet he was not exactly unused to wine... What's more, they had both just come out of church, they had both taken communion, it was not really appropriate...

'I think I'd better start making a move for home.'

'Why?' Arlette inquired. 'You're on your own at present, aren't you?'

'Well yes, I am, but my wife will be back this evening.'

'Oh I see.' Arlette smiled at him in the same way as she had done before, and the effect of her smile was redoubled. 'Whereabouts do you live, Jim?'

'Kensington,' he replied.

'I live in Kensington too. Why don't we share a cab?'

There seemed to be no means of escape now – if, that is, Jim had felt any real desire to escape – and a few minutes later he found himself in the back of a cab, with Arlette sitting alongside him so closely that he could feel the warmth of her thigh against his. It felt delicious – and wrong. He made to move away, but found himself powerless to do so. He turned to look at Arlette, and she turned her face towards his.

'You may kiss me if you'd like to, Jim,' she murmured.

The ensuing kiss was as long as it had been inevitable, and Jim felt ensnared, but happily ensnared.

When the cab reached Arlette's apartment-block they both got out, and Jim no longer even tried to resist Arlette's invitation to come in for a post-lunch coffee and cognac, even though he was perfectly aware that coffee and cognac were not all that was on offer.

Less than half an hour later, Jim was tearfully apologising for the deficiency to which Dilys had been alluding a few days earlier, and which Jim had blamed on prostate surgery; despite Arlette's protestations that it didn't matter, that it was probably because of the wine, and that it would all be fine next time, it was a frustrated, chastened, and guilt-ridden Jim who made his way home to his empty flat.

If Jim had told Arlette that Dilys would be back that evening, it was not because he *knew* that she would be, nor even that he *thought* she would be; it was just a rather feeble way of trying to avoid the temptation to which he had eventually succumbed. It had proved a fairly useful lie in the event, because it had enabled him to run away from a situation which had got out of hand, which had provoked feelings of both embarrassment and guilt, and to avoid the temptation to remain with Arlette for the rest of the night, which is what he really wanted to do.

Now that he was at home, his thoughts that Dilys might conceivably return that evening were replaced by fears that she actually would. It was not that Jim did not want her to return at all, more that a reunion which would in any case have been very awkward was now likely to be even more difficult, because of the mixed emotions with which his more rational self was being bombarded. He tried telling himself to calm down, that for a man fast approaching seventy to behave as if he were a teenager indulging in his first experience of sex was utterly ridiculous, but to no avail; age had no relevance, and neither did experience. He tried to imagine what he would say to Dilys if she were to come home now, inventing answers to all the questions she might ask, as well as to those she almost certainly would not. All his answers seemed unconvincing, and the immediate future looked bleak. When Dilys had left she had been, for some reason, driven by the false notion that Jim had been dallying with Arlette. If she had been suspicious then, what chance would he have now that there was a real basis for her suspicions? Oh God, please God, please don't let her come home tonight!

Jim's unspoken prayer was too late, for no sooner had the thought crossed his mind than he heard a key in the latch, and there, standing before him, was Dilys.

'Hullo,' was all she said, before she flung herself into his arms.

'Hullo,' was all he was able to reply before she removed the possibility of his saying anything else by kissing him full on the lips. Among all the potential situations which Jim had rehearsed in his mind, this particular one had not figured at all, and a great sense of relief came over him, though without alleviating significantly the feelings of guilt which were uppermost in his emotions.

'Have you eaten, Jim?' she asked at last.

'Not since lunch-time,' he replied, relieved at being asked a question to which he felt able to give a truthful answer.

'Then I'll cook a nice meal for us, open a nice bottle of wine, and then we'll have an early night.' And she kissed him again.

'That would be wonderful,' replied Jim at length, feeling that he was off the hook despite only having uttered eight or nine words since Dilys came home, but then being struck suddenly by the possible implications of 'an early night' and an increased awareness of his having broken the sixth commandment (according to Catholic reckoning) earlier in the day.

Dilys busied herself in the kitchen, first pouring a liberal serving of scotch for Jim, and then a slightly weaker-than-usual gin for herself.

'I'm sure you haven't had a proper meal while I've been away, have you?' she asked, but returned to her culinary labours without waiting for an answer, leaving Jim alone with his thoughts.

Needless to say, Dilys's thoughts were not entirely concentrated on the meal she was preparing. She too had been rehearsing possible scenarios for their reunion, and the way she had greeted Jim on her return had been less a spontaneous display of emotion, more a conscious, even calculated, choice of battle-ground, if battle there were to be. She knew Jim well enough to be sure that, even if their 'tiff', as she had described it to Ted, had been of her making, by the time they got together again Jim would have convinced himself that he was at fault, and would have proceeded to grovel in a way that she found frankly nauseating. That was why she had deliberately avoided saying 'sorry', or raising in any way the issues which had led to their brief but, to her at least, painful separation.

She knew that, in spite of his religious convictions, Jim was no saint, and that, deep down, he felt great sympathy with the prayer of St. Augustine: Lord, make me chaste, but not yet. She knew that, despite his protestations to the contrary, he had had a brief fling with a girl in his department at GCHQ several years before, but she had not allowed it to come between them, believing that his feelings of guilt would end it more quickly and more effectively than anything she could say, and she had been right. But she would have been surprised at the speed with which he had been seduced by Arlette. Indeed, her choice of Arlette as an excuse for their little show-down was much more to do with her own feelings of sexual frustration, of feeling neglected, ignored, taken for granted, than with any thought that Ted's ex-wife was a possible rival for Jim's affections. In truth, substituting 'cricket' for 'Arlette' would not really have changed the situation, or Dilys's feelings, to any significant extent.

Her cooking very nearly finished, Dilys went into the drawing-room and replenished Jim's glass, then set the table in the dining-room before opening one of Jim's favourite wines. Ten minutes later they were sitting facing each other across the dining-table.

'You haven't forgotten that it's next week we're meeting Ted and Valerie at Winchester, have you?' she asked, again pre-empting the choice of topic for their conversation, whilst not realising the extent of Jim's willingness to go along with it, let alone his reasons for so feeling.

'No, I haven't forgotten, Ted and I were talking about it while we were in France, and we've got it all sorted out – where we're meeting and everything.'

'Oh, I am impressed,' said Dilys. 'I'm sorry for doubting you.'

'That's all right,' said Jim. 'How were Jemima and the kids?'

Dilys hesitated a moment before answering, because it was a most un-Jim-like question, but then, realising that he too was trying hard to avoid re-opening the wounds caused by their skirmish of a few days ago, decided to take the question at face value.

'They're all fine. It was nice to be able to spend a few days with the children rather than just the odd hour, as it usually is.'

'How's Jemima coping, do you think? It must be even more difficult now the children are a bit older.'

'Yes, I think it probably is, but I think she's doing okay.'

Jemima had been left on her own with two small children a few years previously, when her husband Jeremy had been stricken down by a brain haemorrhage, thus ending a short but extremely successful career as a stock-broker.

The conversation during the rest of the meal consisted mainly of Dilys recounting numerous anecdotes about the children, what they were doing at school, who their friends were, what they liked doing in their spare time, etc. Jim was content to listen, Dilys was content to stick to a subject to which Jim was content to listen, and both of them were studiously evading the issues which were uppermost in their minds.

When the meal was finished, Dilys cleared the table, made coffee, and poured out a glass of cognac for Jim, who settled at once into his favourite leather armchair. Jim rarely did anything about the house, whether it be clearing away, washing up, or even laying the table; as for cooking, apart from a couple of show-off 'party-pieces', it was as much as he could do to re-heat something which had been pre-cooked. Dilys did not resent this too much; it stemmed originally, she thought, from his working-class upbringing, but then had been reinforced by the fact that he was working full-time and she spent most of her time at home. After that, she blamed herself for failing to point out that, now they were both at home, it might be possible to work out a more equitable share of responsibilities. Now, she felt, it was too late, so she just got on with it.

When she had finished clearing up, she went once more into the drawing-room, and found that Jim was fast asleep. She spoke to him; there was no answer. She shook him; he did not move a muscle. She shouted at him; still no response. 'Damn!' she yelled. 'So much for a bloody early night together!'

With that, she switched off all the lights, and took herself off to bed.

The following morning Dilys woke up early, and was surprised to find Jim in bed alongside her; she had not been aware of him coming to bed, and yet she had lain awake for a long time before going to sleep herself. She got up, made some tea, and sat reading for half an hour. Then she heard Jim stirring, and took a cup of tea into the bedroom for him, along with the morning paper which had just arrived.

'Good morning, Jim. Here's a cup of tea. What time did you come to bed last night? I didn't hear you.'

'I didn't notice what time it was, but it must have been early this morning rather than late last night. I'm sorry I dropped off like that. You must have fed me too well.'

'Or watered you too well! Serves me right. Anyway, I must get on. I've got a singing lesson at ten o'clock. What are you doing today?'

'Nothing special, I don't think. I'm not really sure yet.'

'Oh well, there's no need for you to get up yet. As I said, I've got a singing lesson at ten, but I'll be back about twelve. This afternoon I thought I'd like to go and have a look at the Royal Academy Summer Exhibition. Would you like to come too?'

Jim pulled a face. 'No. If it's all the same to you, I think I'll give it a miss. It's probably all piles of old bricks and women with three eyes...'

'You are an old philistine, Jim,' said Dilys. 'Thank God you like music.'

'As long as there's a melody and it harmonises properly.'

With that Jim turned his attention to the morning paper, and Dilys went to take her shower.

At a quarter to ten Dilys went out. Five minutes later, the phone rang, and Jim went to answer it.

'Hello, is that Jim?'

'Yes, it is. Who's that?'

'It's Arlette.'

'Arlette! What are you doing calling me at home? What if Dilys had answered?'

'She's just gone out, hasn't she?'

'Yes, she has, but how do you know that?'

'I saw her go out.'

'How do you know it was her? You've never met her, have you?'

'No, but I've seen her photograph.'

'Where?'

'There's one in your wallet.'

'I know there is, but how did you come to see it?'

'Because you left it in my apartment yesterday, and I had a look inside to see if I could find your phone number. Can I bring it up?'

'No, you mustn't come here!'

'Why not?'

'Nosy neighbours. Do you know that little French *pâtisserie* opposite Gloucester Road tube station?'

'Yes.'

'I'll meet you there in ten minutes.'

'All right. *A bientôt, chéri.*'

'See you in ten minutes.'

Jim, who had still been only half-dressed when the phone rang, hurriedly finished getting ready and rushed out into the street, walking briskly in the direction of Gloucester Road station. There, in the *pâtisserie*, he found Arlette sitting at a table waiting for him, with a coffee-pot and two cups in front of her.

'I've ordered coffee, Jim, I hope that's all right.'

'Yes, that's fine, but I'd rather meet you somewhere less local.'

'Shall we go somewhere less local now?'

'No, this will do for now. Just this once.'

'When shall we meet again, Jim?'

'I don't know. I'm not sure we should.'

'Didn't you enjoy being with me yesterday afternoon?'

Jim, being totally unused to such direct questioning on such an intimate subject, especially from someone he hardly knew, merely mumbled something unintelligible.

'You're not telling me you're the first man in my life to make love to me and not want to do it a second time?'

'I'm not saying anything of the sort.'

'That means you do want there to be a second time. I do too. I'm just asking when, that's all.'

'It's difficult getting away, especially now Dilys is back. Talking of which, she will be back home again pretty soon, so I'd better take my wallet and go.'

'If I can't ring you, how can I contact you?'

'I'll call you if you give me your phone-number. Only for God's sake be discreet.'

'Don't be so afraid, Jim. I'm not going to eat you.'

Jim suddenly recalled Ted saying that Arlette would eat him for breakfast, but the only answer he gave was: 'I know.'

A minute or two later they left the *pâtisserie* and went their separate ways, Jim now in possession of his wallet and Arlette's phone-number, and Arlette in possession of a promise that a phone-call would be forthcoming the moment a window of opportunity opened.

Jim arrived home with just ten minutes to spare before Dilys came in from her singing-lesson.

'Anything of interest happen while I was out?' she inquired.

'No, nothing at all.'

'What have you been up to this morning?'

'Just reading the paper, that's all.'

They had a light lunch, then Dilys got ready to go out again.

'Are you sure you wouldn't like to go to the Royal Academy with me?'

'Quite sure, thanks.'

'In that case I'll take my music with me.'

'Your music?'

'Yes, it's Monday... Rehearsal at 6.15. There's not much point in going from Piccadilly to Victoria by way of Kensington. I might as well go straight there.'

'Oh yes, I see.'

'Jim, are you all right? You seem preoccupied.'

'Me? Not me. I'd just forgotten it was Monday, that's all.'

'Well, that's not like you for a start.'

'Isn't it? Oh well, just put it down to incipient senility. A "senior moment" – isn't that what they call it?'

'Okay, if you like. See you later then. I should be back by nine.'

'Don't you have a longer rehearsal with a concert coming up on Saturday?'

'Not unless something goes seriously wrong or we're doing something new and difficult. But *Gerontius* is standard repertoire, so there shouldn't be any problems.'

'Didn't you say you had a re-audition this week?'

'No, that's next week. They wouldn't do it a few days before a concert. I've got to be there half an hour early next Monday.'

'Do you feel confident about it?'

'As confident as I ever do, which is not very! But I don't intend to let myself be kicked out, that's for sure!'

With that, she picked up her music-case and her handbag, and left.

When Dilys had gone, Jim sat down in his armchair and began to think. He had roughly seven hours in front of him before Dilys came home. Earlier in the day he had promised to call Arlette the moment a window of opportunity presented itself. If seven hours, he thought, didn't represent a window of opportunity, what did? But to call her so soon, wouldn't that give her the impression that he was unduly keen? Well, wasn't he keen? Yes, he was; in fact the previous day's experience, in spite of – or perhaps because of – its anticlimactic nature, made him positively eager to share Arlette's bed once more. But if he did ring, there was no guarantee that she'd be able to see him; she might not even be there. There was only one way to find out, and that was to ring, wasn't it? Yes, of course, but was it a good idea to let her think he was desperate? What was he looking for? A bit of sexual excitement? Or a relationship that would threaten his marriage? For the first time his wife came into the equation, and he had no difficulty in answering that question: he would not give up Dilys for Arlette, or indeed for anybody. Why? Did he love her? Yes, of course he did; he'd been married to her for more than forty years, hadn't he? But Arlette was tempting, wasn't she? And what was it that she had said? She had said that since her marriage to Ted ended, she had felt no need or inclination to marry again. In other words, she was a free spirit, which implied she would be unlikely to put pressure on him to end his marriage. But what if Dilys found out? Well, she wouldn't, would she? Who would tell her? Jim got up from the armchair and went over to the telephone.

Six hours later Jim was making his way home in a state of physical satisfaction but mental disarray. Just as he was about to turn right into the street where he lived, he suddenly paused, thought for a moment, and then turned left instead, not stopping until he reached the Catholic church of St Aidan's, a church which he had never before entered. He went in and knelt down. The church was empty, and almost in darkness. Only the side-aisles were properly illuminated; in the body of the church the only light came from the sanctuary-lamp whose flickering flame cast a dim glow through the red glass in which it was encased. After a moment or two, however, he became conscious of someone being close to him; he looked up, and saw an elderly priest, who appeared to have something to say to him. He stood up.

'Good evening, father.'

'Good evening, my son. I was just coming to tell you that I am about to close the church for the night.'

'Oh.'

Sensing a note of disappointment in Jim's reaction, the priest spoke again: 'Is there anything I can do for you?'

'I was wondering... Is there any chance you could hear my confession, father?'

'Well,' began the priest hesitantly.

'It's really important, father. I must unload myself of the terrible guilt I'm feeling.'

'Very well. Come into the confessional.'

Jim accompanied the priest to the ancient carved-oak confessional-box, opened one of the doors, entered, and knelt down. The priest went in through the other door, and sat opposite Jim, separated from him by a grill through which each of them could hear, but not see, the other.

'Bless me, father, for I have sinned. It is two days since my last confession, father.'

'Two days! What have you done in the last two days that has made your need for confession so great?'

'I have been unfaithful to my wife, father.'

The priest listened while Jim recounted the outline of his sin without entering into graphic detail, then said to Jim in a matter-of-fact way – he was, after all, not hearing this kind of story for the first time: 'And how many times has this taken place?'

'Once, father. No, twice.'

'How long have you been married?'

'Nearly forty years, father.'

'And have you ever been unfaithful before?'

'No, father, never. Well yes, just once, but many years ago.'

'And do you intend to be unfaithful again?'

Jim hesitated, as a biblical quote about the spirit being willing but the flesh weak flashed through his mind, then answered: 'With God's help I will not do it again, father.'

'It will need more than God's help, my son. Even with God's help it will need some resolve from you.'

'I understand that, father, and I will do my best.'

'Then go your way and sin no more. For your penance say five decades of the Rosary.'

'Yes, father, thank you.'

The priest muttered his prayer of absolution, and Jim stood up, left the confessional and went out of the church without looking back. On his way home he quietly said his penitential prayers to himself, finishing them just as he reached his front door. He took out his key, turned it in the latch, went in, poured himself a scotch and sat down, a much relieved man.

Tony Whelpton

Chapter Five

,

The following Saturday two cars made their way along the M3 towards Winchester. The first car, driven by Jim, was about four hours ahead of the second, which was driven by Ted; Jim and Dilys needed to be there earlier, because Dilys would be rehearsing all afternoon, and they were going to have lunch with their son Michael and his wife Jane before Dilys had to go to the cathedral.

Ted and Valerie set out from Crowthorne after lunch, which would give them plenty of time to check in at their hotel and change, before they too made their way to the cathedral to attend the concert.

'What time are we meeting Jim and Dilys?' asked Valerie.

'I'm not sure about Dilys,' replied Ted, 'but we're due to meet Jim at 7 o'clock at the west door of the cathedral. Which door is the west door, I wonder? Did you bring a compass with you?'

'No, I didn't,' laughed Valerie. 'But it's sure to be the main entrance, so all we have to do is follow the crowd. I imagine we won't see Dilys until after the concert.'

'There's a possibility we might see her in the interval, I suppose. That's what sometimes happens at our concerts, but with a more professional outfit like this they perhaps don't allow them to mingle until afterwards.'

'I must say, I'm looking forward to meeting Dilys and Jim after hearing so much about them. It feels rather strange, though, my meeting them for the first time when you've known them since the year dot.'

'I know what you mean,' replied Ted, 'but of course I don't know Dilys anything like as well as I know Jim.'

A few minutes' silence followed, during which time Ted thought about Jim and Dilys. The last time he had spoken to Dilys was when she had phoned him and told him that she'd left Jim, and then ended her call quite abruptly. He had spoken to Jim since, but he could hardly ask him if Dilys had come back to him, because he wasn't supposed to know she'd gone in the first place. He had gone so far as to ask if Dilys was well, to which Jim had answered 'Yes, she's fine', after which they had confirmed meeting arrangements for Saturday, which, Ted concluded, must surely mean that they were back together. On what sort of terms though? There was no point in speculating, because he really didn't have the first idea what it was all about, except that Dilys had suggested there was something Ted might usefully say to Jim, but he didn't know what it was. Perhaps he'd know soon; perhaps he'd never know.

As Valerie had predicted, they only had to follow the crowd to ascertain which was the west door of the cathedral, but, despite the large numbers of people who all seemed to have made arrangements to meet friends in the same place and at the same time, they had no difficulty in spotting Jim; what is more, Dilys was with him. Ted greeted them both, then effected the necessary introductions; Dilys, however, had to leave them almost immediately to join her fellow-choristers for a warm-up before the concert, which was due to begin at seven-thirty.

Ted bought a programme for each of them, and they took their seats in the centre of the nave, about seven rows from the front, an ideal position, thought Ted, in both visual and acoustic terms. After some discussion it was decided that Valerie should sit between the two men; a discussion only resolved when Valerie pointed out that, since they were here to listen to the music, not to talk, then it really did not matter who sat next to whom. As for the question of whether they would see Dilys in the interval or not, it did not arise, for on this occasion the two parts of the oratorio were performed without a break in between.

Choir, soloists and orchestra were all on excellent form, and both Ted and Valerie revelled in the glories of Elgar's music, from the manic chanting of the *Demons' Chorus* to the celestial warmth of *Praise to the Holiest in the Height*. As for

Jim, undoubtedly the meeting of a sinner with his Maker and the travails of the soul prior to being permitted to enter Paradise would have added an extra dimension in the context of his own guilt-ridden anguish of a few days before, but if it were so, there was no external evidence of it either during or after the performance.

When the concert was over, Ted, Valerie and Jim waited for Dilys at the place where they had met earlier in the evening; when she arrived she was noticeably more relaxed than she had been before the concert.

'Valerie,' she said, 'now I feel I can say hello properly. I always get a bit tense before a concert.'

'You didn't appear tense when you were singing,' replied Valerie.

'Oh no, it's fine once we get started. Anyway, let's go to the restaurant – I'm dying for a drink!'

'That's usually my line,' said Jim, after which they moved off, laughing, in the direction of the restaurant.

The restaurant – not surprisingly, since it was Ted who had chosen it – was French, and very authentically French too. Even less surprisingly Jim was delighted to find it so, with the result, as Dilys was not slow to notice – and much to her relief – that he was in a much more affable mood then he had been for a couple of weeks. Valerie, for her part, had been, if not really anxious, a trifle apprehensive, as she often was when she was going to meet someone new, especially someone whom Ted had known for a long time, but in the event the atmosphere was completely relaxed, and within a very short space of time they were all chatting as easily as if they had all been friends for years.

Not unnaturally, much of the conversation, especially during the first stages of the meal, before the effects of an aperitif and several glasses of excellent French wine started to become evident, centred on that evening's concert.

'It must be fantastic,' said Valerie, 'to sing in a choir as good as that.'

'Well, yes, it is,' replied Dilys, 'although we're always aware of our own shortcomings.'

'Are there any?' asked Jim.

'Oh yes, there certainly are, and if we weren't aware of them ourselves, our chorus-master would soon point them out to us – in fact he often does. I mean, we're not professional singers, you know.'

'No,' Ted agreed, 'but you sing to a professional standard.'

'Yes, we do, but I'm sure there are a good number of singers in your choir who are just as good.'

'Yes, there probably are, but there are also some who definitely aren't!' Ted replied with a laugh.

'Doesn't that make it frustrating for the better ones?' asked Jim.

'Yes, it does sometimes,' replied Ted, 'but it's the best choir I've been able to find in our area.'

'Well,' Dilys interjected, 'you know what I told you the other week. We have a lot of out-of-town members. Why don't you apply for an audition with us?'

'I think that's an excellent idea,' said Valerie, even before Ted had time to react. 'When do you rehearse?'

'Monday evenings, 6.15 to 8.15.'

'Oh, so you finish very early then...'

'Yes, we have to, precisely because of the out-of-town members.'

'There you are, Ted,' said Valerie. 'You'd be able to do that and be back home by ten o'clock.'

'Yes,' Ted agreed, 'but you're forgetting one thing.'

'What's that?' asked Valerie.

'The audition, of course. I'd have to pass the audition first!'

All three of Ted's companions wasted no time in assuring him that he had nothing to fear as far as the audition was concerned, but, as he pointed out to them, Valerie was not exactly unbiased and Jim and Dilys had never heard him sing.

'There's one way of remedying that – you could do an audition for us right now!' suggested Jim.

At that the entire party dissolved into hysterical laughter and, in truth, once Ted had assured them that he would think about putting himself forward for an audition, but certainly not there and then, there was little said during the rest of the evening that would have made much sense when examined in the cold, sober light of the next day.

The following morning, after a leisurely breakfast, Ted and Valerie checked out of their Winchester hotel, put their overnight bags in the boot of the car, and set off on their return journey to Crowthorne, this time with Valerie at the wheel, for it was their custom always to share the driving between them, either dividing a long journey into hour-long stints or, when the whole journey would not take much more than an hour, one of them driving there and the other one driving back. Breakfast had been a fairly quiet affair, principally because of the excesses of the previous evening, but by the time they left Winchester their heads had become considerably clearer, and it was Valerie who was first to break the silence: 'Well, I must say, that was a thoroughly enjoyable evening. Didn't you think so?'

'I did indeed. Do you approve of our new friends?'

'Oh yes, they're really good fun, aren't they? I can see why you like them. There's something about Jim that worries me a bit though...'

'Really? What sort of thing?'

'I don't know. It's difficult to put my finger on it. I mean, he's friendly enough, and cheerful enough, but I get a bit of a feeling that underneath that bonhomie there's a bit of a tendency towards depression.'

'What, Jim? Depressive? No, I don't think so. At least I've never noticed anything.'

'Didn't you feel there was a little bit of tension between them?'

'No, I can't say I did. There was nothing I noticed. I think you're imagining it.'

'Mm, maybe I am, maybe I'm not, I don't know. It was more a matter of body language than anything that was actually said. But I really warmed to Dilys. I can't believe she's as old as you say she is. She certainly keeps herself looking young – she must have been strikingly beautiful when she was younger.'

'She was certainly very pretty when she was at school.'

'I bet she was. Weren't you tempted?'

'Huh! She'd never have looked at me! There were scores of boys after her!'

'In which case I'm surprised you weren't one of them...'

'Not me. I was a bit of a slow starter. More interested in cricket than girls at that age – as was Jim, which probably explains why they didn't get together at that time either.'

'What do you think of her suggestion that you might audition for the Bach Choir?'

'I'm not sure,' replied Ted, feeling rather relieved that the conversation had changed tack a little. 'I might give it a go. It's the right time of year to think about it, because a new session will be starting in September, and that means I've got a bit of time to get myself up to scratch.'

'Will that take much doing?'

'Not really, I suppose, but I expect I'll have to prepare a party piece, and that's what will take up most of the time.'

'Did Dilys tell you who to get in touch with?'

'No, but there'll be details on the choir website. I'll find out from there.'

'You can have a look when we get home. I'm going to have to pop out to the supermarket, and you can have a look then.'

Ted had hardly enough time to utter a grunt of agreement before the car came to a halt outside their house; their homeward journey was already over.

A couple of hours later Ted and Valerie were sitting having a light lunch together.

'Well then, Ted, did you have a look at the Bach Choir website while I was out?'

'Yes, I did actually.'

'Oh, well done – I thought it was one of those things you say you'll do and never actually get round to doing until I've nagged you for a week or two!'

'What do you mean? I'm not like that!'

'Not much! Anyway, what did you find out?'

'I found out lots of things. More to the point, there was an online application form, and I've already sent it off.'

'Well done! What happens now?'

'I just have to wait and see. I expect someone will ring me or send me an email.'

'What will you do for your party-piece?'

'Oh, I expect I'll do *O Isis and Osiris* from *The Magic Flute*. That's what I've usually done before.'

'Oh yes, I remember hearing you practise that. It was pretty good – shows off your low notes...'

'That's the idea.'

Just then they heard a beep from the direction of the computer, indicating that an email had just arrived. Ted went over to have a look.

'Oh yes,' he said. 'This is from the Membership Secretary. Someone's going to call me in the next couple of days for a chat, they say. Sounds a bit like an interview by telephone!'

The following day Ted was in the garden mowing the lawn when Valerie suddenly appeared at the kitchen door. Ted switched off the lawn-mower to allow him to hear what she was saying.

'Ted! Telephone for you! Someone from the Bach Choir, I think.'

'Okay, I'll be right there.'

He unplugged the electric lawn-mower, slipped off his shoes, and went into the study to take the call. Fifteen minutes later he emerged.

'That took some time,' said Valerie. 'Did they give you an audition over the phone?'

'All but,' replied Ted. 'She wanted to know all about the different choirs I've sung with and for how long, what pieces I've sung in, what my vocal range is, whether I've ever had singing lessons, how good my sight-reading is – all sorts of stuff.'

'Well, with a professional choir like that, I suppose they have to be pretty thorough. When's your audition going to be?'

'Don't know yet. In fact I don't even know if I'll get one – I suspect it's not her decision. One thing I've found out, though – you don't have to do a party-piece.'

'Oh – so what do you have to do then?'

'Things like scales, arpeggios, intervals – but mainly sight-reading, because they cover such a wide range of musical styles, including new, specially-commissioned stuff, and they don't have much time to learn it.'

'Sounds pretty demanding...'

'Yes, I think it probably is. Very satisfying though. I mean, in some choirs you spend a lot of time just learning the notes – note-bashing, we call it – but with them you're really into the business of making music right from the first rehearsal. I'll have to do some work on my sight-reading though, to make sure it's up to scratch.'

'Is that likely to be a problem?'

'I hope not. It depends what sort of thing they give me to do. If it's a piece of Bach or Handel, or something like that, I should be okay, but if it's somebody modern like Carl Rütti or Judith Bingham, it's a bit less straightforward.'

'But surely they wouldn't expect perfection the first time you saw a piece, would they?'

'I don't know. I would hope not. I'm sure they'd be pretty fair in what they asked you to do. I'll have to ask Dilys to see if she can give me more of an idea.'

Just then the telephone rang. Valerie went to answer it.

'Valerie Bryant. Hello...'

'Hello, Valerie, it's Dilys Fletcher here.'

'Dilys, hello! That's amazing – we were just talking about you.'

'Saying something nice, I hope!'

'Of course,' laughed Valerie. 'No, it was just that Ted was saying he must pick your brains about the Bach Choir audition process.'

'Oh, I see. He is thinking seriously about it, then?'

'Oh yes, in fact he's already sent off an application and been talking to the Membership Secretary on the phone.'

'Oh good. Is Ted there at the moment?'

'Yes, he is. Shall I get him for you?'

'Not for a moment. It was you I wanted to speak to actually. At least, I'm assuming that you're the one that looks after your social diary...'

'Such as it is, yes.'

'I thought it would be. Men are so useless at that sort of thing, aren't they? Anyway, the point is that Jim and I are having a bit of a party to celebrate our Ruby Wedding, and we wondered if you and Ted would like to come.'

'Yes, of course, we'd love to. When is it?'

'September the second – it's a Saturday.'

'Yes, that's fine, we can do that.'

'Oh, that's good – I was afraid you might be away somewhere.'

'No, we should be back from our holiday the previous week.'

'Great! I'll put an invitation in the post for you. Where are you going on holiday?'

'We haven't decided yet, except that it's likely to be somewhere in France. It usually is – not that I mind that. Anyway, I'll pass you on to Ted, and then you can talk about auditions.'

'Okay, Valerie, thanks. Nice to talk to you.'

'You too, Dilys. Here's Ted.'

Ted took the receiver and recounted to Dilys the conversation he had had with the Membership Secretary, and then asked Dilys what sort of music he would be expected to sight-read.

'Oh, I don't really know, Ted. I mean, it's quite a few years since I did mine, and that was with David Willcocks – we had a change of conductor a couple of years ago. I'm not sure what happens these days.'

'But you've recently had a re-audition, haven't you?'

'No, I've got my re-audition next Wednesday, but in any case, re-auditions don't necessarily follow the same pattern. I'm sure you're not likely to have anything ultra-difficult though. You may have one or two awkward intervals to cope with – you know, fourths, sixths, sevenths, and so on, so it would be a good idea to practise those. Oh, and one good piece of advice I remember having before I did mine – make sure you look at the key-signature before you start singing. It's so easy when you're a bit nervous to go straight in and miss something obvious like that!'

'Yes, I can see that. Thanks for that.'

'But tell me – do you have singing lessons?'

'Not these days, no. I did once upon a time. Do you think it would be a good idea?'

'Yes, I think it would, especially if you're really serious about trying to get in...'

'Oh yes. I wouldn't do it at all if I wasn't serious. I don't know of a good teacher round here, though.'

'I can give you the phone number of the chap I go to. He's very good, and he used to be a member of the Bach Choir himself, so he knows what's needed. His name is Andrew, Andrew Barnes, and he lives in Hammersmith.'

When his conversation with Dilys was over, Ted lost no time in contacting the singing-teacher she had recommended, and made an appointment with him for the following week, despite Valerie pointing out that, a few minutes earlier, he had been saying that he was by no means certain that he would get an audition at all. After all, he said, he could always cancel it, and if it should happen that he only had a few days' notice of an impending audition, he might have difficulty arranging a lesson in time.

In the event, it would have made no difference if he had waited, for, no more than two hours later, he received another call from the Membership Secretary, offering him a selection of dates and times for his audition. Although torn between a desire to get it over with as soon as possible, and an even stronger desire to give himself the best possible chance by getting in at least two lessons before the audition took place, he opted for the latter, and chose a date which gave him a full three weeks' preparation time.

Once off the phone, he went back into the sitting-room, where Valerie was sitting reading.

'Well?' she inquired.

'I've got an audition three weeks tomorrow, so I should have time for at least two lessons before it happens.'

'That's really good, I'm pleased. Why don't you call Dilys again and tell her the news?'

'Do you think I ought to?'

'Yes, of course, why not? I'm sure she'd want you to keep her posted.'

'Oh, okay, if you really think I should.'

Ted went back into the study and called Dilys again. 'Hello, Dilys. It's Ted again. I thought you'd like to know – I've got a date for my audition.'

'You've heard already? Well done! When is it?'

'Three weeks tomorrow. And I've spoken to Andrew Barnes, and I've got a lesson with him on Tuesday morning.'

'What – next Tuesday?'

'Yes, 11.15.'

'That's incredible. I've got a lesson with him at 12 o'clock. Why don't you wait for me afterwards and we can have lunch together before you go back to Crowthorne?'

'Oh, great. Er – do you think Jim would mind?'

'No, of course not. Why should he? Valerie wouldn't object, would she? I mean, you won't have time to get back to Crowthorne before lunch, and you've got to eat somewhere.'

'Yes, of course, I'm being silly. I think that's a great idea.'

'I'll see you on Tuesday then, Ted. Bye.'

'Bye, Dilly.'

As Dilys replaced the receiver, Jim came into the room. 'Who was that on the phone?'

'Just now? That was Ted.'

'Again? I thought he rang earlier.'

'Yes, he did. He was just calling to say he'd managed to arrange a lesson with the same singing-teacher that I go to.'

'It sounded as if you were arranging to meet.'

'Well, we were, sort of. It just so happens that his lesson is next Tuesday, just before mine, so we've arranged to have lunch together afterwards.'

'That sounds cosy.'

'What do you mean?'

'What I say. I thought Ted was *my* friend...'

'So he is, but I thought Ted and Valerie were *our* friends now. You don't mind me going out to lunch with Ted, do you? I mean, we've both got to have lunch somewhere, and it would be stupid to go to two separate places when we're both going to be there at the same time. Why don't you come too if you don't like the idea?'

'Oh, no, I wouldn't want to get in the way,' said Jim tersely.

'Oh, don't be so ridiculous, Jim,' replied Dilys. 'If you're going to be like that, I'm going out. I need to get something for dinner anyway.'

Two minutes later she was gone. Not much more than one minute after that, Jim himself picked up the phone and dialled a number.

'*Allô?*'

'*Allô, bonjour, Arlette, c'est Jim.*'

'Jim, how nice of you to call. How are you?'

'I'm fine, thanks. I was just wondering – would you like to meet for lunch next Tuesday?'

'Oh Jim, I'm sorry, I can't. I've got to go to Montpellier again.'

'Oh, drat! It's just that Dilys is going to be out for lunch on Tuesday and I thought it might be an opportunity for us to see each other again.'

'Well, it would be, and there's nothing I'd like better, *mon chéri*, but I've just had a call to say that Tante Julie has died, and the funeral is on Tuesday. I'm flying to Montpellier tomorrow, and I shall probably be there for the whole of next week.'

'Oh, I see, I'm sorry. Er... Does that mean Ted will be in Montpellier too?'

'Oh no, I don't think so. He hasn't been in touch with Tante Julie for years. I expect Sophie will be there, but I haven't had a chance to call her yet to give her the news. Why do you ask?'

'Because it's Ted that Dilys is having lunch with on Tuesday.'

'Is it now! Well I never!'

'What do you mean by that?'

'Oh, nothing. I'm sure it's perfectly innocent. I mean, you were just inviting me for an innocent lunch, weren't you, Jim? Anyway, I must go. I'll be in touch when I get back. *A bientôt*, Jim.'

'Goodbye, Arlette.' And Jim replaced the receiver, for once totally lost for words.

That evening the telephone rang in Ted and Valerie's house. Valerie answered it.

'Hello, Valerie, it's Sophie here. Is Dad at home?'

'No, he's not, Sophie, he's at choir this evening.'

'I thought choir was Tuesday evenings.'

'It is normally, but this is a rehearsal for a small group of them who are singing for a wedding on Saturday. I'll get him to call you when he comes in.'

'No, don't worry, Valerie. But you can give him a message if you would.'

'Yes, of course I will.'

'Just tell him that I had a call from my mother earlier, and she told me that my great-aunt Julie in Montpellier has died.'

'Oh, I'm sorry to hear that. Ted has often talked of her. She was pretty old, wasn't she?'

'Oh yes, she was about 95, I think, and it wasn't unexpected. She'd been ill for a long time.'

'When's the funeral?'

'Next Tuesday. I shouldn't think Dad will want to go, but of course he's welcome to go with us if he'd like to. Peter and I are flying out on

Sunday – we thought if we did that we'd be able to go and have a look at that house Dad and his friend went to look at for us the other week.'

'Are you going to buy it?'

'Quite possibly, but obviously we need to have a look for ourselves to confirm that Dad's enthusiasm was justified.'

'Oh, I'm sure he wouldn't have exaggerated.'

'Oh no, I'm not suggesting that. No, we just need to have a look for ourselves, and then we can get things in motion while we're there. It seems too good an opportunity to miss.'

'Yes, I agree. Anyway, I'll give Ted the news.'

'Thanks, Valerie. I must fly. Nice to talk to you. Give my love to Dad.'

'Thanks, Sophie. Bye.'

When Ted returned, Valerie duly conveyed to him the contents of Sophie's message.

'Will you go to the funeral, do you think?' she continued.

'No, I don't think so. I think I'd stick out like a sore thumb. I know Sophie and Peter will be there, but so will Arlette.'

'I thought all was sweetness and light between you and Arlette now...'

'Ha, ha! That was certainly what she was implying last time I saw her, but I wouldn't trust her as far I could blow her, particularly when she's on home territory surrounded by all her relatives! Anyway, I've just arranged a singing lesson and lunch with Dilys for Tuesday, and I was never close enough to Aunt Julie to justify re-arranging that.'

Before Valerie could make any comment, the telephone rang once more; it was Sophie again.

'Dad! You're not going to believe this... it looks as if we've missed out on that house in France.'

'What? How do you mean, missed out?'

'It's no longer on the market. It looks as if someone has beaten us to it.'

'How did you find that out?'

'Peter went to the agent's website to check on the phone number, with a view to ringing them tomorrow and arranging to go and see it on Monday. Then when he'd made a note of the phone number he decided to have another look at the property details, and it was no longer there.'

'That doesn't necessarily mean someone's bought it.'

'What else could it mean?'

'Any number of things. It could be a fault with the website, or somebody accidentally erasing a file or a link. It happens all the time on the internet.'

'Ever the optimist, Dad, aren't you? I suppose that's possible, but we both think it means we've missed the boat. We should have acted on your recommendation sooner.'

'What are you going to do now then?'

'We'll ring the agent tomorrow morning and find out what the situation is, and then if we really have lost it, we'll have another look to see if there's anything else we fancy. There's nothing more we can do tonight. I'll call you when we've found out what's going on.'

Ted and Valerie were just clearing the breakfast-table the next morning when the telephone rang.

'I'll get it,' said Ted. 'I expect that's Sophie.' He lifted the receiver.

'Hello, Dad.'

'Hello, Sophie. What news? Have you spoken to the agent?'

'Yes, I have, and I'm not best pleased.'

'Why? Has the house been sold?'

'Yes, it has. And she thought she'd sold it to us.'

'Sold it to you?'

'Well... to you actually.'

'What on earth do you mean?'

'When I spoke to the agent, she said it had been bought by a Madame Bryant.'

'Madame Bryant? But Valerie hasn't even been near the place. How could she possibly...'

'No, that's what I said. So I said to the agent, 'Do you mean an English lady, Madame Valerie Bryant?' And you'll never believe what she said...'

'Go on...'

'She said, 'No, a French lady, Madame Arlette Bryant...''

Tony Whelpton

Chapter Six

By the time the day of the singing-lesson arrived, Ted had heard no more from his daughter. Needless to say, this had not prevented him from thinking about the news Sophie had given him a few days earlier, nor, indeed, from talking about it to Valerie – endlessly, it seemed to her, for the conversation always followed the same pattern, and reached the same conclusion:

'I don't know what's got into the woman...'

'So you keep saying.'

'I'm amazed she's got that much money to spare.'

'I know.'

'She will have inherited a lot from her aunt, of course...'

'Yes, Ted.'

'... but even if she can afford it now, why does she want it?'

'I have no idea, Ted.'

'Surely she's not planning to go back to live there permanently...'

'Why not?'

'She likes her life in London too much. And in any case, it's an enormous house. I think she's done it out of spite.'

'Spite? You mean to stop Sophie and Peter buying it?'

'Yes.'

'Why would she want to do that? And how did she know they were thinking of buying it?'

'I don't know. That's what I keep asking myself.'

So the conversation would end – for an hour or so, when it would begin again, taking virtually the same course, give or take a few slight changes of word-order, and each time the questions remained unanswered.

While on the train from Crowthorne to London, en route for his singing-lesson with Andrew Barnes, Ted found himself thinking about it once more. Today, of course, was the day of Aunt Julie's funeral, and Sophie and Peter would undoubtedly be meeting Arlette, either at the funeral itself or, more likely, at the get-together afterwards. Would they, he wondered, tackle her about the matter? Even if Sophie didn't, he felt fairly confident that Peter would. And what would be Arlette's response? She would surely say that she had no idea they were interested in that house, or indeed any other – whether or not that was true.

But if it were true, what complaint could Peter and Sophie have? And if it were not true, how had she found out that Peter and Sophie were even thinking of buying a property? They had not told her themselves, or they would not have been so annoyed about it all. Neither he nor Valerie had said a word about it either. Perhaps the agent had let it out – but that could only have been after Arlette had expressed an interest in the property herself, so that would rule out any likelihood of her action being a deliberate attempt to thwart her daughter and son-in-law.

But who else could have told her? As far as Ted was aware, the only other person who knew about it was Jim, and Ted dismissed that possibility out of hand, for, apart from two brief encounters in Montpellier at which Ted had himself been present, Jim would have had no contact with Arlette, and to Ted's certain knowledge, Jim had not said anything to her about it when they were in Montpellier. Of course Ted had told her that they were in Montpellier to check out a property on behalf of a friend, but he was sure he had not given away any more than that.

That being the case, thought Ted, there was only one possibility remaining: Arlette had acted in all innocence, and, however inconvenient it might be to Sophie and Peter's plans, she was totally blameless and they had no cause for complaint. The thought of Arlette being either innocent or blameless in any circumstances whatever seemed completely alien to Ted, but even he had to admit that it could all have happened by coincidence. After all, as Sherlock Holmes said, once you have eliminated all possible solutions to a mystery, you have to start giving credence to the impossible ones.

Ted's singing-lesson went quite well, he thought, in spite of the fact that he felt rather nervous to begin with – fancy being nervous at my age, he thought, but in truth he was merely reacting in the way most older people do when they find themselves once more playing a role they thought they had left behind many years before. When he emerged from the music-room he was delighted to see Dilys sitting in the drawing-room, but they had time only to say the briefest of hellos before she was called in to have her lesson.

Ted took a seat in the drawing-room and picked up a magazine which was lying on the table, leafing through it in a desultory manner while Dilys went through some fairly routine vocal exercises, but then dropping it altogether and straining to hear more clearly as she began singing the *Habanera* from *Carmen*.

By the time Dilys eventually emerged from her lesson, Ted was quite entranced by the sounds coming from the next room. He realized, of course, that she must have a good voice, or she would not have been able to get into the Bach Choir in the first place, let alone stay there for a number of years, especially since, as with most choirs, the competition is fiercer for the women's than for the men's parts, but he had not even imagined that her voice would be as fetching as the one he had just heard. Once they had taken leave of Andrew and were walking down the road in the direction of a wine-bar where Dilys had suggested they have lunch, he told her so.

'Oh Ted, don't exaggerate, my voice is okay, but it's not that fantastic!'

'Well, I thought it was.'

'I'm glad you did. I would have been very upset if you had thought it was awful, so I won't keep on about it!'

'Something else that impressed me was your French pronunciation – it was faultless!'

'Jim would be pleased to hear you say that – he always helps me when I'm singing in French, and he's such a stickler for getting it absolutely right.'

'Quite right too!'

'Anyway, tell me, how did you get on with Andrew?'

'Pretty well, I think. He's very easy to get on with, and he's very encouraging.'

'Yes, that's what I like about him. He doesn't let you get away with sloppy singing, but he does have a knack of putting you in your place in such a way that you couldn't possibly take offence. Anyway, he told me he thought you had a very good chance of passing your audition.'

By this time they had reached the wine-bar, and general conversation stopped for a while until they had settled at their table and had ordered lunch.

'Well,' said Ted, raising his glass. 'Here's to our auditions!'

'I'll drink to that,' replied Dilys. 'To our auditions!'

'Does Andrew really think I've got a good chance?' said Ted, after his initial sip of wine.

'Yes, I'm sure he wouldn't have said anything at all otherwise. I mean, he's got to say encouraging things to you, but he's not obliged to repeat them to me. I do hope you get in though, it will be awfully nice to have you there as well. But it would be very disappointing if...'

'... if I didn't get in?'

'No, if you got in and I got chucked out at my re-audition...'

'Chucked out! Don't be daft! You're not a demon.'

'A demon? What do you mean?'

'I'm thinking about the demons in *Gerontius*, "dispossessed, aside-thrust, chucked down by the sheer might of a despot's will"...'

'Ha, ha,' Dilys laughed. 'I don't think the conductor of the Bach Choir would regard himself as a despot, and I certainly hope he doesn't think of me as a "low-born clod"!'

'Of course not. You came from quite a good family actually, didn't you?'

The ensuing two-part fit of giggles temporarily put a stop to their conversation, and they ate in silence for a few minutes.

Eventually it was Ted who began talking again: 'How's Jim, by the way? I've hardly spoken to him since Winchester.'

'Oh, Jim's okay. But he's been acting a bit strangely lately.'

'In what way?'

'Well, he's been drinking a lot...'

'I got the impression that was fairly normal behaviour for Jim.'

'Well yes, I know, but he's been drinking even more than usual. And he's been moody – sometimes tetchy, sometimes just quiet. And he wasn't happy about my meeting you for lunch – in fact he seemed quite jealous.'

'Jealous! Did he think I was going to seduce you?'

'You did once...'

'I had the impression it was six of one and half a dozen of the other.'

'I know it was – I just wondered if you remembered.'

'Oh yes, I remember all right! But Jim doesn't know anything about that, does he?'

'No, of course not. It's not the sort of thing I'd talk about with him anyway – he's so strait-laced. It's that Catholic upbringing, you know.'

'Yes, I know, or at least it's his particular variety of Catholic upbringing...'

'Oh, I'm sorry, Ted, I'd forgotten. You're a Catholic too, aren't you?'

'No, not any more. I was brought up as one though.'

'I thought you still were – I'm sure Jim thinks you are.'

'Yes, he probably does. I certainly haven't told him, and he's never asked me, so he probably just assumes that I still am.'

'Yes, that's Jim all right. He's not very keen on change really, so he finds it hard to realize that other people aren't the same. What made you change tack then?'

'Oh, all sorts of things – it's a long time ago.'

'What sort of things?'

'Oh, philosophical things, and the realization that the preaching changed according to the priest's perception of the intellectual level of his audience, which I found patronizing. And being abused by the parish priest didn't help.'

'What! You poor thing! Did you tell your parents?'

'No, I couldn't – I was too embarrassed and confused for one thing, and then they had too much respect for the parish priest. In fact, when they decided it was time that I learned about the facts of life, he was the person they asked to tell me...'

'And did he?'

'No, I told him I already knew all about it, so he didn't insist – I think he was quite relieved. He was certainly embarrassed. And then some time later he refused to give me absolution when I went to confession. He told me I should go to see another priest and tell him what we'd done together. That made me feel guilty too, even though I hadn't actually done anything myself to feel guilty about.'

'Oh, guilt – yes, I know about guilt. Jim suffers from it all the time.'

Dilys hesitated, looked at Ted, then started again: 'Given that you were still a Catholic when we... when we did what we did, I assume you went to confession afterwards ...'

'No, I didn't as a matter of fact.'

'Why not? Didn't you feel guilty?'

'No, not at all. In fact guilt never entered my mind, because it was all so beautiful and I felt so happy. It was because after the business with Father Kerrigan I never went to confession again. I suppose I was still nominally a Catholic, because I was still going to Mass on Sundays, but I was just going through the motions ... I was already on the way out.'

There was a minute or two when neither of them said a word. Then they both started to speak at once.

'Why didn't you ...' Ted began.

'That letter I ...' said Dilys.

They both stopped, laughing rather self-consciously, then Dilys insisted that Ted ask his question first.

'Okay,' he said. 'I just wanted to ask why you never answered any of my letters.'

'What letters?'

'I wrote to you five or six times after you sent me a horrible letter saying you never wanted to see me again.'

'I didn't say I didn't want to see you again.'

'Perhaps not in so many words, but you said you thought it would be better if we stopped seeing each other, which comes to the same thing. So I wrote to you – over and over again – and I never got an answer.'

'I never got any letters, Ted. If I had done, I would have written, believe me. My parents must have intercepted them – I stayed in Scotland, you see, when they went back to Nottingham. Then they decided to sell the house in Caledon Road, and I never even saw it again. They certainly didn't give me any letter from you. But speaking of letters ... That letter I sent you ... I didn't want to send it ... I didn't even want to write it ...'

'So why did you?'

'Because my father made me. We had the most fearful row about it, but it was no good. I tried not to make it a horrible letter. I did my best to show you that I had no regrets about what we did ... I'm so sorry, Ted.'

Ted reached out across the table, took Dilys's hand, and raised it to his lips. 'Don't worry, Dilly. It doesn't hurt any more. But it did for a long time.'

'I know,' Dilys replied. 'For me too. But it's all a long time ago now, isn't it? Water under the bridge and all that ...'

'Yes, it is, so let's talk about something else. I mean, from what you've said about Jim, he's likely to ask you when you get home what we've been talking about, and you can hardly tell him about all that stuff.'

'No, you're right.'

'You know that house in France Jim and I went to look at...'

Ted went on to recount to Dilys what had happened in the last few days – Aunt Julie, Sophie, Peter, Arlette, the house – ending with the suggestion that she might ask Jim if he could recall anything that either of them had said to Arlette that could have let the cat out of the bag. After that, they went their separate ways, Dilys back to Kensington, Ted back to Waterloo to catch the train home to Crowthorne.

At roughly the same time that Ted was speaking to Dilys about the house in Saint-Gély-du-Fesc, Sophie and Peter were about to broach the same subject with Arlette. Aunt Julie's funeral service was now over, and the three of them, accompanied by a handful of friends and acquaintances of the deceased – Tante Émilie was not well enough to come, and there were no other relatives left, it seemed – had gathered together in the bar of the very hotel in which Arlette's dramatic encounter with Ted and Jim had taken place. As long as outsiders were present, it was, naturally, impossible to discuss family matters, but, after what seemed an eternity to Peter and Sophie, they at last found themselves alone. Even so, the topic of the house was not the one with which Sophie chose to begin the conversation. 'I understand that you and Dad are back on speaking-terms,' she said.

'I don't know what you mean, Sophie. As far as I'm concerned, we've always been on speaking terms.'

'Oh, come off it, Arlette,' Peter interjected, 'you've hardly uttered a civil word to each other in years.'

'That's not my fault,' Arlette retorted. 'But what you said to me on the phone about burying the hatchet made such good sense that I thought it was worth swallowing my pride and making a real effort to make things better – for your sake really.'

Then, turning towards Sophie, she added, 'Peter does talk such good sense, you know. He could almost be French.'

Sophie and Peter were both dumb-struck; not that Arlette noticed, because she kept on talking: 'And then, of course, your father had his friend with him – what was his name, Jim, I think – and he was so charming it would have been very impolite to have acted in any other way.'

'Oh yes, Arlette,' muttered Peter to himself. '*Toujours la politesse...*'

Sophie, however, had decided the time had come to go on the attack: 'Of course, you know why Dad and Jim were in Montpellier, don't you?'

'They said something about looking over a property on behalf of a friend – I forget where it was...'

'Saint-Gély-du-Fesc...'

'Ah yes, so it was.'

'You know very well it was,' said Sophie. 'Because I understand you've just bought it.'

'What do you mean, I've just bought it?'

'You've just bought the house in Saint-Gély-du-Fesc that we were thinking of buying, that's what!' said Sophie, whose patience was running out.

'I didn't know you were thinking of buying a house in France – why didn't you tell me? Do you mean Ted and Jim were actually looking on your behalf?'

'Yes, they were,' said Peter.

'Do you mean you chose to ask your father and a stranger to look at it rather than ask me? I think you owe me an explanation...'

'What!' Sophie exploded.

'I am your mother, Sophie,' replied Arlette. 'I feel really hurt.'

'Don't be ridiculous, Arlette,' said Peter, who had decided it was time for him to take a strong line before his mother-in-law was completely swallowed up in a dramatic performance worthy of the Comédie Française. 'Did you or did you not know that Ted and Jim were acting for us?'

'How could I have known? They lied to me, and you didn't say anything about it at all.'

'I see. You just went along to see an estate-agent and, by sheer coincidence, happened to buy the house we had set our hearts on...'

'How could I have known? And how do you know I've bought a house anyway? Who told you that?'

'The agent told us when we called to make an offer. Are you really telling us that you didn't know we were involved?'

'Of course I am. How could I have known?'

'Look, mother, we're going round in circles. Why do you want to buy a house in Saint-Gély anyway?'

'It's a nice place...'

Sophie resisted the urge to scream with frustration, and ploughed on: 'But why do you want to buy a house down here anyway? You're settled in London – are you thinking of coming back to live in France?'

'There's always that possibility.'

'But even if you did, a house like that would be much too big for you.'

'Let me explain.'

'It's time you did.'

'Well, I realized that Aunt Julie was going to leave me most of her money. She's left some to you, by the way, Sophie...'

'Go on.'

'And obviously I needed to do something with it, and taking it over to England seemed a silly idea, considering the exchange rate, and the commission I'd have to pay – given that Blair and his stupid government won't join the euro... That's why I thought buying a house would be a good idea, and the more I thought about it, the more I realized that if I bought a really nice big house I'd be able to let it out when I wasn't using it myself, and you and Peter would be able to stay in it, and then when I eventually die –

Arlette paused for a moment to maximize the dramatic effect – I could leave it to you.'

'You mean you were really just thinking of us all the time...'

'Yes, of course. Now, if you'll excuse me, I have an appointment at the *notaire*'s office at four o'clock.' And Arlette departed abruptly, in much the same manner as she had left the same room a few weeks earlier.

Arlette returned to her room. She had not exactly lied about having an appointment with her lawyer, because she was indeed due to see him at four o'clock – the following day. Once back in her room, she made straight for the telephone and dialled a number. A few seconds later, a man's voice – an English man's voice – answered: 'Hello.'

'Allô, Jim, c'est Arlette.'

'Arlette! What are you doing ringing me at home? I told you it wasn't safe...'

'Yes, but you also told me that your wife was having lunch with Ted today, so I figured it would be safe.'

'Ah yes,' said Jim. 'I'd forgotten I'd told you that.'

'And you'd forgotten you'd asked me out to lunch as well?'

'No, of course I hadn't. Anyway, where are you now? I thought you'd be at your aunt's funeral.'

'Yes, I am – or I have been. It's over now though. It's just that I have a couple of things to tell you about. Or rather one thing to tell you about and one thing to warn you about.'

'Warn me about? That sounds sinister. I'd better hear the warning first.'

'No, it wouldn't make sense if I didn't give you the bit of news first.'

'Okay, go ahead then. But be quick. I don't know what time Dilys will be home.'

'Aren't you allowed to use the phone when she's out?'

'Yes, of course I am. It's just that I'm a bad liar.'

'Well, if she comes in you'll just have to put the phone down. I won't mind.'

'And if she asks who I was speaking to?' asked Jim nervously.

'Just tell her it was a wrong number. Anyway, you remember that house in Saint-Gély-du-Fesc that you and Ted went to have a look at?'

'Yes, of course.'

'Well, I've bought it.'

'You've done what?'

'I've bought it. Or, to be more precise, I'm in the process of buying it.'

'Why?'

'Because I can afford it, and because I thought it would be a nice idea. You liked the house, didn't you?'

'Oh yes, I thought it was a fantastic place.'

'Would you like to visit it again?'

Jim ignored the leading question, or at least chose not to answer it, and said: 'You said something about a warning...'

'Yes, the thing is, Sophie and Peter have found out that I've bought it, and they're not very happy.'

'I'm not in the least surprised.'

'And they're sure to talk to Sophie's father about it.'

'Yes...'

'And they might come to realize that you told me they were thinking of buying the house themselves.'

'How would they be able to work that out?'

'Oh, Jim... Listen, Peter's a lawyer.'

'Yes, so what?'

'Peter's a lawyer,' Arlette repeated. 'And lawyers are so devious.'

'Oh, God!' exclaimed Jim, not out of surprise at Arlette's remark, even if he was thinking that she was pretty devious herself, but because at that moment he heard Dilys's key turn in the lock of the apartment door. 'Dilys is here – I must go.'

Jim replaced the receiver quickly, and went into the bathroom to give himself a few minutes to collect his thoughts before he had to face his wife.

When he emerged, he found Dilys in the kitchen in the process of filling the kettle.

'I'm just making some tea, Jim,' she said. 'Would you like one?'

'Yes, please, that would be very nice.'

Dilys continued with the tea-making process, a little surprised that Jim had made neither comment nor inquiry about her lunch with Ted;

in the light of Jim's initial reaction to the news that she was meeting his old friend she had expected a fairly rigorous interrogation, but in the event none was forthcoming. After a little consideration, however, she decided to raise the matter herself, so immediately after giving Jim his promised cup of tea, she said: 'I had a really pleasant lunch with Ted today after my lesson...'

'Oh yes,' replied Jim. 'I'd forgotten you were seeing him today. How is he?'

'Oh, he seemed fine. A bit nervous about his Bach Choir audition, but Andrew said a lot of encouraging things to him, so I don't think there's any need for him to feel nervous. I think he probably has a tendency to underestimate his abilities. Of course, you know him far better than I do. Is that how he strikes you?'

'Oh, I don't know really. He certainly wasn't the pushy type at school, but I haven't really seen enough of him recently to be able to make that sort of judgement.'

'Anyway, he was good company. Of course it's the first time I've had a conversation with him without you or Valerie being there. He's certainly very easy to get on with.'

'Oh yes, he's always been very sociable.'

'It's a pity you lost touch for all those years.'

'Yes, it is really. We always got on very well together in our younger days.'

With that, the conversation moved on to more mundane matters, leaving Dilys just a little puzzled at the fact that Jim had revealed no sign at all of the jealousy – yes, jealousy was the right word, she was quite sure – which he had evinced a couple of weeks earlier.

When there was a lull in the conversation, however, Dilys felt sufficiently emboldened to raise with Jim the matter which had been most on Ted's mind: 'You know that house in France that you and Ted went to have a look at?'

'Yes, of course, what about it?'

'Apparently Ted's daughter's missed out on it.'

'Really? That's a shame. It's a nice house. They should have acted more quickly.'

'Maybe, but it appears that it's Arlette who's bought it.'

'Arlette?' asked Jim, trying hard to look surprised.

'Yes, Arlette, Ted's first wife.'

'Yes, yes, I know who she is. Well I never!'

'The thing is, Ted is wondering whether she knew Sophie and her husband were interested in that house. He's absolutely certain that he didn't tell her, and he's wondering whether by any chance you let on while you were on your own with her.'

'On my own with her?' Jim repeated.

'Yes, when you were on your own with her before Ted arrived.'

'Oh no, of course not. I didn't even know who she was then,' replied Jim, much relieved at being able to give a truthful answer to a potentially explosive question.

As Peter and Sophie were having breakfast the following morning, Sophie's mobile phone began to ring.

'Oh God, I hope that's not the hospital,' said Peter.

'No, it's a French number. I'll take it outside, so as not to disturb the other guests.'

Peter carried on drinking his coffee. Two minutes later Sophie returned, and said to him: 'Come on, Peter, we've got to get a move on – we're meeting the estate-agent at Saint-Gély at ten o'clock.'

'We're what?' said Peter incredulously. 'Has she found us another house to look at?'

'No, it's the same one. That was her on the phone just now. She was ringing to tell me that the sale had fallen through, and if we were still interested, she could show us round this morning. So I said yes, we could be there by ten o'clock.'

They hastily went back to their room, flung the few things they had brought with them into a suitcase, paid their hotel bill, and twenty-five minutes later they were sitting in their hire-car en route for Saint-Gély-du-Fesc.

Once at the house they soon discovered that it was everything they had expected after hearing Ted's account and, to the surprise of the agent, a sale in principle was agreed in a matter of minutes. In fact Sophie and Peter had rehearsed all the pros and cons several times a week or so earlier, and were only waiting to see the property with their own eyes before proceeding. They did try to find out from the agent what had happened to make the house available once more, but all she could tell them was that she had received a phone-call from the *notaire* at nine o'clock that morning, informing her that the prospective buyer had withdrawn.

Afterwards, as they drove towards Montpellier airport, Sophie and Peter could not help wondering what had happened to make Arlette change her mind about buying the house. At length Peter said: 'There's only one way to find out for certain, and that's to ring her.'

'Yes, you're right, I suppose. She probably won't tell us the real reason, of course. Still, let's see what she says.'

Sophie dialled her mother's mobile number. A few seconds later she was speaking to her, and only a moment or so after that, she had broached the subject of the house, albeit a little tentatively. 'You've decided not to buy the house in Saint-Gély then...'

'How do you know that? You seem to know everything I'm doing these days even before I know myself.'

Sophie refused to be drawn into responding to that comment, and carried on: 'What made you change your mind?'

'You mean it's not obvious?'

'No, it's not obvious at all.'

'Well, I could see how upset you and Peter were at the thought that I should own it and let you use it rather than you owning it yourselves...'

Sophie sighed deeply but inaudibly.

'... so I told the lawyer yesterday evening that I was pulling out and leaving the way clear for you to have it. I was just on the point of calling you to tell you when you rang me.'

'Oh yes,' said Sophie to herself, 'so why didn't you call us last night to tell us?'

By now, however, they had arrived at the airport, and, before taking leave of her mother, Sophie asked one final question: 'What are you going to do with Tante Julie's money if you're not going to buy that house?'

She really expected a reply that was either non-committal or downright indignant, but in fact, to Sophie's surprise, Arlette said: 'I've been thinking about that, and I think I'm going to buy a new place in London – my place is a bit cramped really, you know.'

Chapter Seven

The next two weeks witnessed a frenzy of activity for the Bryant and the Fletcher families in two areas especially: legal and musical. The first was Dilys's re-audition, which she duly passed and which meant that, unless something dramatic and unforeseen occurred, she would be able to continue singing with the Bach Choir for a further three years. The second was that Sophie and Peter finalised their property deal and were now the owners of the fabulous house in Saint-Gély-du-Fesc about which Ted and Jim had raved. Peter himself, who had less experience of the French way of doing things than his wife, was quite incredulous, though Sophie assured him that, perhaps surprisingly for a country so bureaucratic in many respects, it was very normal in France for house sales to be completed quickly once a price had been agreed by both buyer and seller. What is more, they were also pleasantly surprised to find that their offer – 20,000 euros lower than the asking-price – was accepted without demur.

And then at last it was Ted's turn to face the Bach Choir's conductor for an audition in which, to his own amazement and delight, he was successful in his turn, and he lost no time in calling first Valerie, then Dilys, to give them the news, immediately after he left the building in which the auditions were held. Both were equally delighted but – it seemed to Ted, very curiously – were not in the slightest surprised.

Immediately after receiving the call from Ted, Dilys passed the news on to Jim, who made little comment; she then went out to meet their daughter Jemima for one of their periodic shopping-trips. As she emerged onto the street, a car drew up in front of the building next door, where one of the flats had been on sale for quite a time now. Two people got out: a man, whom Dilys recognised as an estate-agent, for she had seen him accompanying other prospective buyers from time to time, and a dark-haired, well-dressed woman, clearly not in the first flush of youth but none the less very attractive, who, to Dilys's surprise, smiled in her direction and said 'Good morning' in an accent that was unmistakably French, before disappearing with the agent into the vacant apartment. Dilys then continued on her way and thought no more about it; there were, after all, thousands and thousands of French people living in Kensington.

A quarter of an hour later, the viewing completed, the agent and his client emerged from the apartment. They stopped for a moment and shook hands, whereupon the man got into his car and drove off, whilst the woman walked off in the opposite direction, not stopping until she arrived at a French *pâtisserie* opposite Gloucester Road underground station.

Once inside the *pâtisserie* she chose a table, ordered a coffee, took out her mobile and dialled a number. When the call was answered she said in a low voice: 'Jim, it's Arlette. I know you don't like me calling you at home, but I know your wife is out, and I have some news for you.'

'Some news? What news? If you mean you've pulled out of the deal at Saint-Gély, I've heard about that...'

'Oh no, Jim, that was two weeks ago. No, I wanted to tell you what I've decided to do instead. It's good news, I think. I hope you'll think it's good news too. Call me when it's more convenient for you, and I'll tell you all about it.'

'Can't you give me some idea now?'

'Well, just a brief idea, but I'm in a public place and there are people I know in here.'

'Okay, so what is it then?'

'I've decided to buy a new apartment.'

'Really? You mean in France?'

'No, in Kensington – in the house next door to yours. I must go – call me soon.' And she switched off her mobile before Jim had time to react.

Jim replaced the receiver and sat down. Then the reaction started: in fact his brain went into over-drive. What on earth was she thinking of? Obviously it was a nice property, and there was absolutely no reason why she shouldn't live there if she chose; what's more, she would be by no means the only French lady living alone in that square. But did she choose it to be near him, or was he flattering himself unduly? No, on balance he thought he wasn't, because, even if she had not spelt it out in words of one syllable, she had made it pretty clear that she would have liked him to visit her in France if she had bought the house in Saint-Gély.

He had rejected that invitation, or at least had chosen to ignore it, for his intentions in that direction were by no means clear-cut. He had been tempted a couple of times, and had succumbed, and he knew himself well enough to be aware that he would be tempted again, but he was wary of entering into any more than a casual, and very temporary relationship. If Arlette were living next door, it was inevitable that he would keep bumping into her whether he wanted to or not, and he would not be able to put the temptation to the back of his mind in the way that he could while she was living in a different part of Kensington.

More to the point, it was also likely that Dilys would keep bumping into her as well – perhaps even get to know her and invite her to meet her Francophile husband, not realising that he and the newly-arrived neighbour were already acquainted in an extremely intimate way.

And then, of course, there was Ted, who had at one time been even more intimately linked to Arlette, and it was probable that he and Valerie would be more frequent visitors now that Ted was going to join the Bach Choir too. It was possible, he supposed, that Ted could make relatively frequent visits without ever running into Arlette, but what about Ted and Arlette's daughter?

Sophie, as was natural, was in regular contact with her mother, and would not only very soon know that she was moving to a new place, but would undoubtedly come to see Arlette there. Once she had, would she not tell her father about Arlette's new apartment – if not going into minute detail, then at least saying roughly whereabouts it was. And what would be Ted's response? Jim could hear it already: 'Why, that must be pretty close to Jim and Dilys's place! What's the actual address? ... Good God, that's incredible, it's next door!' And then, from Ted to Dilys, with a perfectly innocent remark in a post-rehearsal chat: 'I hear my ex-wife's moved in next door to you...'

Jim buried his head in his hands. What could he do about it? Absolutely nothing. But above all, when the news ultimately reached him, he must feign utter astonishment, for how could he have known this was going to happen if neither his wife nor any of his close acquaintances had told him? At length a gleam of light appeared at the end of what had seemed a very long, black tunnel. He must take the initiative himself by telling Dilys and Ted that Arlette was moving in. But how could he do that without letting on that he had been seeing Arlette? That was easy, for, after all, once she had moved in, he was just as likely to bump into her as was Dilys. But to make really sure that that was how it worked out, he needed to know when she would be moving in, or when she would be coming to look over it again prior to moving in. He looked at his watch. Yes, enough time had now elapsed for Arlette to have got back home, but, just as he reached the telephone, the door opened, and in came Dilys.

Sophie, on the other hand, was not the least little bit concerned about what her mother might or might not be up to; indeed, she had all but forgotten Arlette's stated intention of finding somewhere else to live in London, knowing full well that she was a creature of impulse who might very well have forgotten by this time that she had ever expressed any such intention.

Quite apart from that, however, she and Peter had other preoccupations, for in addition to the demands of their extremely busy working lives, they now found themselves the owners of a house in France, with the summer holidays looming and the house only sparsely furnished. One evening, on returning home from the hospital, she called Ted: 'Hello, Dad,' she said when he answered. 'I was just wondering – have you and Valerie got a holiday sorted out yet?'

'No, you know what we're like. We always do things at the last minute anyway, and in the last couple of weeks I've been a bit preoccupied with singing lessons and the like. We were planning to talk about it this evening after supper.'

'Well, we wondered if you would like to spend a couple of weeks at the villa...'

'What, in Saint-Gély?'

'Yes.'

'Love to! But... does it have any furniture yet?'

'Well, that's the point actually. We did negotiate the purchase of a few items, so the place is liveable-in, but Peter and I can't go out there within the next couple of weeks, and we've ordered quite a lot of stuff online. If you and Valerie could be there when it's delivered it would do us a great favour.'

'I can think of nothing better personally, and I'm sure Valerie will have no problems with the idea.'

'And if you'd like to invite Jim and Dilys to join you, there are two bedrooms already fully furnished, so there'd be no problem there either.'

'Oh, okay. I have no idea what their plans are, but I'll talk it over with Valerie and then put it to them as well.'

As Ted had predicted, Valerie readily agreed, which would not have been at all surprising to anyone who knew her, for she was the most amenable of wives, the most amenable of women even. Not that she was particularly self-effacing, and she was certainly not subservient; while not being a regular church-goer she displayed the Christian virtues of humility and charity more than many who made weekly public statements of their adherence to such concepts. As Ted was apt to say, for he was by no means unconscious or unappreciative of her qualities, anyone whom Valerie befriended had a friend for life. Moreover she had many friends, and never ceased to be solicitous of their well-being. Basically, if those around her were happy, she was happy; if they were unhappy, she would not be happy herself until she had done something to alleviate their unhappiness. And on top of all this, she was good fun to be with.

Characteristically, therefore, it was Valerie who immediately telephoned Dilys to ask if she and Jim would like to join them, an invitation which Dilys was quick to accept, even in Jim's absence, knowing full well that for Jim to pass up on a chance to go to France would be akin to an alcoholic refusing a drink after three months' enforced abstinence.

When Jim learned the news, he was predictably enthusiastic. When he had time to reflect, however, he was positively joyous: this, it seemed to him, let him off so many hooks, not the least significant being that it probably meant that all of them would be away at the time that Arlette moved into the apartment next door, and the chances therefore were that they would all hear the news of her move together, at the same time, which would make it much easier for him to manage; he would simply have to express incredulity. Also, it would remove him, for the time being, from the temptations of Arlette, which, he felt, were becoming ever more pressing – not that that meant he was necessarily any less likely to give into them. And on top of this was the undoubted pleasure of re-visiting a place which initially had seemed to him like a paradise on earth, and which he had all but resigned himself to never visiting again, unless, of course, he had become firmly, finally, and perhaps fatally ensnared by Arlette.

Less than a week later, the four friends were on their way.

Tony Whelpton

Chapter Eight

When they arrived at the villa Valerie and Dilys were just as enthralled as their husbands had been on their initial visit. Contrary to their expectations, there was no work to be done when they arrived, other than to unpack their cases and think about what they would eat that evening, for Sophie had made arrangements for someone to go in and clean the house throughout prior to their arrival. Furthermore, the fridge and the larder were already stocked with all the essentials, so there would in reality have been no necessity for them to do any shopping that day at all. Ted suggested, however, that he and Jim should go out and buy something to put on the barbecue that evening.

'I was just thinking,' he said, 'that I'd better make my culinary contribution first, because once Dilys and Valerie have taken over there'll be no going back. If I go first, things can only get better...'

'Or worse,' Jim interjected, 'if you were foolish enough to let me cook anything!'

'Don't you cook then, Jim?' asked Valerie.

'Not at all,' Jim laughed. 'My main contribution to the dining process is to be a willing and appreciative receptacle. Come on, Ted, let's do the shopping, and perhaps Monsieur Durand will buy you a *pastis!*'

'Who's Monsieur Durand?' asked Dilys and Valerie in chorus.

'We'll tell you later,' replied Ted.

'Well, that's a turn-up for the books,' said Dilys to Valerie as the two men disappeared into the distance. 'That's the first time I've ever known Jim volunteer to go shopping – things are definitely looking up!'

'Don't hold your breath,' laughed Valerie. 'They'll probably be three sheets to the wind when they come back!'

'What a good idea,' said Dilys. 'How do you fancy a glass of *rosé* – I saw a bottle in the fridge just now...'

The barbecue was a great success as, indeed, was the entire evening, with Ted's barbecuing skills being praised by all, even by Dilys, which pleased Ted enormously. The two ladies chatted non-stop as if they had known each other for as long as their men-folk had, and Ted and Jim were both in particularly good form – as were the crickets, whose non-stop chirping almost drowned the wine-soaked hilarity which continued long into the night.

The following morning, the only detail of the previous evening's conversation that any of them was able to recall was the matter of by what name the villa should be known, for there was none shown on the gate, nor on any of the documentation that they had seen; the unanimous choice had been *Les Cigales*, because they all felt the crickets had made as much of a contribution to their evening as any of them – possibly, suggested Jim, an even more sensible contribution than they themselves had been in any condition to make. In the sober light of day, however, they decided it would be a good idea to check the other villas in the little road, which itself, of course, bore the name *Rue des Cigales*.

Since there were only three other villas in the road, it was a matter of just a few minutes to settle the issue and, as the others were named respectively *Les Oliviers*, *Les Lauriers-Roses* and *Les Tamarins*, it was quickly agreed that no other name was possible. Five minutes later the postman called, depositing in the mail-box alongside the gate an official-looking letter addressed to '*Madame Sophie Fitzgerald, Villa des Cigales, Rue des Cigales, 34980 Saint-Gély-du-Fesc.*' To universal glee, Jim responded to this with the comment: 'Whoever said French bureaucrats were slow to get on with things?' Various deliveries made to the villa during the next few days finally convinced Ted that Sophie and Peter had simply forgotten to tell them the villa's name – presumably making the assumption that because Ted and Jim had already been there, they already knew what it was.

Throughout the entire fortnight which Dilys, Jim, Ted and Valerie spent at *Les Cigales*, the conversation was non-stop. Sometimes frivolous, sometimes earnest; now hilarious, now serious; at times sober, at other times drunken, but always good-natured, and seemingly in a state of perpetual motion. Nor did it appear to matter who was involved: whether all four of them were present, or just two or three in any of the possible permutations, it was just like being at a never-ending dinner-party, although, as at a dinner-party, the occasional awkward moment arose – as, for instance, when Jim and Ted were having their usual pre-dinner *pastis* on the third evening of their stay, which was a Friday, and Jim said: 'Something I must check out tomorrow are the times of masses on Sunday...'

'In Saint-Gély, you mean?' replied Ted.

'Yes, of course. I don't see any point in going all the way into Montpellier.'

'In that case I can tell you, because I noticed when we were in the village yesterday. Mass is at 11.15.'

'11.15! That's a bit late, isn't it? That's getting close to *pastis* time!'

'Come off it, Jim – it's always close to *pastis* time with you! Anyway, that's the only mass here on Sunday, although there's one at Les Matelles at 9.30, and that's only a couple of miles or so down the road.'

'Well, shall we go to Les Matelles then? What do you think?'

'You can go wherever you like, but I'm not going.'

'What?'

'I'm not going. I haven't been in a Catholic church for well over forty years, except to a wedding or a funeral or something like that. Didn't you realise?'

'No, I knew you'd got a divorce and all that, and I wondered how you'd managed to fiddle that, but you never told me...'

'You never asked me, and there seemed to be no reason to tell you – it's not something I think about a great deal, to be honest.'

'What? You astound me!'

'For God's sake, why?'

'Well, I just remember that you were a Catholic when we were at school, and I simply assumed that you still were. I didn't realise you were a lapsed Catholic.'

'I don't consider myself a *lapsed* Catholic. That seems to imply something fairly recent and something that just sort of happened through laziness or apathy, rather than something which came about as the result of long and careful thought.'

'So you don't believe in God either?'

'I didn't say that. But if I did start going to church regularly, I'd join the Church of England rather than become a Catholic again...'

Jim snorted, as if that made it twice as bad. 'I suppose it was the result of your breaking up with Arlette?'

'No, not at all. It was well before I even met Arlette.'

'What brought it about then?'

Jim took a deep breath. Should he or shouldn't he? He decided he should.

'There were a number of things, but being groped by Father Kerrigan in the cupboard where the altar boys' cassocks and cottas were kept didn't help.'

'Father Kerrigan? I don't believe it!'

'I'm not surprised – my parents wouldn't have believed it either.'

'I'm not sure that I do. You must have imagined it.'

'I certainly didn't, I can assure you. And by all accounts he wasn't the only one at it, was he?'

'Well, I've never come across anything like that, and all the stories you hear these days are always about things that are supposed to have happened in the dim and distant past and so can't be proved.'

'Are you saying I'm a liar?'

'Well, you don't strike me as someone who's been emotionally scarred for life.'

'I didn't claim to have been emotionally scarred for life, but I wasn't happy about it, I can tell you, and certainly some have suffered long-term damage.'

'That's what they say, but I find it hard to believe.'

'Why?'

'Well, it's all been blown up by the press, hasn't it...'

'I have no doubt that the press have built it up a bit, but I know what I experienced, and I also know that I wasn't the only one. There's been so much hypocrisy in the way the Church has dealt with it. But to get back to the original subject, you have the choice of 11.15 at Saint-Gély or 9.30 at Les Matelles. Now have another drink and let's change the subject.'

Jim grunted quietly and acquiesced, and before long everything was back to normal.

The following afternoon, while Valerie was having a swim and Jim enjoying a nap, Ted and Dilys sat by the pool talking about Ted's imminent initiation into the world of the Bach Choir. To Dilys's surprise, Ted had absolutely no idea what pieces they would be working on, so she said to him: 'I'm sure the normal practice is to give you the programme when you get the results of your audition. That way at least you get some chance to look at stuff before you get thrown in at the deep end at rehearsal...'

'Yes, but don't forget I've only been told unofficially so far that I'm in. They said I'll get an official letter telling me the audition was successful, and they'll enclose the programme with that, but it hadn't arrived by the time we came away. What's on the programme anyway?'

'Oh, I haven't got it with me, and there's too much for me to be able to tell you the whole lot. I know we're doing two *Requiems*, the Verdi and the Duruflé...'

'Well, that's a good start. I've done both of those before – not recently, but at least they won't be entirely new. Anything else you can remember?'

'There is something new – new to me, anyway. It's something by Handel – a pastoral ode is how it was described, but I don't know anything else about it, other than the fact that it's based on Milton's *L'Allegro* and *Il Penseroso* – oh, and we're doing it in Paris too.'

'Are we? When's that, do you know?'

'Can't remember exactly – early October, I think.'

'That doesn't give us long to learn it...'

'No, but it is Handel, and it should be a bit more straightforward than some things we have to do...'

'Yes, I suppose that's true. Whereabouts in Paris is the concert?'

'Now *that* I can tell you, because we've been there before. It's the Théâtre des Champs-Élysées.'

'Sounds good. Will you be going?'

'Yes, I expect so. I go on most of the foreign trips, especially the shorter ones, and this one only involves a couple of nights away. Actually, doing a concert in Paris is easier in some respects than doing one in Edinburgh...'

'Will Jim go with you?'

'I doubt it. He doesn't usually, and not many husbands and wives travel with us, except on the longer trips.'

'I'm a bit surprised at Jim passing up the idea of going to Paris. I thought he'd jump at it.'

'Yes, I know what you mean, but he'd be more likely to go if it was in Bordeaux or Lyon than if it was in Paris.'

'Oh, I see – wine-producing regions!'

'I hadn't thought of it that way – perhaps you're right! But no, seriously, I think really he finds Paris holds less charm for him these days than it used to do. Do you think you'll go?'

'Haven't thought about it yet. Well, I couldn't very well think about it before, because I've only just found out about it, but as a matter of principle, if I join an organisation I tend to feel an obligation to join in everything that's going, unless there's a very good reason why I can't. So the answer is probably yes.'

At that precise moment Valerie emerged from the pool and Jim awoke from his nap, and the conversation turned, as it usually did at that stage of the day, to what they would eat that evening and who would cook it. To Ted's surprise, Jim volunteered to do the cooking.

'I thought you said you didn't cook, Jim,' said Ted.

'*En principe*,'[5] laughed Jim. 'It was a French statement – as you know, where the French are concerned there's always a big difference between *principe* and *réalité*, and where my cooking's concerned, virtually the only dish I can cook is *moules marinières* so if everybody's happy to have mussels this evening, I'm happy to cook them. But then that seriously is the full extent of my cooking expertise.'

---

[5] 'In theory'

'In that case you'll have to go to the hypermarket to get them,' said Dilys, 'because the local fishmonger will have shut by this time.'

'That's all right,' answered Jim. 'If Ted would like to come with me we can replenish our wine-cellar, such as it is. We're running a bit low. And we need some more *pastis* too.'

'Oh, I see,' said the two wives in unison, which comment was immediately followed by hysterical laughter on their part, and mock indignation on the part of Jim.

Jim and Ted departed on their shopping expedition, leaving their two wives by the pool. When the two men had gone Valerie and Dilys chatted for a while, and then Dilys said: 'You know, Valerie, I think I fancy a nice glass of cold *rosé*, how about you?'

'What a good idea,' said Valerie. 'I'll go and get some.'

A moment later she re-emerged from the villa carrying a tray on which were a bottle of *rosé de Provence* and two glasses. She filled the two glasses, handed one to Dilys, then went to sit on the sun-bed adjacent to Dilys, where Jim had previously been lying.

'This really is Paradise, isn't it?' said Valerie as she took her first sip.

'Yes, it is,' Dilys agreed. 'I'm so glad Ted and Jim met up again in the way they did – I don't mean because otherwise we wouldn't be here, though of course we wouldn't, but it's making such a difference to Jim.'

'What sort of difference?'

'He was spending too much time on his own really. Since he retired he hasn't really had any male friends, and I think it's made him rather inward-looking and morose.'

'No male friends? Are you suggesting he has too many female friends instead?'

'Good Lord, no! Jim would run a mile from a woman on her own these days!'

Valerie's immediate reaction was to think about Jim's encounter with Arlette in Montpellier, or rather what her initial presumption had been, but Dilys continued talking, and the thought passed.

'No, before he met Ted he was spending too much time on his own, and doing too much drinking...'

'He's doing a fair bit now, isn't he?'

'Ha, ha – aren't we all! But he was spending whole days at Lord's on his own, not speaking to anyone – other than the barman, I suppose – and however passionate you are about cricket, that can't be very good for you. Anyway, he was tending to become moody and snappy, and if he didn't like my reaction he took refuge in the bottle.'

'But he seems pretty relaxed now we're in France...'

'Yes, that's exactly my point. He's a changed man since he met Ted again, and I'm so relieved about that.'

Their conversation was halted abruptly by the arrival of a large van in the lane outside. Two men got out, and one opened the doors at the back of the van while the other rang the bell at the gate of the villa.

'Oh,' cried Valerie. 'It must be one of Peter and Sophie's furniture deliveries. I'd completely forgotten we were here for a purpose...'

Dilys laughed. 'Other than to drink, sunbathe and chat, you mean?'

A few minutes after the delivery-men had left, having installed the delivered items in their designated locations, Jim and Ted returned with the shopping.

'Huh,' said Jim, 'I see you're still resting by the pool...'

'What do you mean?' Dilys retaliated. 'We've only been sitting here for two minutes.'

'Yes,' said Valerie, jumping to Dilys's defence. 'We had a furniture delivery, and we've been lugging heavy wardrobes and stuff about.'

'Didn't the delivery-men do that?' asked Ted.

'No, they didn't,' Valerie lied. 'They just dumped everything outside the door and left.'

'You should have left it for us to see to,' said Ted.

'Yes, I know,' said Dilys, winking at Valerie, 'but we didn't want to leave it standing in the blazing sun. And now we're totally exhausted. Would you be a sweetie, Jim, and get Valerie and me a glass of *rosé*?'

Jim turned and made for the kitchen, muttering under his breath and followed by Ted, who was carrying the shopping. As soon as they disappeared from sight the two ladies begin to giggle uncontrollably, like schoolgirls – but stopped the moment they saw Jim and Ted, now both wearing swim shorts, reappearing with their drinks.

'There,' said Jim, placing the glasses on the table. 'It's lucky we bought a fresh supply of *rosé* because the bottle that was in the fridge appears to have gone – I suppose the delivery-men must have helped themselves to it...' Jim grinned, and winked at Ted. 'I'm going into the pool to cool off a bit, Ted. Are you coming?'

'Yes, I think I will,' answered Ted, and the two friends plunged into the water.

'He doesn't miss much, does he?' said Valerie.

'You can say that again,' replied Dilys, 'but it's nice to see him taking a bit of teasing in a light-hearted manner. We wouldn't get away with that too often at home. Ted's obviously a good influence! Anyway, whatever the reason, I'm very relieved, because this holiday could have been a disaster. I'm going to get him a *pastis* for when he comes out, to ensure he stays in a good mood. Do you think Ted would like one too?'

'No doubt whatever,' said Valerie. So Dilys disappeared to the kitchen in her turn, reappearing with Ted and Jim's drinks just as they emerged from the pool.

'I was thinking,' said Dilys after a while. 'You know we were talking some time back about our Ruby Wedding party?'

'Oh yes,' said Valerie. 'It's not too far away, is it?'

'No, it's only a couple of weeks after we get back – Saturday the second of September. Anyway, Jim and I were talking, and we thought that, although we've never actually met them, we'd like to invite Sophie and Peter – if only to thank them for letting us stay in this wonderful place. Do you think they'd come?'

'Yes, I'm sure they'd be delighted to come if they're free,' replied Ted. 'Would you like me to mention it next time I speak to them?'

'Oh yes, Ted, if you would. I hope they are free – I'm afraid we've left it all a little bit late.'

At that precise moment, Sophie was just arriving home from her day at the hospital. No sooner had she closed the door behind her, and put the kettle on, than the telephone rang.

'Oh Lord,' she muttered to herself. 'I could do without that. Please let it not be the hospital!'

Sophie answered the phone. She soon discovered that it was not the hospital, for the voice she heard was unmistakably that of her mother.

'Sophie,' said Arlette. 'I'm so pleased you're home – I'm so excited!'

'Why, *maman*?'

'I've just got the keys to my new apartment and I wondered if you'd like to pop round to see it.'

'I'm afraid I can't manage this evening. Will tomorrow do?'

'Tomorrow evening?'

'Yes.'

'Yes, that's okay. What time can you be here?'

'Oh, I don't know – any time after six-thirty really, as long as I don't get held up at the hospital.'

'Well, why don't you and Peter come about seven, have a look at the apartment, and then we'll go to have something to eat somewhere.'

'Okay. I'll have to check with Peter, but I expect that will be all right. Are you calling from there now?'

'Yes, I am. Why?'

'I was just going to ask your phone number, then I saw it on Caller Display and so now I don't need to. You'd better tell me the address though.'

'Yes, of course. It's number 62 Lexington Gardens. It's only a few minutes' walk from Gloucester Road tube station.'

'All right. So, all being well, we'll see you there about seven tomorrow.'

Within minutes of Sophie's ending her conversation with Arlette, the phone rang again. This time it was Ted.

'Hello, Dad. This is a nice surprise. How are things going?'

'Pretty well, Sophie, thanks. Very well, actually – we're having a great time.'

Just at that moment a loud outburst of girlish giggling interrupted their conversation.

'Yes,' said Sophie. 'It sounds as if you are! Are you having a party?'

'No, it's just Valerie and Dilys by the pool. They spend half of their time together chortling and giggling.'

'That's good. I'm glad they're getting on well together. What about Jim?'

'Oh, he's fine. He's in the kitchen. He volunteered to do supper this evening – he's cleaning mussels at the moment...'

'I thought he didn't cook.'

'So did I, but he claims *moules marinières* is the extent of his repertoire.'

'Hidden depths, eh?'

'Yes, that pretty well sums Jim up, I think. Anyway, one reason I rang was to let you know that the first lot of furniture arrived today.'

'Oh good. Is it all okay? What did they bring today?'

'To be honest I can't tell you, because Jim and I were out shopping when it arrived, and I haven't checked it out yet. I will do though, and I'll let you know if anything's amiss.'

'Okay.'

'The other thing I wanted to tell you is that Jim and Dilys are celebrating their fortieth wedding anniversary on the second of September, and they're having a bit of a do at their place. They've invited us, and they asked us if we thought you'd like to come too, so I said I'd ask you.'

'Oh, that's nice of them! Yes, we'd love to. September the second, you say? Yes, that looks okay. Where do they live?'

'Kensington. Lexington Gardens.'

'Lexington Gardens! That's amazing! What number Lexington Gardens?'

'Number 64. Why?'

'Because just before you rang I had a call from my mother. She's just moved into 62.'

'She's just done what?'

'Moved into 62 – 62 Lexington Gardens.'

'That's next door to Jim and Dilys! I don't believe it!'

Jim's mussels were a great success, and greatly appreciated by all, despite a little gentle teasing on the part of Ted to the effect that, considering that was the only dish that Jim had learned to cook in the course of the very nearly three-score years and ten that he had been on this earth, he had better learn another dish pretty quickly if he were ever to hear his culinary skills being praised again. The only reference Ted made to his telephone conversation with his daughter was to convey to Jim and Dilys that Sophie and Peter would be delighted to come to their Ruby Wedding celebration; but the fact that he had said nothing to the others did not mean that the news she had given him about Arlette was not at the forefront of his consciousness for the entire evening. It was not until he and Valerie were getting into bed that Ted at last gave voice to his thoughts, although even then it was in response to a question from Valerie.

'What's the matter, Ted? You look very preoccupied.'

'Preoccupied? Me? Well, er, yes... I suppose I am.'

'Are you going to tell me what's bugging you?'

'I'll certainly tell you what's on my mind, but I'm not sure I'll be able to go much further, because I'm totally flummoxed. I don't know what to make of it at all.'

'Tell me what it's about then, and I'll see if I can help.'

'Okay, well, you know I called Sophie earlier on...'

'Yes...'

'And I told her about Jim and Dilys's Ruby Wedding and the fact that they'd like Sophie and Peter to go too...'

'Yes, I know about that, and they accepted the invitation, didn't they?'

'Oh yes, they did, but when I told Sophie where Jim and Dilys live, she told me some astounding news.'

'News? What news? Come on, Ted, get on with it! Honestly, it's like trying to get blood out of a stone!'

'Well, it appears that Arlette has just moved in next door.'

'Next door to Sophie and Peter?'

'No! Next door to Jim and Dilys!'

'Well I never! What a coincidence!'

'Is it?'

'Is it what?'

'A coincidence.'

'Why wouldn't it be?'

'I don't know. It just seems very odd.'

'Yes, I can see that, but I can't see any great significance in it.'

'Well, what's bothering me is what Dilys is going to say when she finds out.'

'Dilys? Why?'

Ted hesitated for a moment before answering, suddenly realising in time that he had never said a word to Valerie about Dilys's suspicions where Jim and Arlette were concerned. 'Well, from what Jim has told me,' he continued, 'Dilys does tend to be a little bit jealous, and...'

'Dilys? Jealous? You've got to be joking! She was telling me earlier that Jim would run a mile if another woman so much as looked at him.'

'Oh yes? How did that topic of conversation come up then?'

'Never you mind. It was just girl-talk while you two were out this afternoon. Do you have any reason to believe otherwise?'

'No, of course not. It's just a succession of funny things really. I mean, how did Arlette know that Peter and Sophie were interested in this house?'

'Arlette says she didn't.'

'I know, but that might not be true.'

'Why not?'

'It just sounds fishy to me. And there are too many coincidences.'

'Coincidences happen.'

'Yes, but I can't help thinking that if Arlette had been in Dilys's position now, she would already have put two and two together and made 793, if not more!'

'But Dilys isn't Arlette.'

'Thank God for that!'

'So let's just take it as coincidence until it's proved otherwise.'

'And say nothing to Dilys and Ted?'

'Say something if you like, but if you do, try not to make it sound as suspicious as you seem to think it is. Anyway, I'm going to sleep now. Goodnight, Ted.'

'Goodnight, darling.'

Within a matter of seconds Valerie was fast asleep. Ted, for his part, lay awake for two hours or more. What was going through his head was the scepticism in the face of coincidence which Jim himself had recommended so vehemently, and which, if he were to exercise it now, would lead to the finger of suspicion pointing at Jim. Eventually, however, he decided to say nothing whatever about Arlette's move to Jim and Dilys – which was exactly what his initial resolution had been.

When Ted awoke the following morning, his attitude was totally different. It was not that he had forgotten what had transpired the previous day, nor the anxiety which had ensued. It was more that the clear light of day – and, no doubt, the fact that he was no longer feeling the effects of the previous night's alcoholic consumption – had made him realise that the news which his daughter had conveyed to him did not necessarily presage the end of the world. To begin with, he had no reason to think Arlette had the remotest idea of where Jim lived. What is more, she would clearly have inherited a good deal of money from her aunt Julie, and it made sense to invest it in property. Also Ted was aware that Arlette loved living in Kensington, and he had seen for himself how attractive Lexington Gardens were; she would still be close to her existing friends, and close too to all the places she was wont to visit. Finally, London was a big place, with lots of people living there, and you could go for months on end without bumping into your neighbours. The more he thought about it, the less sinister it seemed, and the more he felt inclined to subscribe to the coincidence theory.

Having reached that conclusion, Ted very quickly came to another: there was not really any reason why he should not mention it to Jim and Dilys. In fact he resolved to tell them as soon as the occasion arose, because the longer he delayed, the more difficult it would be to explain why he had not mentioned this extraordinary coincidence earlier, for they would all know that he had learned of it from Sophie the previous evening.

When Ted and Valerie went downstairs to meet the others for breakfast, they saw that Dilys was already sitting on the terrace, drinking coffee. Jim was obviously not yet up, although there was nothing unusual about that, because he was normally the last one of the four to emerge in the morning.

As Dilys got up to greet Valerie and Ted, her mobile started ringing. She made an apologetic gesture to her friends, while simultaneously indicating to them that there was a whole jug of coffee available, and then answered her phone: 'Hello...'

'Hello, mummy. It's Jemima.'

'Jemima! What a nice surprise! It's a bit early for you though, isn't it? It must be only about 7.30 in London.'

'Yes, I suppose it is a bit early, but I wanted to tell you about Emily.'

'Emily? What about her?' asked Dilys, displaying a grandmother's anxiety.

'She had an accident last night, and I spent a good part of the night at the hospital with her.'

'Oh no! Is she all right?'

'Yes, she's okay now, so don't worry. She just broke her arm, that's all.'

'That's all? How did that happen?'

'Well, we thought at first it was worse, but she was just a bit concussed.'

'Where did this happen? At home?'

'No, not at our home, anyway. We were actually just outside your house. We just popped round to check that everything was okay there. I parked the car, and I was just getting out. Emily was quicker than I was, and ran across the road...'

'Without looking? Silly girl!'

'No, she did look, and there was nothing coming. But there was a removals van parked outside the house next to yours, and there was a cyclist on the pavement that she couldn't see because of the van, and he knocked her over.'

'Oh, poor lamb! You say this cyclist was on the pavement?'

'Yes, a young man, head down, going full tilt. She didn't stand a chance.'

'Just wait till I tell Jim. You'll hear the eruption from there! He's always raving about cyclists riding on footpaths.'

'But that's it, isn't it? They're not footpaths any more. Anyway, we were very lucky, because the lady who is moving in next door to you – which is why the van was there – she saw it happen, and she took us inside and let us wait there until the ambulance arrived.'

'That's kind.'

'Yes, she was really sweet. She's French, actually – although I noticed from some mail that had come for her that she has an English surname. I suppose she must be married to an Englishman.'

'How long did you have to wait for the ambulance?'

'Only about fifteen or twenty minutes. But Arlette gave Emily a glass of orange...'

'What did you say?'

'A glass of orange.'

'No, before that. The lady's name...'

'Oh, the French lady... Her name's Arlette. Anyway, Arlette gave Emily a drink, and...'

'And what's Arlette's surname?'

'Oh, I can't remember. No, wait a minute, it was O'Brien, or something like that... No, it wasn't, it began with a B... Bryant, that's it! Arlette Bryant, I remember.'

217

'Well, well, well!'

'What do you mean by "Well, well, well"?'

'Well, you know the friends we're here in France with...'

'Ted and Valerie, yes...'

'Their name is Bryant. Arlette is Ted's first wife.'

'Well I never! What a coincidence! Anyway, she was very nice, and terribly helpful.'

Dilys's conversation with her daughter continued for another few minutes until Dilys saw Jim arriving, whereupon she took her leave.

During the time Dilys had been on the phone, Valerie and Ted had laid the table for breakfast on the terrace, and, having been joined by Jim, were chatting while waiting for Dilys to finish her conversation.

'Sorry about that,' said Dilys on rejoining her friends. 'That was my daughter Jemima.'

'I thought she was my daughter as well,' Jim interjected.

'Oh, Jim, of course she is,' replied Dilys, rolling her eyes in mock exasperation. 'I'll start again. That was our daughter Jemima.'

'It was a long call,' said Jim. 'What was all that about?'

Dilys proceeded to tell them all about Emily's accident, a narration which lasted much longer than Jemima's phone-call, largely because it was interrupted by a long tirade from Jim – as Dilys had predicted – on the subject of cyclists refusing to obey the law of the land, a tirade whose vehemence grew in intensity before eventually subsiding in a series of smaller after-shocks.

'There's one detail in Jemima's story I haven't mentioned yet,' said Dilys, after Valerie and Ted had each expressed their sympathy over what had happened to Emily, 'and that's the identity of the lady who's just moved in next door and who was so helpful to Jemima.'

'Oh?' said Jim. 'Does that have any particular significance?'

Ted and Valerie exchanged a quick glance, and then once more gave all their attention to Dilys.

'Yes, it does actually,' replied Dilys. 'Because she's French, and her name is Arlette Bryant.'

Only one of the three people to whom these words were directed evinced any surprise, and that was Jim.

'Really? Are you sure?'

Dilys assured him that there was no mistake.

'Well, well, she certainly is a surprising woman, isn't she! Did you know anything about this, Ted?'

'As a matter of fact I did,' Ted affirmed.

'I have to say I'm a bit surprised you didn't mention it. How long have you known?'

'Only a matter of a few hours. Sophie told me when I was on the phone to her last night, but it was rather late when I found out, so I decided to leave it till breakfast, and then when breakfast-time came, Dilys's news seemed rather more urgent, wouldn't you say?'

Jim readily accepted this explanation, feeling inwardly that he had gone far enough, and had nothing to gain by expressing further surprise at the fact that Ted's ex-wife and his only-recently-acquired lover had become their new next-door neighbour.

After breakfast the two men sat together by the pool while their wives strolled down to the village to do the shopping for that evening's meal. Naturally, Dilys and Valerie spent most of their time together talking about Arlette; their husbands talked about cricket.

'Is the fact that Arlette is living next door to us likely to make any difference to us?' asked Dilys. 'What I mean is, will it stop you and Ted coming to our Ruby Wedding party?'

'I don't see why it should,' replied Valerie. 'I know Arlette isn't Ted's favourite person, and he wouldn't trust her any further than he could blow her, but they're not exactly at daggers drawn all the time, and it's not as if it's a long time since they saw each other – and last time she was all sweetness and light.'

'So I believe, but she does appear to create chaos wherever she goes, doesn't she? Do you think she does it on purpose?'

'Oh, God! Who knows? Maybe she does, I don't know. I mean, obviously I don't know her all that well. I mainly know her through what Ted has said about her, and if she was applying for a job, any testimonial Ted wrote for her would rule her out at once! But as far as I'm concerned, if you become friendly with her because she's living next door, I don't see why that should affect our friendship, do you? But it might not be a good idea to arrange any intimate dinner-parties with Ted and Arlette both there!'

Dilys laughed, but reflected inwardly that she had no intention whatever of arranging any intimate dinner-parties involving Arlette, whether Ted was there or not.

During the remainder of their stay at *Les Cigales* the topic was not raised again, which did not mean that it did not loom large in the consciousness of more than one member of the party.

As far as Ted was concerned, his thought-processes were driven by the basic mistrust which came to the fore whenever he was obliged to have anything to do with his ex-wife. For a number of years it had lain dormant, but in the last couple of months or so – ever since he had run into Jim at Lord's – it had been virtually ever-present. He was, of course, very pleased that he had rekindled his friendship with Jim, and not only because it meant a renewed acquaintance with Dilys, although that was certainly an added bonus; and of course, he had finally got an answer to the question that had bugged him for such a long time when he was younger – why his initial relationship with Dilys had foundered almost as soon as it had begun. But at the back of his mind was a certain uneasiness, caused by the mystery surrounding Arlette's sudden interest in the house that Sophie and Peter were planning to buy. He did not, of course, know anything about the way Jim's relationship with Arlette had developed, and would have been astonished – incredulous even – if someone were to tell him what had occurred. But basically he felt uneasy that a not-so-pleasant element of his past life seemed to be interfering with the pleasure he was deriving from a much more welcome re-visitation of the past.

Dilys too felt uneasy, although she had, if anything, even fewer grounds than did Ted to be suspicious of Jim. For her it was more a matter of intuition – a reflex stimulated in a flash by Ted's inadvertent revelation that Jim and Arlette had been in the hotel bar together before Ted's arrival and the subsequent dramatic exit of Arlette. But this too was driven by the internal workings of her own psyche, as she would have admitted to herself in a quiet, reflective moment; growing old she certainly was, but she was still conscious of her own sexuality, and did not feel ready to consign that part of her being to a securely-locked cabinet labelled 'The Past'. The fact that Jim appeared to have reached that point first did lead to occasional outbursts of anger, which in fact were nothing more than expressions of sexual frustration, and when she did think about it in a rational way she convinced herself that if Jim was not interested in making love to her, he was unlikely to be interested in making love to someone else – especially his best friend's ex-wife.

As for Jim – perhaps surprisingly, for such a cerebral man – he was confused. But, as Dilys had pointed out on more than one occasion, he was driven by a desire – no, a compulsion – to adhere to the requirements of a religious doctrine which the vast majority of his co-believers would now consider outdated. Paradoxically, the preoccupation with sin which characterized this doctrine, with its insistence that all men – and women – were sinners, appeared to encourage the very behaviour that it was designed to discourage, and Jim found it all too easy to succumb to the temptations of the flesh, especially when they came in the form of an attractive and eager representative of the culture which in some ways he had come to regard even more highly than his own. On a more practical level, he kept wondering how matters would develop now that Arlette would be living next door. But he realised too that all his speculation, all his analysis and all his plans were ultimately useless, because at the heart of it all lay Arlette, her intentions and her behaviour.

Valerie was the least worried of them all. She was above all pleased that Ted had renewed his acquaintance with his old friends, and in particular that he was now about to embark on a new chapter of his life as he joined the Bach Choir. She was delighted to have met Dilys, and to have found her a stimulating and agreeable companion. She had thoroughly enjoyed their holiday at the *Villa des Cigales*, and the idea of

Arlette lurking mysteriously in the background did not cast as dark a shadow on her as it did on the others. Over the years she had heard a lot about Arlette, mostly from Ted, of course, and therefore what she had heard was for the most part not very complimentary, but nothing that she had experienced would have suggested to her that Arlette constituted even a minor threat to the equilibrium of their happy band. Whether her judgment was well-founded or not, remained to be seen.

Chapter Nine

During the week that followed their return home from their holiday in France, there was virtually no contact between the two couples, largely because Dilys was busy preparing for the Ruby Wedding lunch-party which was due to take place on the following Saturday. For once Jim was involved in the preparation too. In reality his culinary skills were rather better than he tended to claim, and were by no means restricted to the *moules marinières* with which he had been so successful at Saint-Gély, although he rarely exercised them, and his unwonted helpfulness in terms of organising the event only materialised after Dilys had painstakingly pointed out to him that their hurriedly-arranged holiday in France had led to her having far less time than she really needed to prepare for the big day. Even then she felt relieved that she had asked Jemima to lend a hand – she should also have enlisted Valerie's help, she was beginning to think – because Jim's idea of helping for an hour, except in those fields which especially attracted him, seemed to involve her in at least half an hour's preliminary explanation of what was required. In addition, Jim was less than happy with the timing of the event, for it clashed with the final match of the England-West Indies test series, and he was only slightly placated by the fact that the match would be at Kennington Oval, not at Lord's, and for some reason Jim appeared to think that anywhere south of the Thames would involve a lengthy and time-consuming journey, whereas if anything, the Oval was probably nearer Lexington Gardens than Lord's was.

A certain amount of time was taken up too by discussing the weather prospects for the day of the party, for the forecast was not particularly promising. The original intention had been for the entire party to be held in the communal garden in the middle of the square, and they had accordingly booked it for the purpose a few months previously. As the day of the party approached, however, they started to worry about the weather and, in particular, about the difficulty of moving food and drink back inside if it should begin to rain once the party was under way. Given the shortage of time remaining to them, Dilys diplomatically refrained from reminding Jim that she had raised this matter a couple of months earlier, and he had promised to think about it. The issue was finally settled when, with only two days to go, Jemima suggested that they hire a marquee – which had been Dilys's original idea – and, despite Jim's initial resistance on grounds of cost, this is what they resolved to do.

During that week Jim and Dilys did not set eyes on Arlette; indeed they were so preoccupied that the thought of her never crossed their minds, not even Jim's. On the Friday, however, the day before the party, Arlette was just arriving home from the shops when she saw a group of workmen carrying tables and chairs into the garden, where stood a large marquee which had not been there when she went out that morning. She asked one of the men what was going on.

'Oh, it's for a party, love.'

'A party? For the residents? Nobody told me about a party. When is it?'

'Tomorrow I think, love. But it's a private party, I think. If you want to go, you'd better get on the right side of your neighbours sharpish, you know what I mean?'

'Which neighbours?'

'Oh, some people at 64 – hang on a bit, let's have a look.' He pulled out a piece of paper from his pocket, looked at it, and continued: 'Fletcher. Mr and Mrs Fletcher, that's who it is.'

'Fletcher? Ah, Mr and Mrs Fletcher, I see. Thank you.'

And Arlette went into her flat rapt in thought.

Shortly before nine o'clock the following morning Jemima and one of her friends arrived at Lexington Gardens, bearing the ingredients for a number of dishes which now needed nothing more than assembling prior to being served at the lunch-party, along with two or three desserts which were all ready to serve and merely needed to be placed in the fridge. Dilys and Jim had already been up for nearly three hours, and at last everything appeared to be falling into place. At about the same time, Valerie and Ted were leaving Crowthorne, for they were due to go to Hampstead before making their way to Kensington: they would be spending the night with Sophie and Peter, and needed to drop off their overnight bags at Downshire Hill first. Also on their way were Jim and Dilys's son Michael, who was travelling up by car from Winchester, along with his wife Jane.

At about 11.45, half-an-hour before the first guests were expected, Jemima was mixing a *vinaigrette* – the very last element of their preparation – when she said to Dilys: 'Is this all the wine vinegar you've got, mummy? I don't think there's going to be enough.'

'Damn!' said Dilys. 'I knew there was something I'd forgotten to put on my list. I'll get Jim to go and get some. Jim!'

'Yes!' said Jim, whose answer was somewhat half-hearted because he was sitting watching the test match on television.

'Jim, we've run out of wine vinegar. Would you mind popping down to the delicatessen to get a bottle?'

Jim grunted, got up from his armchair, and switched off the television, feeling rather peeved at being disturbed because once more West Indian wickets were tumbling, he had just seen the great Brian Lara clean bowled first ball for the first time in his long international career, and the

West Indies currently stood on 32 for 3; but Jim did not complain too much because even he realised that he was going to have to stop watching fairly soon anyway, and originally he had thought that he would not be able to see any of that day's play at all.

When he returned from the shop, the bottle of vinegar clutched safely in his hand, Michael and Jane had just arrived, and were getting out of their car. He stopped to greet them, but before they reached the steps leading up to the front door, Arlette emerged from next door.

'Jim, hello! How nice to see you!' said Arlette, and she kissed him, French-style, on both cheeks.

Jim, trying hard to conceal the embarrassment he was feeling, introduced Arlette to his son and daughter-in-law, apologised to Arlette for being unable to stop and chat, and led Michael and Jane into the house.

Once they were inside the house, Jim felt extremely relieved to find that it was still a hive of activity, with much still to do and little time to do it in, because it meant that neither Michael nor Jane mentioned the latest encounter with Arlette, as they all threw themselves into the task of helping Dilys get everything ready in time, which was just as well, because almost as soon as she had just finished applying the final touch, the guests started arriving.

Most of the guests, thirty in number, knew each other already, which made the early stages easier, the only introductions needed being those involving Ted, Valerie, Sophie and Peter, and cries of amazement and admiration rang out as they stepped into the marquee and saw the food which Dilys had just finished setting out, with two whole poached salmon forming the centre-piece.

'Dilys, how fabulous!' cried one. 'Just look at those salmon – they look divine!'

'Not responsible,' replied Dilys. 'Poaching salmon is Jim's province.'

'Game-keeper turned poacher,' quipped Jim.

'I thought *moules marinières* was the extent of your competence,' said Ted. 'That's what you told us when we were in France anyway.'

'I only do things that are easy,' retorted Jim, 'and poaching salmon is an absolute doddle if you have a big enough fish-kettle.'

A number of voices were raised in protest.

'No, seriously,' Jim continued. 'I've been doing this for years for special occasions, and I'd be much more likely to make a mess of making an omelette!'

'What's the secret then, Jim?' asked Valerie.

'I'll tell you the secret in two words,' said Jim. 'Jane Grigson.'

'Jane Grigson?'

'Yes, Jane Grigson's *Fish Cookery*, Penguin Books, page 220. If you can read, you can poach salmon to perfection – it's dead easy, it really is!'

Not everybody appeared convinced, despite Jim's protestations, but an hour or so later, once they started eating, all were convinced by the results, much to Jim's obvious embarrassment and to Dilys's private delight – not because she liked Jim to be embarrassed, but because she felt that Jim was more in need of praise than he was normally willing to acknowledge.

From this point onwards Dilys was able to concentrate on socializing with her guests, because the serving of drinks and food was now in the hands of four university students, children of friends who were also at the party. Like the accomplished hostess she was, Dilys moved quietly from one group of guests to another, making especially sure that any necessary introductions were made, and even more quietly ensuring that the waiters and waitresses were doing their job efficiently but unobtrusively; she had also previously arranged that Jemima would look after Sophie and Peter during the initial stages of the party, whilst Michael and Jane were allocated the task of looking after Valerie and Ted.

Scarcely had the first nibbles of the canapés that Dilys had painstakingly prepared been taken, along with the first sips of champagne, than an almighty clap of thunder shook the marquee, followed by the sound of rain falling in torrents, which produced very varied reactions among those present: most of the guests were simply relieved that they had arrived before the rains came; Dilys was relieved that she had been able to persuade Jim that a marquee would be a good idea, whilst Jim was actually pleased that it was raining, because it meant that his expenditure had not been in vain.

For a while the buzz of conversation intensified, partly to compete with the sound of rain on canvas, partly because of the excitement which a sudden thunderstorm tends to provoke; but gradually, as the rainstorm gave way to a steady but prolonged drizzle, the volume of voices also fell, as the conversation reverted to matters other than the weather.

'I was hearing from my parents about your wonderful villa in France, Sophie,' said Jemima. 'It sounds absolute heaven!'

'Yes,' replied Sophie. 'We're looking forward to spending some time there ourselves soon – we've only seen it once, and that visit lasted less than an hour! At least we know now that it's a house that works, because Mum and Dad and Jim and Dilys don't appear to have been confronted by any problems.'

'Other than incipient alcoholism,' added Peter.

'I'm not sure that *incipient* is the right adjective,' laughed Jemima. 'Not as far as my father is concerned anyway!'

'Are you really worried about him?' asked Sophie, her medical persona coming to the fore.

'No, not really, I don't think. He does knock it back a bit at times, but I don't think it constitutes a major health problem.'

'How's your little girl, by the way?' asked Peter, sensing that a change of subject was called for. 'I understand she had an accident...'

'Yes, she did, poor little thing, she broke her arm. But she's coming along fine now, and she's very proud of her plaster-cast – it's been autographed by all her class-mates at school, and by her class-teacher as well!'

'Is she here today?' asked Sophie. 'I thought we might see your children here ...'

'No, I didn't think it was the sort of occasion they'd enjoy. They're staying with their other grand-parents. They only live about half a mile from us, so it's quite convenient, and they're always pleased to have them to stay. You heard about Emily's accident then?'

'Yes. Actually we heard about it twice – once from Dad when we phoned him in France, and once from my mother – Arlette...'

'Oh yes, of course, I was forgetting Arlette was your mother – she was terribly helpful, I don't know what I'd have done without her, she was so sweet.'

'Yes, she can be,' laughed Peter, 'but my problem is normally less one of not knowing what I'd do without her, than one of knowing exactly what I'd like to do *with* her!'

'Oh Peter! Take no notice, Jemima!'

'Well, I did say she can be kind, didn't I?' said Peter, defending himself. 'And so she can be – but she can also be extremely awkward.'

At that moment they were joined by Dilys, and Jemima's brother Michael.

'Who can be extremely awkward?' asked Michael.

'My mother-in-law,' replied Peter.

'Valerie? I can't imagine her being awkward.'

'No, Valerie's my step-mother,' said Sophie. 'We were talking about Ted's first wife, Arlette.'

'She's just moved in next door to Jim and Dilys,' added Peter.

'Oh, I see! So that was the French lady Dad introduced me to just as we arrived this morning. Seemed affability itself, especially where Dad was concerned – flung her arms around him and kissed him on both cheeks! You'll have to keep an eye on her, Mum!'

But Dilys had already turned away, smiling weakly, and, pretending not to have heard, moved on to another group of guests.

Jemima turned to her brother and said sharply: 'Michael, really! You ought to be more careful about what you say...'

'Careful? Me? What on earth do you mean?'

'I mean you shouldn't make remarks like that to Mummy. Didn't you see the way she reacted?'

'Yes. She smiled and then went to talk to somebody else. She obviously realised it was a joke even if you didn't.'

Jemima sighed and looked despairingly at Michael.

'Do you mean Mum is really worried that Dad might go off with Arlette?' said Michael, choosing to ignore Jemima's reaction. 'Come off it, sis, you can't be serious!'

Jemima also chose to ignore her brother, and turned instead towards Sophie.

'I'm sorry, Sophie,' she said. 'We shouldn't be embarrassing you by talking about your mother like this...'

'It's all right, Jemima,' Sophie replied. 'I saw Dilys's reaction too, and for whatever reason

Michael's remark appeared to have touched a raw nerve. Arlette may be my mother, but I know she can be something of a loose cannon. Even I wouldn't trust her! I expect Dilys has been wondering how it came about that Arlette suddenly turned up living next door too. Especially because we've all been wondering how she found out about that house in France that we were after, and that she suddenly decided to buy.'

'I'm sorry, I don't know anything about that,' protested Michael.

But before anyone could enlighten Michael on the matter – not that any of them apart from Michael felt particularly inclined to keep talking about it – an announcement was made to the effect that lunch was ready, and their little group made their way towards the long table on which the food had been laid out, and nothing else was said on the subject.

As Ted and Valerie were waiting to be served, Dilys came up to them, smiled, and said: 'Ted, I wonder if you would do me a great favour?'

'Of course,' replied Ted. 'What's the favour?'

'Well, Jim was supposed to have asked Michael ages ago if he would propose a toast to our forty years, and he forgot to ask him. When eventually he got round to asking him – about five minutes ago, would you believe? – Michael said he couldn't really do it at such short notice.'

'Do you mean you want me to have a go at Michael to persuade him otherwise?'

'No, I wondered if you'd do it instead.'

'Me? What on earth makes you think I could do it – at even shorter notice!'

'Oh come on, Ted!' said Valerie. 'You know you love making speeches. You've spent the best part of your life on your feet haranguing people...'

'In the classroom, yes, but...'

'But nothing! Yes, Dilys, of course he'll do it, won't you Ted?'

'If you really want me to, Dilys, of course I will. I'm just not sure that as a relative newcomer into your lives I'm the right person to be talking about your forty years together. But if you're really stuck...'

'Yes, we are! And we'd both love you to do it.'

'Okay,' said Ted. 'I'll try not to say anything too indiscreet.'

'I'm sure you won't,' said Dilys. 'There'd be a much greater risk of that happening if Michael was doing it. I'll tell one of the serving-girls to tip you the wink when it's time.'

She kissed Ted on the cheek, saying 'Thank you, Ted – bless you!'

'You'd better tell that serving-girl to keep my glass topped up all through lunch then!' said Ted. 'I'm going to have a busy lunchtime!'

An hour passed, and Ted had almost forgotten what Dilys had asked him to do, when he suddenly felt a tap on his shoulder. He turned round and saw one of the young waitresses mouthing silently at him: 'It's time'. So he stood up, tapped loudly on a glass to achieve relative silence, and began.

'Ladies and gentlemen. For some reason it has fallen to me to propose a toast to our good friends Dilys and Jim. It came as a great surprise to me to be asked, because Valerie and I have only recently joined their circle of friends. But then it occurred to me that in fact there is nobody here, not even Jemima or Michael, who have known them as long as I have. Actually, now I come to think of it, I was friendly with Jim even before he met Dilys. What's more, I believe I met Dilys before Jim did – perhaps if I hadn't been the shy, timid boy that I was, we might have been celebrating a different occasion today! But a missed opportunity usually opens up the way to alternative opportunities, and I can't complain about the way my life has panned out, so I'll just congratulate Jim on his good taste and his good fortune, and Dilys on having the good sense to marry a man who is not only a member of the MCC, but also a first-rate salmon-poacher.

'So, ladies and gentlemen, I invite you to raise your glasses and join me in toasting the fortieth anniversary of our good friends – Dilys and Jim!'

'Dilys and Jim!' The cry echoed round the marquee as the guests responded to Ted's toast, and then burst into prolonged applause.

Then Jim rose to his feet and made a short but appreciative reply, after which the guests left their tables and resumed drinking, mingling as they had done prior to the meal. Jim immediately moved towards Ted and thanked him for his kind words, and then went on to join another group. A few minutes later Dilys also came up to Ted to express her thanks, and then, when she was absolutely sure that no one but Ted could hear her words, she said quietly: 'Who was this shy, timid boy, Ted? I seem to remember you taking your opportunity with both hands...'

Chapter Ten

Just two days after Dilys and Jim's Ruby Wedding celebrations, it was time for Dilys to resume and for Ted to begin rehearsals with the Bach Choir. With the rehearsal due to begin at 6.15, they had arranged to meet in a café near Victoria at 5.15, so they could have a chat over a cup of tea, after which Dilys would take Ted to the hall where they rehearsed, and introduce him to a few of his new colleagues.

After they had been served, Ted asked Dilys how she and Jim had enjoyed their party.

'Oh, very much indeed,' replied Dilys. 'It was lucky we had the marquee though. Just imagine what it would have been like if we'd been out in the open air when that thunderstorm struck!'

'How long did it take you to clear up afterwards?'

'Oh, not too long really. The servers were all very efficient, and they'd been clearing up as they went along.'

'Ah, typical students then,' said Ted.

'Fortunately not,' laughed Dilys. 'They knew how to stack *and* empty a dish-washer, and they only had a little to drink themselves!'

'What did you and Jim do after everyone had gone?'

'We had a row.'

'Oh no! What about? No, I'm sorry, I shouldn't ask.'

'Oh, it's all right, Ted, don't worry. It's the sort of thing that often happens after occasions like that, if not actually *at* them. It was something that Michael said that started it off – I'll tell you about it another time. We'd better make a move, or we'll be late.'

So Ted paid the bill, and they made their way to the rehearsal.

Shortly after Dilys had left the house on the way to meet Ted, Jim also went out, but only with the intention of going as far as the post-box at the corner of the road. When he returned, he was just about to start mounting the steps outside his house when he heard a familiar voice nearby: 'Jim! Jim! How nice to see you!'

Jim turned to face the direction from which the voice was coming, and saw Arlette standing at the entrance of the house next door.

'How was the party?' Arlette asked, thereby cleverly ensuring that their encounter developed into a conversation rather than a quick exchange of greetings.

'It went very well, Arlette, thanks,' Jim replied.

'It's a good thing you had a tent to hold the party in. Wasn't that thunderstorm terrible!'

'Yes, it was quite a downpour, wasn't it?'

'I hate thunderstorms! They frighten me to death, especially if I'm alone. I bet they don't frighten you, do they, Jim?'

'They don't *frighten* me,' Jim replied, realising that he now had no option other than to enter into a real conversation, only the second one he and Arlette had had since she moved in next door – the first encounter, of course, being 'the subject of the comment made by Michael, which had led in turn to the row about which Dilys would soon be telling Ted. 'They don't actually frighten me,' he resumed, 'but I don't really like them. Although I do remember an occasion when we were in the south of France, just on the edge of the Alps, when there was a spectacular thunderstorm which carried on for hours, and which kept rolling round and round the valley as if trapped by the mountains. It was phenomenal.'

'Talking about the south of France, how did you enjoy your holiday in Saint-Gély-du-Fesc?'

'Oh, we enjoyed it very much,' said Jim.

'I'll tell you what,' said Arlette. 'Why don't you come in and tell me about it, and then I can show you my new apartment. You haven't seen it yet.'

Jim began to murmur something about another time, but Arlette interrupted him. 'I know Dilys is out, because I saw her go. And I really need some help to understand how the hot water system works – it must be the same as yours, I think.'

So saying, she turned and started going into the house next door to Jim's, and Jim, to his own surprise, found himself following her.

Ted was immensely relieved to find that, although the standards required by the Bach Choir's chorus-master were demanding, especially where intonation was concerned, he was by no means unable to cope. What was more, the standard was so high that he no longer felt frustrated by extended periods of 'note-bashing', because each individual was proficient enough technically to enable them to start making real music from the outset, whereas with some of the choirs to which he had belonged in the past that might not happen until the final rehearsal, or indeed the performance itself – and sometimes not even then!

He enjoyed some friendly exchanges with one or two of his fellow-choristers, though necessarily short ones, as he had expected, because they were kept pretty busy during the two hours of the rehearsal – half an hour less than he had been used to at Reading. But he was pleased to be presented with details of the forthcoming trip to Paris, and he had put his name down straight away, because it had already been discussed while he and Valerie had been in France with Jim and Dilys.

After the rehearsal was over Ted and Dilys decided to have a quiet drink together before going their separate ways. They began by talking about the rehearsal, and then about the Paris trip, which was due to take place towards the end of October, some of the pieces which they were due to perform having been sung through that evening for familiarization purposes: the real work on them was yet to come.

Ted had already decided not to make any reference to the conversation they had been having earlier, but it was Dilys who brought the matter up again.

'You know I was saying earlier that Jim and I had a row after the party... Well, I'll tell you what it was about.'

'No,' Ted protested. 'You don't need to. It's none of my business.'

'It might be,' Dilys countered. 'Because it does involve your ex-wife.'

'Arlette?'

'You don't have any other ex-wives rampaging around, do you?'

Ted laughed – less at the suggestion that he might have other ex-wives than at what he thought was an appropriate choice of verb to describe Arlette's customary behaviour.

'No, I don't, thank God! But I thought you told me it was something that Michael said that sparked it off.'

'Well, yes, it was. But Michael's remark involved Arlette. Apparently when Michael and Jane arrived, Arlette was just coming out of next door, and when she caught sight of Jim she greeted him with a kiss...'

'What, a proper kiss?'

'Oh no, French-style – kiss on the cheek, you know...'

'That's no big deal though, is it?'

'No, of course not. But it was what Michael went on to say then that upset me. He said "You'll have to keep an eye on her, Mum!"'

'Oh, Dilys, surely that was just a joke!'

'Yes, of course it was, but it followed soon after another conversation I'd been involved in...'

'Yes?'

'I was with some of our neighbours, and they started talking about this new French woman who had moved in next door. Then one of them said "I'm surprised not to see her here today"!'

'I'm glad she wasn't!'

'I know, I'm sure you are, Ted.'

'What did you say to her then?'

'I said that he hardly knew her. And then this neighbour went on to say that she had seen Jim and Arlette having coffee together in a *pâtisserie* in Gloucester Road.'

'What! Do you think that's true?'

'Yes, I do. In fact I know it's true, because I asked Jim about it later.'

'And what was the answer?'

'He said he'd just bumped into Arlette one day when he was on the way back from the post-office, and she had suggested that they have a coffee together.'

'Seems feasible.'

'Yes. Anyway, I asked him why he hadn't told me about it at the time. That was when he flew off the handle. He said he didn't know he was supposed to give me details of every little thing he did every day, and then he retired to his study with a bottle of whisky, slamming the door behind him. I didn't see him again until the following morning.'

'Oh dear, that wasn't a very good end to your special day.'

'No, it wasn't. But it's the sort of thing that happens now and then. And then the following morning Jim feels awfully guilty and apologises – but I never end up getting an answer to the question that caused the problem in the first place!'

'But you can't seriously believe that Jim is carrying on with Arlette?'

'I suppose I don't *seriously* believe it, but she just makes me uneasy, that's all.'

'Yes, I can believe that, but listen,' said Ted. 'Arlette is my ex-wife, and we have a lot of history behind us, some of which – but only some – I've told Jim. Now Jim is a gentleman, and, although I'm not saying he doesn't believe what I've told him about Arlette, he simply doesn't have any reason to treat her any less politely than he would any other woman who was pleasant to him. Don't you see?'

'Yes, I suppose I do.'

'I mean, look at you and me. We could have been seen together in two different drinking-establishments today, couldn't we?'

'Yes, of course we could. And to prove that it's all absolutely innocent, I'd better do this.'

With that, Dilys stood up and kissed Ted on both cheeks. 'And now we'd better go home,' she continued. 'You don't want to miss your train.'

So Ted and Dilys walked together to the underground station, said goodbye, and went their different ways.

Jim, having had only a cursory glance around Arlette's apartment despite having spent more than four hours in her company – and certainly not having inspected the water-system – arrived home only half an hour before Dilys. He made a quick sandwich, had a glass of scotch, and went to bed. When Dilys eventually arrived home he first of all pretended to be asleep, and then appearing suddenly to wake up, he said sleepily: 'How was your evening, Dilys?'

'Oh, it went very well,' she answered. 'I had a quick drink with Ted afterwards, and he enjoyed it too.'

'Thank God you didn't come home straight after the rehearsal!' said Jim to himself.

'You're in bed early,' Dilys resumed. 'Did you eat?'

'Oh, I just had a sandwich, that's all. I was feeling shattered for some reason, so I decided to turn in, I'm sorry. Would you like me to get up and make you a cup of tea?'

'No thanks, Jim,' said Dilys, a little surprised at Jim's uncharacteristic offer. 'If you're tired, you go back to sleep, and I'll come to bed in a few minutes. Sleep well.'

'Good night,' said Jim.

When Dilys came to bed ten minutes later, she thought Jim was asleep, but in reality he stayed awake that night for a long time after Dilys succumbed to sleep, turning over in his mind all that had happened that evening, and wondering where it was all going to lead him – in this life, and, as the night progressed, in the next...

In Crowthorne, Ted and Valerie just sat for half an hour over a cup of coffee, talking about the rehearsal. Ted showed her the plans for the Paris concert, and told her about the few people he had met so far, about the music and the atmosphere. He told her about the wine bar which he and Dilys had visited and, of course, about Dilys herself, although he made no mention of the row which had broken out between Dilys and Jim, nor about Dilys's suspicions. In his case it was not a matter of keeping things from Valerie, as it might have been if Jim had been in the same position; it was more that Dilys had confided in him, and his natural instinct was to respect that confidence.

After all, if Dilys wanted Valerie to know about it, the relationship between the two wives was already such that she would bring up the subject herself, which, thought Ted on reflection, she might very well do, feeling perhaps that a woman's interpretation of the situation would naturally be different from a man's.

Two days later, Dilys went out at about 10.30 in the morning, having arranged to meet Jemima for a day's shopping.

'I'll stay out for lunch, of course,' she said to Jim as she left. 'There's some of last night's supper left in the fridge – you can have that for lunch if you like. It'll just need three minutes or so in the microwave.'

A few minutes after she had gone, Jim picked up the phone and dialled a number. He heard it ring out a few times, and then a voice replied:

''*Allô?*'

'Hello, Arlette, it's Jim here.'

'Jim, *mon chéri, quel plaisir!*[6] How are you?'

'I need to talk to you, Arlette. Can I come round and see you?'

'Of course you can, Jim. You know I'm always pleased to see you.'

'I'll be there in two minutes.'

'Okay. *A bientôt, chéri.*'[7]

A few minutes later Jim arrived at Arlette's flat and rang the doorbell. The door opened at once, and Arlette greeted Jim with a kiss – not the peck on the cheek with which she had greeted him on the day of the party, but with a real lover's kiss.

'No, Arlette,' Jim protested. 'That's not why I've come. I want to talk to you.'

---

[6] 'Jim, darling! How nice!'
[7] 'See you soon, darling.'

Arlette looked crestfallen.

'Oh, Jim! Of course you can talk to me. But why do you refuse my kiss? Don't you want me any more?'

'I didn't say that,' said Jim. 'Let's sit down and talk.'

Arlette said nothing, but went to sit at one end of a *chaise longue*, making sure that there was plenty of room for Jim to sit beside her. Jim ignored the implication, and sat down in an armchair nearby.

'Oh, Jim,' said Arlette, clearly disappointed. 'You are so serious this morning. Why are you so cold?'

'I'm not cold,' said Jim. 'But I am serious. And I'm serious because it's a serious situation that we've got ourselves into. And I think it's going to have to stop.'

'Stop? Why? Don't you like making love to me?'

'Yes, of course I do. And that's the problem.'

'Why is it a problem if you like doing it?'

'Because of Dilys.'

'Does Dilys know?'

'No, she doesn't. At least I don't think she does.'

'Why aren't you sure?'

'How can I be sure? I can hardly say to her "Do you know I'm having an affair with Arlette?"'

'Of course you can't. That would be indelicate.'

'Isn't it indelicate of me to make love to another woman?'

Arlette ignored the question and pursued her own train of thought. 'If Dilys already knew about it she would say so. And if she knows about it and doesn't say so, she doesn't care.'

'No...' Jim began.

'That means she either doesn't know or she doesn't care. So where's the problem?'

'Well...'

'You've already said you like making love to me, and you say Dilys doesn't know. So will you tell her?'

Jim looked horrified. 'No, of course I won't.'

'Well, I won't tell her, so where's the problem?'

'What we're doing is morally wrong. You know it is. You go to church, you know what the Church's teaching is.'

'As I understand it, the Church's teaching is pretty contradictory...'

'No, it's not. It's perfectly clear. "Thou shalt not commit adultery." What can be clearer than that?'

'It depends what you mean by adultery. If it means what you seem to think it means, it has obviously changed since God gave that commandment to Moses.'

'Of course it hasn't changed!'

'If you think that, you clearly haven't read the Old Testament very well.'

'What do you mean?'

'Just look at people like Abraham, the father of God's chosen people, and Solomon, the fount of all wisdom. They had lots of wives, and scores of concubines as well.'

'That was a long time ago.'

'But not as long ago as the Commandment you're quoting. My interpretation is that if you're not hurting anybody, and you don't have any evil intent, then it's not a sin.'

Jim tried to intervene to the effect that what she was saying bordered on heresy, but Arlette carried on: 'You've already said that Dilys doesn't know, and if she doesn't know, you can't be hurting her.'

'But the potential is there for hurting her.'

'I think I could tolerate potential pain...'

'You know what I mean...'

'Yes, I do know what you mean, and I think you're wrong. And at the moment, you're not hurting Dilys, but you *are* hurting me.'

'I'm sorry, I don't want to hurt you.'

'Then don't. Real pain hurts more than potential pain.'

With that, Arlette burst into tears, Jim moved towards her to console her and assure her that he didn't want to hurt either her or Dilys, and eventually her sobs subsided.

It was three hours before Jim returned home, during which time the philosophical discussion was not resumed.

Once Jim was home, he put his lunch in the microwave, as Dilys had suggested, but ate only half of it, and that without much enthusiasm. Eventually he decided to discard what he had been unable to eat, being careful to put it into the bin in such a way that Dilys would not notice that he had thrown half of it away. Then he went and had a shower, and settled down in an armchair to watch some fairly uninteresting cricket on television, and promptly fell asleep.

He awoke with a start about an hour later, his slumber disturbed by the ringing of the telephone. He went to answer it, and found it was Valerie calling.

'Hello, Jim. I told Dilys I'd give her a call to arrange a date for you both to come and spend a weekend with us. Is she there?'

'No,' replied Jim. 'I'm afraid she's not. She's gone out shopping with Jemima, so Heaven knows what time she'll be back. Do you have a date in mind?'

'Yes – in fact we almost agreed on a date at the weekend, but we didn't have our diaries to hand. Actually it wouldn't have made any difference if we had, because we could hardly have a planning conference in the middle of your party! We were talking about three weekends from now – the weekend of the 23rd/24th. Will you tell her that looks okay from our end?'

'Yes, of course I will. Thanks, Valerie.'

'Thanks, Jim. Bye.'

'Bye.'

With that, Jim settled back in his armchair to continue watching the cricket – and was still asleep when Dilys came home about 6 o'clock.

'Hello, Jim,' said Dilys. 'Sorry to wake you! Had a good sleep?'

'Yes,' said Jim. 'I sat down to watch this cricket match, but it was so boring I must have dozed off.'

'Did you have lunch?'

'Yes, I had what you suggested.'

'Was it okay?'

'Yes, it was fine, thanks. Oh, by the way, there was a call for you from Valerie. She wants us to go there the weekend of the 23rd.'

'Oh, that's great. Suits me fine. I'll give her a ring now and confirm it. You get back to your fascinating cricket match.'

Jim grunted, and settled in his armchair once more.

Tony Whelpton

Chapter Eleven

During the two weeks or so which followed, the lives of the Fletchers and the Bryants continued fairly uneventfully. Two further Bach Choir rehearsals were held, with Dilys and Ted continuing to meet for tea first and for wine after, which they clearly both enjoyed, quite unaware that at more or less the same time Jim and Arlette were enjoying other, less innocent delights, in the course of which Jim neither called into question the morality of what they were doing, nor investigated the distinctly suspect chronology of Arlette's Old Testament justification of what the vast majority of modern Europeans would consider shameless adultery.

Then, on Saturday morning, as Valerie and Dilys had agreed, Dilys and Jim travelled by train to Crowthorne, where Ted picked them up and drove them to his house, where Valerie already had lunch waiting for them. Fortunately the weather was fine; it was one of those balmy late-September days of which one dreams but which seem to materialise ever more rarely. Valerie had prepared a dish of cold meats of the kind the French call an *assiette anglaise*, which,

255

accompanied by a carafe of *rosé*, was perfect for that sort of day, and which evoked for all of them memories of the days they had spent together at the *Villa des Cigales*, and it was precisely reminiscences of those days which dominated their conversation throughout the whole of lunch and a good portion of the afternoon.

Prior to Jim and Dilys's visit, Valerie had been fretting about the food she would prepare for them, not so much Saturday or Sunday lunch as dinner on Saturday evening, because she had already had some experience of Dilys's culinary skills at the Ruby Wedding party, in addition to having been somewhat intimidated by Ted's fulsome praise of the meal he had enjoyed with Jim and Dilys shortly after their meeting at the test match. Ted had done his best to persuade her that there was no competition involved, but she felt under pressure nevertheless, and it was with great relief that she heard Dilys enthusing over the main course she had prepared, which involved pieces of chicken cooked with sherry vinegar, cream and tarragon.

'This is absolutely divine, Valerie,' she said. 'You must give me the recipe!'

'Oh, it's no big deal,' Valerie replied. 'It's a Delia Smith recipe – nothing special.'

'It still has to be cooked properly,' said Dilys. 'And in any case, I often use Delia Smith recipes myself – though I must admit, I don't always tell people where I've got them from!'

'I don't disagree with you, Dilys,' Ted interjected, 'but Jim was maintaining the other day that if you could read, you could cook, weren't you, Jim?'

'I didn't quite say that,' Jim protested. 'I was talking about poaching salmon, and doing that is an absolute doddle.'

'A couple of months ago,' said Ted, 'you were claiming that you had no cooking skills at all, and then you surprised us first of all with your mussels, and then with your poached salmon, both of which were exquisite. How many other "doddles" have you got up your sleeve?'

'None whatever,' replied Jim.

'Not quite true,' Dilys countered. 'He does quite a passable cheese sandwich!'

'I look forward to trying it,' said Ted, as they all dissolved, as they often did, into uncontrollable laughter.

After dinner Ted said to Jim: 'I suppose you would like to go to mass tomorrow morning, Jim? I've checked out times, and there's one at 10 o'clock. I'll drop you off there if you like, and pick you up later.'

'Why not come with me?' said Jim.

'You're not thinking of trying to convert me back to the faith of my fathers, are you, Jim?'

'Not in the slightest. I realise that's a lost cause. I just thought it would save you two journeys.'

'Actually,' said Valerie, 'that's not a bad idea. It will get you two out from under our feet, and you can go and have a drink afterwards, while Dilys keeps me company as I prepare lunch.'

To Ted's surprise, he found himself agreeing to go to mass with Jim.

Once the two men had left, Valerie and Dilys sat over coffee for a while before Valerie started to prepare lunch.

'How long have you and Ted been married, Valerie?' said Dilys.

'Only half as long as you and Jim,' replied Valerie. 'Twenty years ago last March. I wish I'd met him earlier, and then I could have saved him from the clutches of Arlette!'

'That's true – but then there would have been no Sophie! Had you been married before?'

'Yes, briefly. Very briefly.'

'Oh, that sounds painful.'

'Yes, it was, very. It still is when I think of it.'

'I'm sorry, don't...'

'No, it's okay. It's probably not what you're thinking. I met a young R.A.F. officer just after I finished university. Colin, his name was. He was a flying instructor, and we got married about a year after we first met. We were very much in love, and very happy, and then less than a year after the wedding, he and some of his pals were doing formation aerobatics, getting ready for a Battle of Britain commemoration show, and Colin and one of the others collided. They were both killed.'

'Oh no, Valerie, that's awful!'

'Yes, especially when you think they were doing it in memory of the pilots who were killed in the Battle of Britain. I'd love to know how many young men have been killed in their memory in exactly that way. I don't suppose they keep the statistics, but it must be quite a few...'

'How old was he?'

'25. But that wasn't the end of it. I was pregnant, and I lost the baby.'

'That's terrible! It's the worst thing imaginable for a woman to lose her baby! I'm sorry to have brought it up.'

'No, it's a long time ago now. It was terrible at the time, of course. And then I had to give up being an R.A.F. wife and make some sort of career for myself.'

'What did you do?'

'I went into publishing. I had a degree in English, you see, and I didn't feel confident enough to go into teaching. To begin with I was just a dogsbody, but after a while I became a copy editor, and then eventually a commissioning editor.'

'And you kept on doing that until you retired?'

'If only! No, about five or six years after I married Ted, our company was taken over by an American firm, and a lot of us lost our jobs. Of course by that time I was the wrong side of 50, and I was never able to land another job. I managed to do a bit of free-lance proof-reading, and stuff like that, but it wasn't like having a real job. It could have been worse though. I mean, if I'd never met Ted...'

'How did you and Ted meet?'

'Oh, it was at an educational conference – I was working for an educational publisher, you see. It's funny, when Colin died, and the baby went too, I made a solemn oath to myself that I'd never get married again. And then as soon as I met Ted, I forgot all that!'

'Well, it must have been a good twenty years after you took that oath, so it doesn't really count as a broken vow...'

'No, but it did mean that I'd left it too late for Ted and me to have our own family.'

'Of course. Oh, Valerie, what a hard time you had!'

'I used to think so, but now I'm older I realise that there aren't many people who haven't got some sort of tragedy buried deep within them somewhere. Anyway, come on, I need to start doing lunch!'

Ted could not even remember the last time he had set foot inside a Catholic church, although he did not share that thought with Jim. Once there, he was very surprised to find that much had changed since the time when he had been a regular mass-goer, to the point where, he felt, the service had become almost indistinguishable from the Church of England Eucharist that he very occasionally attended. But he was much more surprised, when the moment came for the congregation to take communion, that Jim did not approach the altar-rails to take communion himself; more than that, he did not even present himself, arms crossed, to receive a blessing from the celebrant, as did some of the congregation who, for whatever reason, did not want to receive communion.

After mass was over, he and Jim repaired to a nearby pub, where they each ordered a pint of ale – the first time, Ted reflected, that he had seen Jim drinking anything alcoholic other than wine, *pastis* or whisky. Once served, they withdrew to a small table in a quiet corner of a spacious garden behind the pub, with access restricted – an anachronism really, thought Ted – to Lounge rather than Saloon customers.

'Cheers, Jim,' said Ted, raising his glass, immediately after they had sat down. 'Welcome to Crowthorne!'

'Thanks, Ted,' replied Jim. 'Cheers!'

They sat in silence for a minute or two. Then Jim said: 'Ted, there's something I want to talk to you about...'

'Go on then,' replied Ted.

'It's a bit difficult to know where to start. I suppose I want your advice really.'

'Okay,' said Ted, a bit lost for words.

'Well,' Jim began falteringly, 'we've known each other for a long time, haven't we?'

'Yes, we have.'

'Even though there were a number of years in between, when we weren't in touch...'

'Yes...'

'It's just that there's no one else I can talk to about this...'

'Why not Dilys?'

'Good God, no! She's the last person I could talk to about this. I could talk to a priest, I suppose, but I'm no longer confident that a priest would be able to understand or advise me properly...'

'Okay, Jim,' said Ted, realizing for the first time that a really important topic was about to be broached. 'Try me.'

Jim took a deep breath and continued: 'I'm having an affair with Arlette.'

'You're what?' answered Ted, overwhelmed by astonishment more than anything else.

'I'm having an affair with Arlette, and I feel trapped. I don't know how to get out of it.'

'I don't know how you got *into* it! Didn't I say she'd eat you for breakfast?'

'Yes, you did, but I thought that was just the remnants of past unhappiness and bitterness speaking.'

'Well, there was an element of that, certainly, but there was a much more substantial element of solid truth. How did this come about?'

Jim began to relate to Ted the circumstances of their initial encounter at the French church in Leicester Square, culminating in Arlette's move to the apartment in Lexington Gardens.

'Did you know she was going to move in next door?'

'No, I didn't. She didn't tell me until it was a *fait accompli*. If I'd known that was what was in her mind I would have done everything in my power to stop her.'

'Of course – which is why she didn't tell you about it until it was signed and sealed.'

'Yes, I see that now.'

'What are you going to do about it then?'

'I don't know what to do. That's why I'm asking you.'

'Okay then. Let's start with a couple of fundamental questions. I'll try to be as neutral and as matter-of-fact as I can. First question – do you want to leave Dilys?'

'No.'

'Sure?'

'Absolutely.'

'Absolutely's a big word.'

'Yes, I know it is, but it's the right answer to that question.'

'Okay. Second question – do you think Dilys would stay with you if she found out?'

'Yes... No... I don't know. How would she find out?'

'You might tell her.'

'No I wouldn't.'

'You're telling me...'

'Yes, but that's different. I couldn't tell her.'

'Somebody else might.'

'Who?'

'Arlette, for instance.'

'No, she wouldn't tell her.'

'How do you know?'

'She told me she wouldn't.'

'You obviously trust her more than I do!'

'I've got no reason to think she's lying.'

'Okay. Let's leave that for a minute. Do you remember when we first went to Montpellier, and you were saying how sceptical you were about coincidence?'

'Yes.'

'Do you think it was coincidence that you and she bumped into each other coming out of church?'

'Yes.'

'Okay, perhaps it was. Do you think it was coincidence that she chose an apartment next door to you?'

'Yes... Well, maybe.'

'Maybe, but unlikely. Do you think it was coincidence that she came out just as you and Michael were arriving for the party?'

'Probably. Don't you?'

'Possibly, but there are an awful lot of coincidences starting to build up, especially when you include the coincidence of her choosing to buy the house in France that we were looking at.'

'Maybe.'

'Okay, let's look at it from another angle. Sorry to be personal, but having an affair is a very personal matter. Is your attraction to Arlette totally sexual, or are you in love with her?'

'What does "in love" mean?'

'What a question! I suppose I mean are you attracted by her more as a woman than as a person?'

'If she wasn't a woman I wouldn't have gone to bed with her!'

'Knowing you, I'm not surprised about that! But to put it bluntly, is it just a matter of sexual gratification?'

'I don't know...'

'Would you have responded to her in the way you did if she hadn't been French?'

'No, I suppose I wouldn't.'

'And would you be going round to see her for the pleasure of her company if all that was on offer was tea and biscuits?'

'No, I wouldn't.'

'Okay, Now I'm not going to ask the next question that comes into my mind, because it would involve going into private matters involving *two* of my best friends, not just you and Arlette. So I'll just give you a matter to think about, and to think about very deeply and seriously: other than flattering your ego by at least claiming that she finds you desirable, and also by being French, what do you get from Arlette, that you can't get from Dilys, that is worth running the risk of losing Dilys altogether?'

'I don't need to think about it. I know the answer already. The answer is nothing.'

'In that case, you've got to stop seeing her.'

'I know, but how, when she's living next door? If she were living in her old place it would be a great deal easier.'

'If you can't just do it by will-power, you might have to go away for a few weeks – stay with us, for instance, or with Michael.'

'But if I did that, how would I explain it to Dilys?'

'Ah.'

'That's a great help!'

'I didn't say I knew all the answers. I just said I'd ask you some questions.'

'I suppose I could engineer a row with Dilys and use that as an excuse for going to stay with Michael...'

'I thought the object was to stay with Dilys. Are you going to achieve that by hurting her in the way that would?'

'No, I see what you mean. No, I couldn't do that!'

'Thank God you've got some sense, Jim! But look at the time – it's time we were getting home for lunch. Now that it's clearer in your mind what you want to achieve, it's up to you to work out how to achieve it.'

'Yes, Ted, I know. Thanks for your help. It is a lot clearer now. You should be in marriage guidance!'

'Not likely! It's difficult enough dealing with your own relationships without having to sort out other people's!'

Later that night Ted found it difficult to sleep. The weekend had been a very enjoyable one, but Valerie was exhausted, and was asleep as soon as her head touched the pillow. Ted, however, started thinking about the conversation he had had with Jim in the pub. It had not been an unpleasant conversation, but, needless to say, the subject-matter of it was such that it certainly cast a cloud over his weekend, and, he supposed, over Jim's, although Jim had been his usual convivial self at lunch. It was, Ted reflected, as if

Jim had just been to confession and was now feeling cleansed of the sin that had been weighing him down. That was clearly why he had not taken communion, and, equally clearly, Ted thought, the notion of sinning weighed more heavily on him than the notion of hurting Dilys.

Ah yes, Dilys! She would be devastated if she found out. At the moment there was only a potential cloud hanging over her, but it was a thunder-cloud which would need very little to cause it to burst. And then, of course, the repercussions would be widespread, affecting him and Valerie as well and, with Arlette on the loose, who else?

Ted had already decided not to say a word to Valerie about it. For one thing, Jim had spoken to him in confidence, just as if he were in the confessional, and Ted found himself bound just as much by the seal of confession as a priest would have done. Actually, thought Ted, there was very little to tell, for apart from Jim saying that he was having an affair with Arlette, virtually no factual details had emerged, not because Ted had wished to avoid any suspicion of prurience – which obviously he did – but because their conversation had been very French in style: it had been a detached, unemotional, philosophical examination of the principles which lay behind the one fact that was under discussion, and of what possible routes lay ahead of the clearly unhappy Jim.

Of course tomorrow would be Monday, which meant Bach Choir rehearsal, which in turn meant he would be seeing Dilys. How would what he now knew affect their conversation? As far as he was aware, Dilys knew nothing of the affair. But he was equally well aware from things that Dilys had said to him that she had her suspicions, and it would take only the slightest hint dropped by Ted for her to feel that those suspicions were justified. Therefore he would have to be extremely careful in what he said to her.

But Jim was his friend too, and he wondered when their next conversation would be, and what would be the nature of it? And what were Arlette's intentions? He suspected that she was just playing around, and toying with Jim, just as a cat toys with a mouse. But what if she wasn't? Should he get in touch with her himself? Not a good idea, he told himself at once: what possible good could come out of it?

At last Ted dropped off to sleep. The next thing he knew, the sun was flooding through the window, and Valerie was standing by him with a cup of tea.

'Ted! You're awake at last! I thought you'd never wake up!'

'Why? What time is it?'

'It's nine o'clock. It's not like you to sleep as long as this, especially as we had such an early night...'

'Yes, that's weird. Can't think why I slept so long. Must have been a relaxing weekend, I suppose...'

'Huh! It might have been relaxing for you – it was damned hard work for me!'

'Yes, I know it was – I didn't mean that, I'm sorry,' said Ted, thinking within himself that he could think of better ways of relaxing than his Sunday morning chat in the pub with Jim had been.

When Ted did meet Dilys later that day she made no reference to the suspicions she had voiced before, and, of course, neither did he. Instead they both expressed their pleasure at the weekend they had just spent together, and there was no way in which their conversation differed from their normal weekly chats. At the same time, however – and at various points during the rehearsal – Ted found himself thinking about Jim and wondering where he might be at that specific moment, for it was obvious to him, even if was not to Dilys, that Dilys's absence for a guaranteed period of time every Monday would provide a first-class window of opportunity for a would-be adulterer.

That was why, only half-way through the rehearsal, he resolved to make sure that he and Dilys had a drink together afterwards, for that would give Jim enough time to return and sort himself out before Dilys got home, in the event that he had taken as little notice of Ted's advice the previous day as he had of the priest's injunction to 'go and sin no more' after his earlier confession, at the very start of his relationship with Arlette. As things turned out, it was Dilys who proposed they go to the wine-bar again – which was just as well, because, in another part of London, Jim and Arlette were laying the foundations of Jim's next confession.

Over the course of the next few weeks Ted heard nothing from Jim, although he did continue to see Dilys before and after rehearsals. Again Dilys made no reference to her worries about Jim, and at least Ted was a little reassured by that, because if things had come to a head, either she would have said something about it, or she would not have been there at all. They talked instead about the rapidly-approaching trip to Paris, of which they had now been given more details, including the information that they would both be staying at the Hôtel Keppler, a stone's-throw from the Arc de Triomphe – a hotel which Ted already knew, because he and Valerie had stayed there together on a number of occasions in the past.

The concert would take place on Saturday evening 21st October, but, with a rehearsal due to start at 10 am on Saturday morning, it would clearly be sensible to fly out the day before, especially since Parisian time was an hour ahead of London time. As Ted and Dilys were not subject to the same constraints as younger members of the choir who would be working on Friday afternoon, and hence would be obliged to catch an evening flight, they decided to meet at Heathrow and take a flight in the early afternoon.

Dilys duly left Lexington Gardens just after 1 o'clock, having had an early lunch with Jim. Not more than ten minutes after she left, Jim was ringing Arlette's doorbell. But to his surprise, she was elegantly dressed and carrying a small suitcase. On seeing Jim, she said: 'Oh Jim, it's you – I thought it was my taxi.'

'Your taxi? Why? Where are you going? You know that Dilys is away in Paris this weekend. We were going to spend most of the weekend together.'

'Yes, *mon chéri*, I know we were, but something turned up, and now I've got to go away for the weekend. I must have forgotten to tell you. Sorry!'

Before Jim could respond, Arlette's taxi did arrive, whereupon she closed her apartment door, picked up her weekend case, gave Jim a hasty peck on the cheek, and said: 'Must go! Have a nice weekend! Bye!'

And she was gone, leaving Jim to return to his own empty apartment.

Once Ted and Dilys were installed in their rooms at the Hôtel Keppler, they met, as they had arranged, in the hotel bar. To their surprise, there were no other choir members in evidence – nor, indeed, had they spotted any on the plane; it would appear that most, if not all, would be arriving on later flights. Ted ordered a *kir* for each of them, and they began to discuss where they would eat that evening.

'I'm not sure that we can afford to go somewhere where the cooking's likely to be as good as yours, Dilly. But I do know a place not far from here which is eminently affordable, and the food is not half bad.'

'Flatterer!' Dilys laughed, and went on: 'That sounds good to me. Where is it?'

'It's a *bistro* in the Boulevard de Latour-Maubourg, which is within easy walking-distance of here. It would take no time at all.'

'Okay. If you say it's good, I'm sure it is.'

'I'd better pop into Reception to ask them to ring the restaurant in case they're booked up. We wouldn't want to arrive there and find ourselves obliged to walk around for ages trying to find somewhere else because they have no tables.'

Ted went out of the bar into Reception, coming back only three or four minutes later, to tell Dilys that he appeared to have secured the last available table. About half an hour later they were on their way towards the *bistro* which, as Ted had promised, was not more than about five minutes' walk from the hotel.

To Dilys's delight and Ted's relief, the food was just as good as Ted had predicted. But Dilys, it seemed to Ted, did not seem to be quite her normal, sparkling self, and at about half past ten they were on their way back to the hotel – not that that was such a bad idea, because a late night might mean they would be insufficiently alert to deal with the following morning's rehearsal. Ted saw Dilys back to her room, and said goodnight with a chaste kiss on the cheek, whereupon Dilys suddenly burst into tears.

'Oh, Ted, oh, Ted!' she sobbed. 'I'm so unhappy!'

'Dilly!' said Ted. 'What on earth's the matter?'

'Oh Ted, it's so awful! I don't know what to do!'

And she began to sob even more uncontrollably.

'Is it something you can tell me about?' asked Ted.

'I'll try. I'd like to, if you don't mind...'

'Of course. If there's anything I can do, I will.'

'I'd just like you to listen,' replied Dilys. 'You're my oldest and most respected friend, and I feel I can trust you more than anyone else.'

'Even Jim?'

'Especially Jim.'

With that, she opened her bedroom door, and Ted followed her in.

Once inside, Dilys just stood there, with Ted facing her, and dissolved into tears again.

'I think you'd better sit down, Dilly,' said Ted.

Dilys sat on the edge of the bed, and Ted sat in an armchair three or four feet away.

'Okay,' said Ted. 'Go ahead. Tell me what it's all about.'

He then heard the statement that he had been dreading hearing from Dilys's lips for a few weeks now: 'I've discovered that Jim is having an affair with Arlette.'

'What? I don't believe it!' cried Ted, feeling rather hypocritical as he pronounced the words, but still convinced that he ought not to reveal the fact that he already knew.

'It's true, Ted, they've been meeting while we've been at rehearsals.'

'How do you know?'

'I found a note in the breast-pocket of one of Jim's shirts I was putting in the wash. It said 'See you round here on Monday evening as usual. A.''

'That's not proof of an affair.'

'Oh, come on, Ted, don't be naïve! Jim wouldn't be going round to Arlette's flat to play tiddly-winks, would he?'

Ted dismissed any temptation to smile at the incongruous thought of his ex-wife playing tiddly-winks with anyone, least of all Jim, and said: 'Have you spoken to Jim about it?'

'No, not yet. I only found the note this morning, and if I'd raised the matter then, it would have meant my missing the plane.'

'You shouldn't jump to conclusions before you've spoken to him, you know,' said Ted unconvincingly.

'I don't need to ask him, Ted,' she replied. 'I've known for some time deep down. For a long time he's been making me feel less than a woman, and now I know he's preferring her company to mine, I don't feel like a woman at all.'

Ted looked at Dilys, and thought that he'd rarely seen anybody more like a woman than she was.

'I think I'd better go,' he said, getting to his feet.

'Please don't go just yet, Ted,' she said pleadingly. 'I've never felt so unhappy.'

Suddenly Dilys was full of tears again. Ted put his arms around her and kissed her tenderly on the cheek. She looked at him, their eyes met, then their lips, and before long they were lovers again, as they had been fifty years before.

It was six o'clock the following morning when Ted awoke to find Dilys still in his arms, and his hand on her right breast. He gently removed his hand, and Dilys too opened her eyes, looked up at him and smiled.

'I'm not sure we should have done that, Dilly,' he said.

'I am,' she replied. 'But we're not going to do it again. I said last night I didn't feel like a woman any more, and now I do. I didn't mean things to turn out the way they did, but I'm glad they did. You were the first man ever to make me feel like a woman, after all, and a woman never forgets her first lover, unless she's been a lot unluckier than I was.'

'But Jim has hurt you by sleeping with somebody else, and now I've...'

'No,' Dilys interrupted. 'I know what you're going to say. You're going to say that you've hurt Valerie by sleeping with me. But it's different.'

'Why is it different?' asked Ted.

'Well, look,' Dilys began. 'I don't have the first idea what your and Valerie's sex life is like. It's none of my business, and I wouldn't ask. But I know you both well enough to be aware that you're the most stable and secure partnership I know, and you're totally devoted to each other. And I love you both.'

'That means,' she continued, 'that if I thought what we did last night was likely to damage that relationship, I wouldn't have let it happen. That perhaps makes it sound as if it was all premeditated, but it wasn't. It was totally spontaneous, and utterly beautiful, just as it was all those years ago.'

'I know,' Ted began, 'but...'

'No, wait, Ted. I've never talked to anyone like this before, and now I've started, I might as well finish. Jim and I haven't made love for the best part of two years. Some people would say that's normal for somebody of our age, but there's so much twaddle talked about sexuality in older people, and in older women in particular, and it drives me insane. There have been times when I've been screaming because I was so desperate to make love to Jim and I couldn't get any response. If a man imposes his sexual desire onto an unwilling woman it's called rape, and it's appalling, of course it is, but what is it called when a man imposes his sexual apathy on a woman who's hungry for his love? What I'm trying to say is that by sleeping with Arlette, Jim nearly tipped me over the edge, but by sleeping with me, you've pulled me back again.'

'There are some people who would say that you've used me,' said Ted.

'Perhaps I have,' replied Dilys. 'But do you feel used?'

Ted looked up, and saw her smiling face, in stark contrast to the desolate image she presented a few hours before, and said: 'No, Dilly, I don't, but I won't be saying anything to Valerie about it.'

'No, of course you won't, and neither will I, but I will ever be grateful to her for lending me her gorgeous husband for a few hours, even if she wasn't aware of it. Now we'd better get up – we've got a rehearsal to go to.'

'Just one thing more though,' said Ted. 'Are you still going to confront Jim?'

'Oh yes,' she replied. 'I certainly am. And when I do, he'll feel so guilty he'll be begging for forgiveness. Then I'll tell him I love him too much to let him go, and I will forgive him, but for his penance he's going to have to start making love to me again.'

'I never had penances like that when I went to confession,' laughed Ted. 'If I had, I might never have stopped being a Catholic!'

The rest of the day passed amazingly quickly, and the concert was very well received by a capacity audience. As was usual after a concert, Ted and Dilys felt exhausted, but when they arrived back at the hotel, they decided to have just one more winding-down drink before retiring to their – separate – beds.

Once they had settled down with their drinks in a quiet corner of the bar, they chatted about various aspects of the rehearsal and of the concert itself. When that topic was exhausted,

Ted finally said: 'Now listen, Dilly. I know we've agreed not to talk any more about what happened last night, but there's one thing I've got to ask you arising out of that, which is really very, very important.'

'All right, Ted,' replied Dilys. 'Go ahead.'

'I'm sorry, Dilly, but I've got to ask you this. How long have you had that lump in your breast?'

'Ah, you noticed it,' Dilys replied.

'Well yes, of course I did. But how long have you had it?'

'Oh, quite a while.'

'How long is quite a while?'

'Oh, I don't know. About a year, I suppose...'

'A year! Have you consulted anybody about it?'

'No.'

'Why not, for goodness' sake?

'I suppose I was too frightened.'

'But it's not something you can allow yourself to be frightened of and then do nothing about.'

'Yes, I know really.'

'Does Jim know about it?'

'No, he doesn't.'

'Now look, Dilly, I want you to be responsible about this. You're not an empty-headed young girl, you're an extremely intelligent and level-headed woman...'

'Don't be cross with me, Ted, please!'

'I'm not cross, Dilly, I'm worried. And so should you be until you get it checked out. I want you to promise to do something about it tomorrow.'

'Tomorrow's Sunday.'

'Well, Monday then.'

'I'll see.'

'Dilly! I'll ring you up every day and badger you until you do!'

'What will Valerie think if you start phoning me every day?'

'Oh, honestly! I'll tell her about it then, and she'll keep badgering you!'

'And what will you tell her about how you found out about it?'

'Oh, Dilly! Look, for God's sake, this is really serious! You've got to get it checked out. If you like I'll give you Sophie's number, and then you can call her and have an informal chat about what to do about it if you like. But you must do something about it, Dilly, you really must!'

Dilys leaned across the table and kissed Ted on the cheek. 'All right, Ted, I will.'

'Promise?'

'Yes, promise. I'll get in touch with somebody on Monday. I know I should have done something about it before, but there was nobody I felt I could talk to, and nobody I felt cared enough about my body to be interested.'

'But now you do.'

Dilys smiled again, and said, 'Yes, now I do.'

'And you'll let me know the outcome of any tests you have, and so on?'

'Yes, I will. Bless you, Ted, you're a lovely man.'

'Not as lovely as you, Dilly. Just look after yourself.'

With that, they said good night, and went to bed.

The following morning they flew back to London, and the topic was not mentioned again; Ted did not even remind Dilys of the promise she had made the night before – he was confident enough now to know that she really meant what she said.

When they arrived at Heathrow, Ted and Dilys said goodbye, Ted went to catch the train to Reading, whilst Dilys took a taxi to Kensington, arriving in Lexington Gardens well before Ted arrived home.

She got out of the taxi, paid the cabbie, climbed the steps leading to the front door, and rang the doorbell. She was not particularly surprised that no one responded: it was Sunday, and Jim had probably stayed out for a drink after going to church – or, of course, he might be with Arlette, but she dismissed that thought almost as soon as it entered her head, because he knew roughly at what time she was likely to arrive home, and would not be so careless.

She put down her weekend case, located the latch-key in her handbag, and let herself in. She went first into the bedroom to deposit her case, then to the bathroom. A few minutes later, as she passed the door of Jim's study on her way to the kitchen, the sight which met her eyes made her blood freeze. After what seemed to her like an eternity, her paralysis gave way to a paroxysm of screaming, to which no one responded. Finally she made her way to the telephone, and dialled Ted and Valerie's number. She heard the phone ring a couple of times, and then Valerie's voice.

'Valerie!' she screamed. 'Valerie! It's Dilly! I don't know what to do! I don't know what to do!'

'Dilys!' said Valerie. 'What on earth's wrong? What's happened?'

'Oh, Valerie!' she cried. 'It's Jim! It's Jim! I don't know what to do! It's Jim! Jim's dead!'

Tony Whelpton

Chapter Twelve

When Valerie received Dilys's phone-call, with its dramatic news, she too was at a loss to know what to do. She tried to ask Dilys for more information, but all she could hear was the sound of sobbing, which lasted for several minutes until the phone went dead. She had no idea whether Dilys had spoken to anyone else before calling her; if she had, it was clear that no one was with her yet, and it was also clear that, since the phone was apparently still off the hook, she had not called anyone since. She thought of calling Ted, who must have been well on the way to arriving home, since Dilys was already in Kensington, but then she remembered that, for some reason she had never been able to fathom, he never took his mobile with him on trips abroad. She could have called Jemima or Michael, but she did not have their numbers. She switched on her computer and searched for the phone numbers of people called Fletcher in Winchester; she found several, but none of them appeared to be called Michael.

At that moment Ted arrived, much to Valerie's relief. She rushed to the door, opened it, and rushed out, so that when they met he was still only halfway up the path.

'Ted! Thank God you're here! Come inside, quick! Something terrible's happened!'

Ted followed her inside, where she told him about Dilys's phone-call, and her own feeling of helplessness.

'Have you tried ringing Dilys back?' he asked.

'No, I haven't. Perhaps I should have done.'

Ted picked up the receiver, dialled the number, and then, after waiting for well over a minute, decided that no one was going to answer, so he replaced it.

'I think I'd better ring the police,' he said. 'Then I'll drive up to London and see what's going on. At least with it being Sunday the traffic shouldn't be too bad.'

Ted then called the local police, who appeared to have some difficulty understanding why someone in Berkshire would call to tell them about the death of somebody in London, but he did eventually manage to persuade them to pass the information on to the Metropolitan Police. With that, he jumped in the car and made his way towards Kensington.

Fortunately he had been correct in his conjecture that the traffic would be fairly light, and about an hour later he arrived in Lexington Gardens to find a police car parked outside number 64. He went up to the door and rang the bell; a minute later a policewoman answered the door. Ted explained to her about the phone-call Valerie had received, and why he had come, and she let him into the apartment, where he found Jemima, sitting alone in the drawing-room. There was no sign of Dilys, but he could hear voices coming from the main bedroom, and a solitary male voice coming from the study, which he assumed was that of a policeman dictating notes into a voice-recorder.

Jemima greeted him and began to put him in the picture. Gradually it became clear that after calling Valerie, Dilys had run into the street screaming; a neighbour – fortunately not Arlette – came out to see what was happening, and took her inside; it was the neighbour who had called first the police and then Jemima, who had come straight over.

'Where's Dilys?' asked Ted. 'Is she all right?'

'No, she's in a terrible state,' replied Jemima, 'so I called the doctor, and he's with her at the moment. I expect he'll give her something to calm her down. It must have been such a shock, finding Dad lying on the floor like that...'

'She found him on the floor then? I'm sorry, Jemima, I don't know any details at all, because your Mum only told Valerie that Jim was dead and that she didn't know what to do.'

'Oh, well... I'll tell you as much as I know. She found him on the floor, there was a glass of whisky and an open bottle of whisky on the desk, and alongside them was a packet of sleeping-tablets.'

'Oh no! He didn't... Oh, I'm sorry, Jemima, you don't have to talk about it, I'm sorry.'

'No, it's all right, Ted, honestly. Don't forget I've already been through something of the sort when Jeremy died. But the big difference this time is that it looks as if he did it himself – Mum certainly thinks he did anyway. The police aren't saying a lot, but that's how it looks to me too.'

'Did he leave a note?'

'Not as far as I know. But there's a police-sergeant in the study now looking round, and they say a police doctor is on his way too.'

At that precise moment the doorbell rang and the policewoman went to the door. When she returned, she was accompanied by a man carrying a black bag, who was evidently the police doctor, for he was directed immediately into the study, and took no notice of Jemima or Ted.

'What I don't understand,' continued Jemima, 'is why Dad would want to do away with himself. He had moments when he could be a bit morose, but I've never known his morale to sink as low as that – have you?'

'No, I can't say that I have,' said Ted, 'but that doesn't prove that he wasn't ever depressed.'

'The really strange thing, though, is something my mother said – in between the sobs and screams, I mean. She kept screaming "That bloody woman! That bloody woman!" I have no idea who she was talking about, have you?'

Ted had a very good idea who she was talking about, but decided it would not be particularly helpful at that moment to reveal what was in his mind. As it happened, the conversation stopped at that point because the bedroom door opened and Dilys's doctor appeared. He made to speak to Jemima, then noticed Ted and hesitated.

'It's all right, doctor,' Jemima reassured him. 'This is Mr Bryant – he's a close family friend – you can speak freely.'

'Thank you,' said the doctor. 'I just wanted to say that I've given your mother a sedative – she's a lot calmer now. Here's a prescription in case she needs more, but I've left her enough to see her through tomorrow anyway. I think when the police have finished here it would be a good idea if she went home with you for a while – unless you're staying here with her, that is. Oh, and there's just one more thing – while she's taking these sedatives she should steer clear of alcohol. Give the surgery a call if you need me to see her again.'

With that, the doctor took his leave and departed. As soon as he had gone, Jemima said to Ted: 'There's no way I can stay over here – I've got nobody to look after the kids. I just hope she'll be willing to come with me.'

'If she won't,' said Ted, 'I'll stay up here and keep an eye on her – that's assuming she agrees to that. We obviously can't leave her alone, especially since the doctor says she mustn't drink.'

'Who mustn't drink? Who says so?'

Jemima and Ted turned, and saw Dilys emerging from the bedroom.

'You, Mum. The doctor says that because of the medication he's given you, you mustn't drink.'

'Oh, I see. I won't take any more pills then. Quite honestly I think a glass of wine would do me far more good.'

'I'm sure you're right, Dilly,' said Ted. 'But you've already had the pills, so you'll have to wait a bit for a drink.'

'Ted! I'm sorry, I hadn't realised you were there! How sweet of you to come!'

With that she immediately started to cry again.

'Come and sit down,' said Ted, and she obediently sat on the sofa beside him.

'The doctor thinks it would be a good idea if you came home with me, Mum,' said Jemima.

'Oh no,' replied Dilys, 'I can't do that – the police are still here.'

'I mean when the police have gone.'

'No, darling, I shall be all right here. I need to stay here really. I feel a lot calmer now. I shall probably cry a bit, but that's no bad thing, and I won't start being hysterical again, don't worry. I'm sorry I made it hard for you.'

'Now look,' said Ted. 'I can understand your wanting to stay here, but you need someone to keep an eye on you, and Jemima needs to go home to see to the children. Would you like me to stay with you?'

'Oh Ted, would you? Are you sure? Would that be all right with Valerie? ... Oh, poor Valerie,

I must call her, I must have upset her so much the way I behaved...'

'Valerie will understand,' Ted assured her. 'In fact if you'd like her to come and keep you company she'd be delighted.'

'No, Ted, you'll do – for now, anyway. And you knew Jim better than Valerie did – we can talk about him more easily.'

'Whatever you like, Dilly. I just want to make sure you're all right.'

'I shall be all right, don't worry.' She paused, and an angry look spread across her face. 'But if I ever get my hand on that bloody French woman next door...'

'There, there, Dilly, not now,' said Ted.

'What's this all about, Mum? What French woman?' asked Jemima.

'She means my ex-wife,' explained Ted.

'Why? What has she done?'

Before Ted could change the direction the conversation was heading, Dilys answered: 'She killed my husband, that's what!'

'She did what?'

'She killed my husband! She and your Dad were having an affair.'

'What! I don't believe it!' said Jemima, totally dumbfounded.

'Your mother *thinks* they were having an affair. She doesn't *know*...'

'I know they were, Ted! I have proof. And I think Jim knew that I'd found out. That's why he killed himself.'

Before either Jemima or Ted could say anything else, the study-door opened, and the police-sergeant and the pathologist emerged. The pathologist left straight away, but the sergeant stayed behind to speak to Dilys and Jemima. Seeing Ted, he hesitated before speaking, but this time it was Dilys who was the one to reassure him that anything he wanted to say could safely be said in front of Ted.

'Well, Mrs Fletcher,' he began. 'I'm afraid we're going to have to take Mr Fletcher with us. There will have to be a post mortem, you see.'

'Yes, of course,' murmured Dilys. 'Of course there will.'

'Somebody will be back to talk to you in the morning, and of course you'll be kept fully informed of all that happens. There's just one thing I will say now, though. We're not actually sure at the moment how your husband died – the post mortem will tell us that – but I think I can assure you that your belief that he killed himself is not supported by the evidence.'

'You say he didn't do it himself? But what about the pills? And the whisky?'

'The thing is, Mrs Fletcher, the amount of whisky in the glass corresponds exactly with the amount missing from the bottle, and since there's no sign of another bottle anywhere, it looks as if he hadn't yet drunk any. As for the pills, although the packet had been opened, no pills appear to be missing. So, unless there's something else we haven't noticed, at least I think I can reassure you on that score.'

The police-sergeant quietly indicated to Ted that it would be a good idea to get Dilys to move out of the drawing-room while his men removed the body, so Ted said to Dilys: 'Come on, Dilly, I'll make a cup of tea for all of us – but I need you to show me where everything is first.'

When Dilys and Ted returned to the drawing-room with three cups of tea, the policeman had already gone and, although Dilys probably realised that Jim had gone too, she made no reference to the fact. After a moment's silence, however, she said: 'Well, it's a relief to know that he didn't do it himself. I couldn't bear the thought of all the torment he must have gone through before he decided to end it all. But whatever turns out to be the cause of death I shall still blame Arlette...'

'That bloody woman, you mean,' said Ted. 'Yes, I think I shall too, though it's a long time since I stopped calling her names as flattering as that – I usually use far worse terms...'

A flicker of a smile appeared on Dilys's lips – just for a split second – and then she said: 'Jemima, darling, I think you'd better go home and see to the children. Don't worry about me – I'll be all right with Ted. And Ted, you'd better call Valerie.'

'Okay, Mum,' said Jemima, 'if you're sure. But I'll just wait until Ted has spoken to Valerie, just in case he can't stay after all.'

'I'll ring her now, then,' said Ted, 'but I can't see her saying no.'

As Ted had predicted, Valerie raised no objection to his proposal to spend the night at Lexington Gardens; if Ted had not made the suggestion she would have done so herself, for she recognised the distressed state that Dilys was in, and thought it would make it even more difficult for her if she were to be left completely alone. As it was, Valerie would herself come up to London the following day and do whatever she could to help Dilys through at least the early stages of her grief.

By the time Jemima had gone home it was already about 9 o'clock in the evening, and it suddenly occurred to Ted that neither he nor Dilys had had a bite to eat since having a sandwich on the aeroplane on the way back from Paris. He pointed this out to Dilys, but she said she had no appetite, and didn't need anything.

'But you need something, Ted,' she said. 'Let me get you something to eat.'

'No,' replied Ted. 'If you're not going to eat, then neither am I. Why not let me get you a bowl of soup – that would do you good.'

'Oh, all right, then,' she agreed finally. 'I have some packets of soup that I usually keep for Jemima's children when they're here. They should be in the cupboard just above the microwave – unless Jim helped himself to them while I was away. He's so lazy, you know.'

Dilys suddenly realised what she had said, and burst into tears again, her inadvertent use of the present tense recalling her to the reality of her predicament. Ted put his arms around her, and she stayed in that position for a full five minutes before her sobbing eventually subsided and she began to regain her composure.

'I'll get you that soup, Dilly,' said Ted sympathetically. 'But I'm here to be useful to you, not to be entertained.'

'I know. I just keep thinking of Jim and how he must have suffered.'

'We don't know that he suffered at all,' Ted countered. 'It may very well have happened quite suddenly, with no warning and no pain.'

'That's not really what I mean,' said Dilys. 'I'm thinking about his state of mind – the guilt I'm sure he was feeling over the business with Arlette. I know the police-sergeant said he thought Jim didn't do away with himself, but whether he did or not, I'm sure he felt quite wretched about it, because he always did if he thought he'd done something wrong. But of course you don't think he was having an affair with Arlette anyway, do you?'

'Well... No, I didn't exactly say that. I said "How can you be sure?" You didn't seem to me to have much evidence to go on, at least at first.'

'What do you mean?'

'I mean that to begin with you were just reacting to a vague feeling that might or might not have been justified. But when you found that note...'

'You seemed to think I was over-reacting to that too...'

'I was just trying to protect you, Dilly, that's all.'

'Had Jim said anything to you about Arlette?'

Dilys's question came out of the blue, and Ted could see no justification for continuing to conceal the truth.

'Well, yes, he had. But he told me that he felt trapped, and was looking for a way out...'

'But why did he want her and not me?'

'That's a question he couldn't answer either. And I think the simplest answer is to say that she's French and you're not. It may seem a bit glib and simplistic to say that, but don't forget I married her – a long time ago, admittedly – and that was certainly something that influenced me. When you have a love-affair with a country in the way that both Jim and I had when we were young, there's a tendency to prefer anything that comes from that country to anything that comes from your own, even if it runs counter to common-sense to do so.'

'Do you think it was Jim who started it?'

'No, I don't. I think it was Arlette who made a play for him.'

'Are you sure?'

'I'm not a hundred-per-cent sure, no, but from what Jim told me about the way things happened, I'm as sure as it's possible to be without having been there.'

'But men are easily led, aren't they?'

'Yes, I have to say they are – but I have to say also that, for every man who's easily led, there's usually a woman doing the leading!'

'But even if Arlette did lead him on, I'm sure Jim would have been consumed with guilt afterwards – I mean, it's that Catholic thing again, isn't it? But look, you were brought up as a Catholic …'

'Yes, you know I was.'

'Of course I do, and I remember you told me you didn't feel guilty after we first made love as youngsters. But did you feel guilty after our first night together in Paris?'

'No, I didn't.'

'Not at all?'

'Not at all.'

'Why not?'

'Because over the years I've come to have a much more rational view of things. To begin with, guilt is a destructive emotion that doesn't get you anywhere...'

'You can say that again!'

'That doesn't mean I don't sometimes feel guilty. But for me to feel guilty I would also have to feel that I'd done something mean, something malicious, something evil even...'

'Have you ever done anything malicious or evil?'

'Not as far as I know – not deliberately anyway. I'd never hurt anybody deliberately.'

'I can't imagine you hurting anyone, Ted. You're such a good friend to everyone. You know, you meant the world to Jim.'

'Really?'

'Oh yes, didn't you know? No, of course you wouldn't, because you wouldn't think of it, and Jim would never have told you. But he told me...'

There was a moment's silence, then Dilys continued: 'Ted, there's something I want to ask you...'

'Go on, then, ask away...'

'I'm frightened of being on my own tonight.'

'I know, Dilly. That's why I'm here.'

'Yes, I know it is. But I don't want you to leave me.'

'I'm not going to leave you.'

'Oh God,' said Dilys. 'This is so difficult! I didn't find it at all difficult the other night when I asked you to make love to me! And now I don't want to make love to you but I do want you to come to bed with me and hold me and comfort me. I just don't want to be on my own, and I want the comfort that being with you would give me. I'm not talking about anything sexual, it's just comfort I need. I might not sleep, but I might want to talk – would you mind that?'

'I wouldn't mind that in the least.'

'Oh Ted, you're such a wonderful friend! Come on then, let's go to bed – but, promise – no sex!'

'Of course not,' replied Ted. 'We're British!'

For the first time since she discovered Jim's lifeless body lying on the study floor, Dilys nearly laughed. Then she got up, and led Ted to the bedroom.

Once they were in bed, Dilys and Ted continued to talk about Jim and Arlette, but as tiredness began to take its toll, their conversation became more and more repetitive and more and more fragmented. At last it stopped altogether and both of them went to sleep.

At some time between three and four o'clock, Dilys woke with a start, sat bolt upright, and said: 'Ted! Ted! I've been so stupid! I've been so stupid!'

Ted, only half awake, merely grunted.

'Oh Ted! I'm sorry, I must talk to you!'

Ted, who had momentarily all but forgotten where he was now sat up in bed, though still not fully awake. 'What is it, Dilly? What's the matter?'

'Oh Ted,' she said, 'I feel so guilty! I am stupid!'

'Why do you feel guilty?' asked Ted. 'I'm only keeping you company, like you said...'

'Oh, it's not that, silly! I don't feel guilty about that! I feel guilty about Jim!'

'Why should you feel guilty about Jim?'

'What have we been talking about ever since Jemima went home?'

'We've been talking about Jim.'

'And?'

'What do you mean?'

'Jim and who else?'

'We've been talking about Jim and Arlette.'

'Exactly. That's why I feel so guilty.'

'I don't see why.'

'We've been talking about Jim and Arlette, and a little bit about Jim and me, but we should have been talking about Jim, Ted! Just Jim. Not Jim and Arlette, not Jim and you, not even Jim and me. Just Jim. I'm sorry, I am so stupid. I just couldn't see the wood for the trees. He's gone, Ted! He's gone for good, and I'll never see him again.'

'I know, Dilly,' said Jim, still rather confused.

'And all I can think about is my hurt feelings – my hurt pride – because he might have preferred somebody else's company. And for how long? For a couple of weeks or so? Perhaps a month, who knows? But he gave me forty years. And all I've been able to do is think about that couple of weeks and forget all about the forty years! How could I be so bloody insensitive!'

'Oh Dilly,' said Ted. 'Don't be so hard on yourself. You're only human.'

'I know, and a lot of humans are totally lacking in sensitivity, totally lacking in gratitude – but the fact that they're human doesn't make it right.'

'So... Can I make a suggestion?'

'Yes?'

'I'll go and make us a cup of tea, and then we'll sit here and talk about Jim. We've still got half the night left...'

With that, Ted got out of bed, reappeared a few minutes later carrying two cups of tea, and they talked about Jim and no one but Jim, until finally, some time after six, they both sank into a deep sleep.

Ted was awakened by a sudden blaze of light; through the narrow slits which were all his eyes appeared willing to become, he could vaguely make out a shape standing over him, silhouetted against the source of light.

'Ted! Ted!' said the shape's voice softly.

With a great deal of effort he managed to open his eyes just a little further, slightly more awake now, and realised that the shape was Dilys, now fully dressed, and standing in front of the window through which the sun was shining, holding a cup of tea.

'Ted! It's nine o'clock. Here's a cup of tea for you.'

She put the cup down on the bedside table, then leaned over and kissed him on the forehead.

'Breakfast in half an hour!' she announced. 'I've put a towel in the bathroom for you.'

With that, she left the bedroom, closing the door behind her.

Ted sat up in bed, had a few mouthfuls of tea, but decided that having a shower would do more than the tea to wake him up. After showering, he dressed, finished his tea, and opened the bedroom door. An aroma of bacon being grilled and eggs being fried greeted his nostrils, so he made for the kitchen.

'I'm sorry I slept so long, Dilly,' he said. 'You look as if you've been up for ages.'

'I have,' she replied. 'But it's all right, I found plenty to occupy myself. I realised, for instance, that I hadn't even got round to unpacking my weekend bag after we got home from Paris.'

'That's a point,' said Ted. 'Neither have I. I put it down in the hall when I got home, and then I rushed out and jumped in the car and came up here. I expect Valerie will have sorted it out though. Talking of Valerie, if it's half past nine now, I should think she'll be here before too long. But what time did you get up then?'

'Oh, about seven o'clock, I think.'

'You should have woken me too.'

'No, I'd kept you awake long enough as it was. You go and sit down, breakfast's just about ready.'

As they sat having breakfast together, Dilys said: 'You know, Ted, I can't think how I would have got through last night if you hadn't been with me. I needed to talk. I needed to express all the jumble of thoughts that were buzzing inside my head, and you were absolutely wonderful.'

'I didn't say much,' said Ted.

'You didn't need to,' Dilys replied. 'I had enough to say for both of us. But you did listen, and what you did say was full of good sense and incredibly helpful. And I can't think of anyone else I know whom I could have talked to about Jim in quite the same way. It was such a shock coming home yesterday and finding Jim in the way that I did, but talking with you – pretty well all night, I suppose, I'm sorry about that! – talking with you seems to have enabled me to make the transition from that initial state of shock to a state where I know I'm going to be able to cope with the next few days.'

'It's still not going to be easy for you, you know,' said Ted.

'No, I know it's not, I'm not kidding myself. I'm sure I shall have an outbreak of hysterics from time to time, but I don't feel alone any more. I'm not saying the shock has gone, I'm not saying that I'm not full of grief, but I do know that I have the rock of your friendship to support me, and that means such a lot.'

The doorbell rang before either of them could say anything more. Ted went to the door, and returned a few minutes later accompanied by Valerie.

As soon as Valerie saw Dilys she threw her arms around her, and both of them dissolved into floods of tears; not a word was said, nor was it necessary. At length they released each other, and Valerie said: 'I'm sorry, Dilys, I promised myself I wouldn't be like that. I was determined to be strong for you.'

'It's all right, Valerie, don't worry,' Dilys replied. 'I don't mind my friends crying like that – it's perfectly normal. I've done a lot of crying, so has Ted – and there'll be a lot more tears shed yet. But that doesn't mean I'm not in control, I am – and I've got your wonderful husband to thank for that.'

Ted, a little embarrassed, began to protest, but Dilys cut him short.

'No, Ted, let me. Your poor husband, Valerie, has been a tower of strength. I kept him talking nearly all night, and, by the time morning came, thanks to him, my feelings of utter desolation had gone, and I felt ready and able to face the world. I'm not saying I don't still feel lousy inside, but if it hadn't been for Ted, it would have been a whole lot worse. He's amazing. Thank you for lending him to me.'

Needless to say, whereas Valerie took Dilys's words at face value, they had a slightly different connotation for Ted. But if he felt any embarrassment arising from his awareness that it was the second time in a couple of days that Dilys had used those words, he did not show it.

A few minutes later, the doorbell rang again; this time it was Dilys's son Michael. Another five minutes, and Jemima arrived, followed shortly after by a police officer, who stayed only long enough to confirm to Michael, who had taken him into the study to speak to him privately, that Jim's death had been referred to the coroner, and that until the coroner had been satisfied as to the cause of death, they would be unable to make any but the most sketchy and provisional arrangements for the funeral. When the police officer had gone, Michael relayed to the others what he had been told.

'So,' Dilys said when Michael had finished, 'how long will we have to wait?'

'At the moment,' Michael replied, 'no one has the remotest idea, not even the coroner, but the coroner will certainly order a post mortem.'

'And an inquest?' asked Dilys anxiously.

'Not necessarily,' replied Michael. 'Whether there is an inquest depends on what the pathologist says. If the pathologist says death was due to natural causes, the coroner can authorise the registration of the death, and the funeral can go ahead. If it's not as straightforward as that, the coroner can insist on an inquest, and then it will take as long as it takes.'

'How do we find out the result of the post mortem?' asked Jemima.

'As I understand it,' said Michael,' the police will be told, and then they'll send somebody round to tell us. But until that happens, there's not a lot we can do.'

'Oh yes, there is,' said Dilys. 'We know there's going to be a funeral at some point, so we can at least go ahead with planning what form it's going to take.'

'Yes, we can do that,' said Michael,' but before we do, I'd better check Dad's will. I'm his executor, and I have to apply for probate before any of the provisions of the will can take effect, but at least I can see if he's expressed any particular wishes about the form his funeral will take.'

Fortunately they did not have to wait very long to find themselves in a position to proceed with the process of organising the funeral. Within forty-eight hours they received word that the coroner had decided that no inquest was necessary, for the pathologist had determined that Jim had in fact succumbed to a heart attack, and that the presence of the whisky and the sleeping-tablets was a total irrelevance. As a result the police ceased to be involved, and the family were able to arrange a fitting funeral, along the lines which Jim had indeed detailed in his will, and which, Ted was not surprised to learn, involved a full *Requiem* mass at Brompton Oratory, and appropriate music by Bach, Mozart, Fauré and Allegri.

During the days preceding the funeral Ted and Valerie spent as much time as they could with Dilys, realising that, with Michael and Jemima being almost fully occupied with administrative matters to do with registration of death, probate, negotiations with undertakers and church, and a hitherto unimaginable number of other things, they were in the best position to help Dilys to go through the motions of coping with everyday life.

Ted and Valerie spent the night before Jim's funeral at Sophie and Peter's house in Hampstead. Earlier in the evening they had participated in a relatively low-key ceremony at Brompton Oratory, during the course of which Jim's coffin was received into a side-chapel, where it would rest until the mass itself began at 10.30 the following morning. Only members of the family and a few very close friends were in attendance, which meant that their expressions of grief could be less muted than they would be the next day when they would be subjected to more public gaze. Even so, Dilys was sufficiently in control to be able to take Ted and Valerie on one side afterwards, and say: 'Valerie, when we get here tomorrow morning, Jim's immediate family will gather in this chapel and follow Jim into the church. But Michael, Jemima and I were talking earlier, and we all think that you and Ted have been so wonderful since Jim died that we feel you've become part of the inner family, and so we'd like you to join us if you would. Do you mind?'

'Mind?' said Ted. 'It would be a privilege.'

'It would indeed, my dear,' Valerie added, taking Dilys in her arms as she did so, and the two friends remained locked in this embrace for a whole minute, sobbing quietly together, before Dilys pulled away and said: 'And now we must press on – there's a lot to do. But it's going to be a lot easier tomorrow with you and Ted helping me.'

In the morning Ted and Valerie went to the Oratory by taxi with Sophie and Peter. When they arrived, a full half-hour before mass was due to begin, they were amazed to find the church already well on the way to being full. They were met by Michael, who took Sophie and Peter to the pews which had been reserved for them, whilst Ted and Valerie went to the chapel, where they found Dilys and Jemima kneeling with heads bowed, one on either side of Jim's coffin.

At about a quarter past ten they were joined by the priest who would say the mass, accompanied by an impressive number of acolytes, one bearing a crucifix, one bearing a thurible which already contained burning charcoal, to which the priest would add a scoop of incense before the procession began, and four others who removed from their stands four orange candles which had been surrounding the coffin, and who then took their places in the procession behind the thurifer. Then came the priest, followed by the coffin, borne by four former colleagues of Jim's, as specified in his will, with Dilys immediately behind, flanked by Jemima and Michael, and Ted, Valerie and Jane bringing up the rear.

As soon as the church clock struck the half-hour the procession moved off and the choir began singing the first of Jim's prescribed pieces, Fauré's *Cantique de Jean Racine*:

> *Verbe égal au Très-Haut,*
> *Notre unique espérance...*[8]

This was a work which Ted had often felt he would like to be sung at his own funeral, and, as many experienced singers find, he had great difficulty preventing himself from joining in, almost as if he felt the choir would be unable to manage without his support. If he had been able to see Dilys's face rather than the back of her

---

[8] 'Word co-equal with the Highest, our only source of Hope ...'

head, he would have noticed that she faced precisely the same problem.

Once they were settled in their allocated seats the mass began, following the old Tridentine rite which Jim had requested, and to use which a special dispensation had to be granted by the bishop, but, punctuating the ceremonial was Jim's choice of music, selected, Ted reflected, from works which would have been extremely likely to figure among those Jim would have chosen to take to the proverbial desert-island: *Hostias et preces* from Mozart's *Requiem*, the final chorale from Bach's *St. John Passion*, and, as Jim's coffin was carried out of the church, Allegri's *Miserere*, with its soaring treble line symbolising the flight of the departing soul pleading for God's forgiveness.

Once the mass and the subsequent interment were over, all the family and a sizeable number of other guests repaired to Lexington Gardens, where Michael had arranged for a marquee to be erected once more in the garden – albeit a larger marquee this time – but, needless to say, the occasion was much more sombre than the one which had taken place only a few weeks before, although more than one person who had attended both functions made allusion to the absence of the expert salmon-poacher and, as one often finds on such occasions, there was by no means a total absence of laughter as various people recalled their memories of Jim.

Throughout the entire proceedings, both in the church and afterwards, Dilys conducted herself with the quiet calm and dignity which those who knew her well had frequently witnessed on fairly formal occasions, although most of them knew perfectly well that what was going on inside was totally different, as she moved from one group to another, chatting amicably and gracefully accepting their condolences.

Ted and Valerie also moved from group to group, and their conversations were made easier by the fact that they had met a number of the guests at Jim and Dilys's Ruby Wedding party, and also, of course, because that occasion was too recent to have allowed most of the guests to have forgotten all about whom they had met and what they had talked about. It was a particular pleasure too for Ted and Valerie to meet for the first time Jim and Dilys's grand-children, of whom they had up to then heard a great deal but seen nothing.

It was not until fairly late in the proceedings that Ted and Valerie found themselves alone with Sophie and Peter. Almost immediately Sophie said to her father: 'Dad, did you notice who was sitting right at the back of the church?'

'No,' replied Ted, 'I can't say I did. I'm afraid I wasn't taking much notice of who was there. Why?'

'I just hope Dilys was as preoccupied as you then,' said Sophie.

'What do you mean?' asked Ted, puzzled. 'Who was it?'

'Who do you think it was, Ted?' Peter interjected. 'It was Arlette, of course, dressed all in black and all alone, and she must have left before the end, because she'd already disappeared by the time we came out.'

'Good God!' Ted exploded. 'How dare she show her face after what she's done! You're right, Sophie, I hope Dilys didn't notice! And I hope to God she doesn't turn up here!'

To Ted's relief his fears were ill-founded. Moreover he would have been even more relieved the following day if he had been present when a small white van drew up outside the house next door to Dilys's, and a man got out of the van and erected a notice-board outside the apartment only recently acquired by Arlette. The notice read 'For Sale'.

Tony Whelpton

Chapter Thirteen

Despite Ted's promise to Dilys when they were in Paris that he would badger her incessantly about the lump in her breast if she did not make an immediate appointment to have it checked out, the threatened badgering did not in fact take place; events had rather overtaken them, to put it mildly. But Ted had not forgotten, and he spent much time when he was on his own wondering when it would be appropriate to bring up the matter again.

But if Ted had not forgotten, neither had Dilys, and no more than a week after Jim's funeral, without any prompt from Ted, and without mentioning the matter to anyone else, she made an appointment with a doctor at her local surgery – not the doctor who had cared for her on the day she had discovered Jim's body, but one of his female colleagues, whom she knew rather better, even though in the past she had never needed much in the way of medical attention, other than for everyday, routine ailments.

The doctor showed Dilys into her consulting-room, invited her to sit down, and then said: 'Mrs

Fletcher, I was so sorry to hear about your husband. How are you coping?'

'Pretty well on the whole, I think,' Dilys replied. 'I'm very lucky in having some very good friends who have made it so much easier.'

'That's good. Are you still taking the tranquillisers?'

'No, I'm not. I stopped taking those about three days after Jim died.'

'Are you sleeping okay?'

'On and off. I suppose it's not bad really, but I do have wakeful periods every night. But it's not really a problem.'

'What can I do for you today then?'

Dilys told her about having become aware that she had a lump in her right breast.

'When did you first notice it?'

'Oh, quite a while ago.'

'A week?'

'No, more.'

'A month? Two months? How long?'

'Oh, I don't know – a couple of years, I suppose.'

'Have you had it looked at before?'

'No.'

'I'd better have a look now then.'

After a brief examination the doctor continued: 'Well, Mrs Fletcher, there's actually very little I can tell from that sort of examination. In fact I have to tell you that it's virtually impossible for any GP to make any sort of diagnosis, and that's why we have a number of very strict guidelines that we're obliged to follow. As a result, because there's certainly something there, and because of your age, and because of the length of time that it's been there, then the guidelines say that I have to refer you for specialist examination as a matter of urgency.'

'As a matter of urgency? Do you think I have cancer then?'

'The honest answer is I don't know. There's no way I can tell – I can't say yes, and I can't say no. All I'm saying is that, because you tick those particular boxes, the guidelines say you must be examined properly as a matter of urgency.'

'I see.'

'So I'll make contact with the hospital and they'll be in touch with you to confirm your appointment.'

'Okay. Just one thing – I do have private medical insurance...'

'For once it might not make any difference – you could end up seeing the same consultant on the same day in a case like this. But it's up to you.'

'Well, I have paid for it, so I might as well use it.'

'All right, I'll get that sorted for you.'

Dilys thanked the doctor and left. Only ten minutes after she arrived home the telephone rang; it was the hospital already, offering her an appointment in a week's time – with an apology that it was impossible to see her any sooner.

Feeling a little dazed at the speed at which everything was happening, Dilys made herself a cup of coffee, and sat down. After a minute or two's reflection, she picked up the phone and called Valerie. 'Hello, Valerie, it's Dilys.'

'Hi, Dilys, how are you getting on?'

'I'm fine, thanks, Valerie. I just thought I'd give you a ring to say hello. I couldn't remember if I'd told Ted that I would be giving choir a miss for a couple of weeks...'

'Yes, I'm sure you did – I think he said something about that. He's not in at the moment though, but I'll tell him. What are you up to at the moment?'

'Oh, not a lot. Actually there's no shortage of things I ought to be doing, but I'm feeling rather tired at the moment...'

'I'm not surprised. Are you not sleeping well?'

'Actually I am, but I still feel tired. I expect it's a reaction to everything that's been going on.'

'I expect it is, yes. Have you seen the doctor again?'

'Yes, I have actually – well, not the one that gave me the tranquillisers, my usual one.'

With that, Dilys's composure disappeared, and, between fits of sobbing, she related to Valerie what the doctor had said.

'Try not to worry about it too much, Dilys,' said Valerie. 'The odds are still in your favour, and, as Sophie has often said to me, it's a pre-arranged process that has to be followed, and in most cases it turns out to be nothing – but the vast majority of women assume the worst right from the very start.'

'Yes, I know you're right. I suppose I'm just very emotional at the moment.'

'Of course you are. But if it's any help, I've been in that position too, and I was scared to death. Luckily it turned out that the lump was just a benign cyst, and they drained it and that was the end of it. And that's what often happens – in fact it can be even less of a problem than that.'

Dilys, now feeling a little calmer, professed herself to be reassured, and they talked about other matters for a few minutes before Dilys rang off.

Two or three minutes later Ted came in.

'Hello, Ted,' said Valerie. 'You've just missed Dilys. She couldn't remember whether she told you that she was going to miss choir for a couple of weeks.'

'That's funny,' Ted replied. 'She told me at least three times, if not more. In fact I remember telling you.'

'That's what I thought. But I don't think that's why she rang really. I think she's scared.'

'Scared? Of what? Of being alone, I suppose.'

'No, she'd just come back from the doctor's, and she's apparently got a problem.'

Ted realised at once what this was about, but still said: 'What sort of problem?'

'She's apparently found a lump in her breast and it's got to be investigated.'

'No wonder she's worried. I remember how you were. Did you tell her about yourself?'

'Oh yes, of course I did, but she's obviously still worried, and she'll continue to be until it's properly sorted out, because no two cases are ever the same.'

'Well, if there is a real problem, I hope she ends up in good hands. I should imagine she can afford to go privately.'

'Yes, but I'm not sure it would make much difference. What was going through my mind, though, was whether it might be a good idea for her to come and spend a few days with us. It's going to be an anxious time for her, waiting for this hospital appointment, and being in that apartment all on her own isn't going to make it a lot easier, is it?'

'No, you're right. I think that's a very good idea, if she'll agree to it. Why don't you ring her back and see what she says – I think she'd appreciate the suggestion coming from you.'

Valerie called Dilys without delay, and both she and Ted were delighted that she accepted their invitation without hesitation. It was duly arranged that Ted would pick her up in two days' time – Friday – and then would drive her direct to the hospital for her appointment the following Wednesday. Once that arrangement had been made, Valerie telephoned Jemima, and invited her and the children to join them on Saturday morning; they would stay over, and return to Wimbledon on Sunday afternoon. To make the party complete, Valerie then phoned Michael and Jane, and arranged that they too would join them for dinner on Saturday and lunch on Sunday.

Later that evening, just as Valerie and Ted were finishing their meal, the telephone rang: it was Dilys. 'Valerie,' she said, 'I've just heard that you've invited Jemima and Michael for the weekend too. That's absolutely wonderful! But what a houseful you're going to have!'

'That's all right,' Valerie reassured her. We've got plenty of room.'

'It's not so much the room I was thinking of. I was thinking of all that work for you!'

'Not half as much work as you had for that Ruby Wedding party!'

'Oh well, I did have help though...'

Valerie laughed. 'I didn't say I wouldn't allow you to help a little bit!'

'No, I won't help a little bit. I insist on doing more than that. What I suggest is that I look after the meal on Saturday evening, and you look after Sunday lunch. What do you say? I mean, we can still help each other, can't we?'

Valerie was about to protest, but thought better of it, realising that it would not only be a great help to her, but that it would probably be very good for Dilys too.

When Ted arrived at Lexington Gardens to pick up Dilys, he was surprised to find that, as well as a medium-sized suitcase and four zip-up dress covers, each containing two dresses, she had three or four carrier-bags which, he discovered, contained everything she would need to prepare Saturday evening's dinner. He took the suitcase and the carrier-bags to the car, then went back up to the apartment to fetch the rest. He was just about to pick up the dresses when Dilys stopped him.

'No, Ted, I'll take the dresses. You carry this, it would be a bit heavy for me.' She indicated a sizeable cardboard box.

'What on earth's that?' Ted exclaimed.

'It's a case of champagne.'

'Champagne! Heavens, Dilly, you didn't have to go to those lengths!'

'No, no,' she protested. 'It's a present from Jim.'

'A present from Jim? What do you mean?'

'Well, I had a nice surprise yesterday when the mail came. There was an official-looking letter addressed to Jim, and when I opened it I found it contained a cheque for £500 – one of his Premium Bonds had come up!'

'No! I don't believe it! That's incredible! But doesn't that have to count as part of his estate?'

'Yes, of course it does, but most of it's coming back to me, so I can certainly afford half a dozen bottles of champagne. And anyway, it's what Jim would have wanted. It's just a pity he's not going to be with us.'

'He'd certainly help us to drink it!'

'No, I don't mean that. He was always complaining about his Premium Bonds. He'd had them for years, and never won a sausage!'

The three friends spent a quiet evening together, enjoying one or two drinks and a simple meal. Ted and Valerie were pleased to find that Dilys appeared to be quite relaxed; they talked a lot about Jim, though without Dilys becoming unduly upset, and also about her forthcoming medical investigation, which she also seemed to be taking in her stride. Ted was especially happy that they were able to persuade her fairly easily that her best way forward in the circumstances was to carry on with her normal life, including a return to Bach Choir activities, and even taking part in a performance of Bach's *Christmas Oratorio*, which was due to take place in mid-December.

The following day Jemima and her children arrived shortly before lunch. It was the first time Ted and Valerie had really had a chance to meet the children, Jonathan, who was ten, and his sister Emily, who was two years younger, other than in the rather stressful circumstances of Jim's funeral, and the first time too that they had had the pleasure of observing Dilys fulfilling the role of a clearly well-loved grandmother.

Fortunately the weather was kind to them that weekend; it was cold, but sunny, and they made the most of it by taking the children to Windsor for the afternoon, which excited them greatly, even though they were not rewarded by a glimpse of anyone from the royal household, despite Emily's hope and Jonathan's conviction that they would see the Queen herself. Jonathan's disappointment was quickly alleviated, however, when Valerie made toasted crumpets for them when they came in from the cold.

Michael and Jane arrived shortly afterwards, and it was not long before the first bottle of Jim's Premium Bond champagne was broached, followed quickly by the second; it was perhaps just as well, Valerie observed, that Dilys had done most of her meal-preparation in advance, and that what remained to be done was neither labour-intensive nor intricate, although Michael pointed out, in a manner which instantly reminded Ted of Jim, that the success of his mother's cooking was in direct proportion to the quantity of alcohol she had consumed. Whether that was true or not, the succulent duck-breasts she served them, accompanied by a red wine sauce enriched with chocolate and Agen prunes, were a tremendous success, as had been the much simpler starter of Parma ham and celeriac *rémoulade* that had preceded them. As for the remainder of the evening, that drifted by in a sea of hilarity which Valerie found reminiscent of the happy days they had spent with Jim and Dilys in the south of France.

After breakfast on Sunday morning, Michael and Jane went back home to Winchester. Since the weather was still surprisingly good for the time of year, Ted took Jemima and the children out for the morning, whilst Valerie busied herself with lunch. When Dilys discovered that Valerie was preparing a traditional English roast dinner, she insisted on helping with the vegetables, on the grounds that a meal of that kind required much more manual labour than she had needed to put in herself the previous evening. Valerie protested to begin with, but not too vehemently, partly because she could see the validity of Dilys's argument, partly because, although her hang-over from Saturday evening's excesses was not extreme, it was still there; and in any case, she always enjoyed Dilys's company, and found her easier to talk to than anybody else she knew apart from Ted, especially since she had told her about the tragedy of her first marriage.

To Valerie's delight, Sunday lunch was a great success as far as the children were concerned: they made it perfectly clear that they preferred cooking of that kind to the fancy things that their grandmother liked to make. Jonathan in particular revealed a marked predilection for Yorkshire puddings, and would seemingly have eaten nothing else, had it not been for his mother's firm insistence that he eat something else too.

Shortly after lunch Jemima and the children departed, and the remainder of the day was quieter and more relaxed, as was the first half of the next. But in the afternoon Ted resumed his normal Monday routine of catching the train to London, en route for the Bach Choir rehearsal. For the first time, however, he was not doing that journey alone, for Dilys had decided to act immediately on her decision to resume choir activities, and caught the train with him; it gave both of them a great deal of pleasure to visit their usual café before rehearsal and their usual wine-bar after, and then to make their way back to Crowthorne together.

At last Wednesday arrived – the day of Dilys's hospital appointment. Ted and Valerie drove her up from Crowthorne and dropped her off at the hospital, where Dilys was met by a receptionist. Once she had found her file, the receptionist showed her into a small waiting-room.

'Would you take a seat, Mrs Fletcher? A nurse will come and see you first, and then you'll see the doctor after that.'

Dilys hardly had time to sit down before the door of the waiting-room opened again, and a nurse appeared. 'Hello, Mrs Fletcher. I'm Josephine Lewis. Would you like to come with me, and we'll have a little chat before you see the doctor.'

Dilys stood up, and obediently followed the nurse into a small consulting-room, where again she was invited to sit down while the nurse asked her a series of questions, first of all to establish that she had the right notes and then, Dilys assumed, since she asked the very same questions her doctor had asked, to verify that her doctor had accurately recorded the results of her own questioning.

'Now, Mrs Fletcher,' said Nurse Lewis. 'The doctor wants me to do an ultrasound scan.'

'Ultrasound? Is that the same as a mammogram?'

'No, it's not. To be honest, it's rather less uncomfortable for you. Sometimes we use one, sometimes we use the other – they give us slightly different information.'

Dilys said no more, partly because she was afraid she was already getting out of her depth, partly because of a natural tendency she had always had to trust someone who was supposed to be an expert, and the nurse began the ultrasound examination. She appeared to be examining both breasts, not just the one in which she had the lump, and then both armpits too. Initially Dilys was a little surprised by this, but quickly persuaded herself that this must be the normal routine – after all, once the equipment was in use, you might as well do the job thoroughly, she thought to herself. Once she had finished, the nurse told Dilys to get dressed again, made a few notes, and then said: 'Thank you, Mrs Fletcher. I'll just take these in to Dr Fitzgerald, and she'll be out to see you in ten minutes or so.'

'Dr Fitzgerald?'

'Yes, she's your consultant,' said the nurse, after which she left the room.

Dilys sat for what seemed like several hours, although when she looked at her watch she discovered that only fifteen minutes had elapsed between the time the nurse had left the room and the time Dr Fitzgerald entered.

'Dilys Fletcher – would you come this way please?'

Dilys looked up and saw a smiling, familiar face.

'Sophie!' she exclaimed. 'It's you!'

'Yes, I'm afraid you've drawn the short straw! Come in and have a seat, Dilys.'

Once they had settled, Sophie continued: 'Something I must ask you first, Dilys – are you comfortable with having me for your consultant?'

'Of course I am! Why wouldn't I be?'

'Because some women would be embarrassed if they were being treated by someone they knew, especially when it's to do with an area like this.'

'Not me! I feel a lot more comfortable knowing that it's you than I would be if I was dealing with a stranger!'

'That's okay then. But I'd still better assure you that anything that's said between us stays here – I mean I won't talk about your case to Dad and Valerie.'

'Oh Sophie, I know you wouldn't. But even if you did, it wouldn't matter. They were very good friends already, but since Jim died they've been the best friends ever.'

'I'm glad to hear it. Anyway, let's get on. I understand you're wondering why you had an ultrasound scan rather than a mammogram.'

'Yes, I am actually.'

'Most people do. But it depends on the case and what we already know about it. In your case it's perfectly clear that there is a lump in your right breast, and the ultrasound tells us immediately if it's solid, or if it's filled with fluid, which the mammogram wouldn't.'

'What difference does it make?'

'If it's full of fluid it's more often than not a benign cyst, and we can drain it. And that could be the end of the problem. Not necessarily, but it could be.'

'And what about mine? Or do I have to wait for the results to come through?'

'No, you don't have to wait, I have them already. And the answer is no, your lump doesn't contain fluid. It's solid.'

Dilys's face fell. 'Oh! Does that mean I have cancer?'

'The fact that the lump is solid doesn't necessarily mean it's malignant, no. There are a number of other things we need to look at first.'

'Is that why the nurse was looking under my arms?'

'Well, yes. Your GP wasn't sure – in fact it can be very difficult to be sure simply by touch – but she thought she might have detected something under your arm too.'

'That's lymph nodes, isn't it?'

'Yes, that's right.'

'And was she right?'

'Yes, she was, I'm sorry to say. But that still doesn't necessarily mean it's cancer.'

'But the odds are getting shorter, aren't they?'

'If by that you mean that someone with a lump which has spread to the lymph nodes is more likely to have cancer than somebody with no lump at all, yes.'

'Where do we go from here then?'

'We can only really find out exactly what's happening if we do a biopsy. Now there are a number of different types of biopsy, and I think that what we need to do with you is an excision biopsy.'

'Excision?'

'It basically means the lump's got to come out.'

Sophie went on to explain that today she would have a chest x-ray, a blood test, and a fine-needle aspiration of the lymph nodes, which would enable them to determine whether they needed to be taken out when they removed the lump; in a week or two she would spend a night in hospital, the lump in her breast would be removed under general anaesthetic, and then it would be subjected to tests so that they could determine its nature.

'This is all starting to sound very serious,' said Dilys. 'I suppose there's no easier way, is there?'

'No, I'm sorry, Dilys, there isn't − if there were, I'd use it, believe me. And you're right, it is serious. But just remember, we don't know how serious it is yet.'

'But what do you think?'

'I don't know yet, Dilys. But you've got to prepare yourself for at least the possibility that we might not like what we find.'

'I don't much like what you've found already! But if it's got to be done, it's got to be done. Let's get on with it.'

Over at their house in Crowthorne, Ted and Valerie were sitting over a cup of tea, as they usually did about four o'clock in the afternoon when they were both at home, when Valerie said: 'I wonder how Dilys got on today. I think I'll give her a ring to find out.'

'That's a good idea,' replied Ted. 'I've been thinking about her a lot too. I should think she'll be back from the hospital by now.'

'Yes. That's what I thought. In which case she might very well want to talk, but feel nervous about making the first move – I remember what I was like!'

Without further ado Valerie got up and went over to the telephone. She heard the number ring out a dozen times or so, after which the answerphone cut in, whereupon she replaced the receiver, feeling that no useful purpose would be served on this occasion by leaving a message.

Ten minutes later she tried again, but with the same result. But her third attempt was more successful, and it was with some relief that she heard Dilys's voice at the other end of the line.

'Hello, Valerie,' said Dilys, once she realised who was calling. 'I just noticed you'd called, so I was going to ring you back in a minute or two – I've only just got in...'

'Well, shall I call you back in about ten minutes then?'

'No, no, it's okay – I expect you want to hear my news.'

'How did you get on?'

'Well... it began with a surprise – a nice surprise, I have to say...'

'That's good...'

'Because when the consultant came in,' Dilys went on, 'it turned out to be Sophie!'

'Well I never! That's incredible!'

'And lucky too, because it made everything so much easier. Even talking about difficult things turned out to be easy, because she was so nice. It was strange in a way meeting someone you already know pretty well, but acting in her professional capacity. She's terribly good at her job, you know – well, I suppose there's one aspect of her job that I haven't experienced yet, and that's the actual surgical bit, but if she's as good at that as she is at everything that goes before, I'm not too worried.'

'Oh,' said Valerie. 'Does that mean you're going to need surgery then?'

'Yes, I'm afraid it does. She doesn't know whether it's malignant or not yet, because she doesn't know the results of the biopsy, but the lump's got to come out whatever.'

Dilys went on to relate to Valerie all that had happened already, and all that was likely to happen – which, of course, Valerie needed to rehearse to Ted as soon as her conversation with Dilys ended.

Shortly after she had finished talking to Valerie, Dilys heard the door-bell ring. When she opened the door she found that it was Jemima, who had decided to drop in to see her mother and be briefed in person rather than by telephone, so Dilys made some tea and sat down with her daughter, to go once more through the details of all that had been done, and all that had been said.

When Dilys had finished telling Jemima about the fine-needle aspiration, which was the last thing that had happened at the hospital, Jemima said: 'How long will it be before you get the results of the biopsy?'

'I've got an appointment to see Sophie again in a week's time. She said things should be a bit clearer then.'

But just then the door-bell rang once more. When she opened the door this time, Dilys was amazed to find that it was Sophie. She showed her in, saying: 'I've never had this sort of service from a specialist before!'

Sophie smiled briefly, and said: 'It's not just because you're my friend as well as being my patient. I know it's an anxious time when you're waiting to know what's what, and if I have a patient who lives as close to the hospital as you do, and I have time to drop in and have a word personally, then I think it can be better than doing it by telephone.'

'Come in, Sophie,' said Dilys. 'That's really kind of you! I'm doing well for visitors today – Jemima is here too.' But her unexpressed thought was, 'The hospital's not all that close to Lexington Gardens, and it's certainly not on Sophie's route home to Hampstead! How many patients has she ever called on like this? I wouldn't mind betting that I'm the first – she must have bad news for me!'

Sophie greeted Jemima, and said, 'I'm glad you're here, Jemima. It would be a good idea if you stayed with your mum while I tell her what we've found out. If that's okay with you, Dilys?'

'Oh yes, of course it is,' replied Dilys. 'Do I take it that means it's bad news?'

'I'm afraid it's not good, Dilys. The cells we removed from your lymph nodes turned out to be cancerous, so when we remove the lump from your breast we're going to have to remove the lymph nodes as well.'

'I see,' Dilys replied. 'Does that mean it's very advanced?'

'Not necessarily. We shall need to do more tests to determine what sort of treatment you need, and, of course, to find out whether it has spread anywhere else – which, of course, we hope isn't the case.'

'But when you've removed the lump and the lymph nodes, if it hasn't spread anywhere else, isn't that the end of it?'

'It could be. In fact I hope it is, but we'd still have to treat you as if it were still there, just in case.'

'I see. What sort of tests do you need to do then?' asked Dilys.

Sophie briefly described the various tests and scans they might do, and then talked about hormone and biological treatment, radiotherapy and chemotherapy, doing her utmost to appear reassuring.

'I've brought some leaflets for you too,' she went on. 'They will explain everything to you, but if there's anything you don't understand, give me a ring. I don't believe in keeping patients in a state of ignorance, it's just not fair. Some people say they'd rather not know if the news isn't good, but when it comes down to it there are very few cowards about really, and I know you're not one of them. The worst aspect of coping with something like this comes from fear, and the best way of coping with fear is to keep the patient informed – that and having proper support, which is where you come in, Jemima, and, I guess, my Dad and Valerie too.'

'How long will it take to get it all sorted out?'

'It's difficult to say really, but even in the best-case scenario, it will take you quite a bit of time to get back to normal – it's not going to go away in a couple of weeks. Having said that, we sometimes find that even women who have a very advanced stage of cancer manage to lead fairly normal lives. You can never tell. Everybody's different.'

When Sophie had gone, Jemima went over to Dilys and hugged her. 'Are you all right, mum?'

'Yes, darling, don't worry, I'm okay. I'd rather the news were different, but that's how it is. And I have this strange feeling of having been here before, because having had this lump for so long before I did anything about it, I've gone over all sorts of possible scenarios in my head, including this one.'

'Are you sure you can cope? Would you like to come back and stay with me for a while?'

'Not until I've had the operation, I don't think. I suppose when I come out I'll need a bit of looking after, and it would be easier for you if I were at your place then. Would that be okay with you?'

'Yes, of course it would, mum.'

'But until I go in to have my op, I'm sure I can cope here. I've got a lot of things to sort out here first. And do you know what? For the first time since your father died I feel almost glad that he's not here – he would have found it so hard to cope with this, so I'm glad he doesn't have to. Try not to worry too much about me. I shall have my moments, but if I suddenly burst into tears it doesn't mean that I've given up hope and I can't cope any more.'

With that, mother and daughter fell into each other's arms and cried in unison.

Dilys was determined that she would carry on with her everyday life as normally as possible in the time that remained before her operation. As things turned out, this period was to be quite short, because just two days after her consultation with Sophie, Dilys learned that she would only have to wait one week more before undergoing surgery. This had the effect of concentrating her mind even more, and she enlisted the help of Ted and Valerie in the matter of sorting out the apartment, especially where Jim's possessions were concerned.

On the second day Ted and Valerie were there, Ted noticed a removals van outside next door, and then caught a glimpse of Arlette, who appeared to be directing operations, accompanied by a well-dressed man, clearly her junior by some years. Ted took care to keep out of sight, but he heard enough to become aware that they were speaking French and, moreover, were expressing themselves in a way that implied a high level of intimacy.

That evening, back home in Crowthorne, Ted received a phone-call from Sophie, who appeared to be in an unusually agitated state, which made him suspect that she had some bad news regarding Dilys, before he realised that if she had, it would not be him that she was ringing.

'Sophie! What's wrong? You sound really upset!'

'No, not upset,' Sophie reassured him. 'But exasperated, yes!'

'Exasperated? Why?'

'Why do you think? That mother of mine, of course!'

Ted sighed. 'Oh, I see. What has she been up to now?'

'She's moved in with a Frenchman who can't be any older than me, and she says they're going to get married.'

'Good God! That woman never ceases to amaze me! Where did she get him from?'

'Apparently he's the owner of a French *pâtisserie* in Gloucester Road.'

Tony Whelpton

Chapter Fourteen

The few days that remained before Dilys's operation was due to take place passed incredibly quickly. Ted and Valerie, seeing that Dilys needed their help every day, had thought of staying in Hampstead, not just for that week, but during the whole of the period that Dilys would spend in hospital. But the more Ted thought about it, the more he became aware of the problems that it would engender, because it would mean, for instance, that when Dilys had the operation, her surgeon would return home afterwards – to spend the evening with her patient's best friends. They decided forthwith that this would put too much pressure on all of them, but especially Sophie, and the matter was resolved when Dilys suggested that they should stay in her apartment at Lexington Gardens.

The operation, when it finally took place, appeared to have been successful from a strictly surgical point of view. As she had promised Dilys, Sophie did not discuss the matter with Ted and Valerie in any great detail, and they were sensible enough not to ask, but Dilys herself was perfectly satisfied that Sophie was keeping her totally informed of what was going on. Also, Sophie continued to stress that what happened now depended more on the tests they were about to do than on the surgery she had just performed, and Dilys would see her seven days after the operation, in order to review the results of those tests. In the meantime, when Dilys came out of hospital, she went to stay with Jemima in Wimbledon.

The week following her operation seemed interminable to Dilys, principally because she realised how much depended on the results of her tests. At last the waiting ended, and she found herself once more in Sophie's consulting-room.

'Hello, Dilys,' said Sophie. 'How are you feeling?'

'I've felt better,' replied Dilys, 'but I suppose it could be worse.'

'How have you been sleeping?'

'Not too badly really, but I still feel incredibly tired, even though some nights I sleep for twelve hours solid.'

'And what about eating?'

'To be honest, I haven't really felt too much like eating. In fact for much of the time I've been feeling quite sick. I suppose that's because of the anaesthetic, isn't it?'

'Mm, it could be, but normally I would expect you to have got over that by now. Have you had any other aches and pains of any kind?'

'I've had a bit of tummy-ache, that's all...'

'Show me where...'

Dilys pointed to an area just below her rib cage. 'Round about there.'

'Do you have it now?'

'Not at the moment, no.'

'Stand up a moment, and then bend forwards a bit, as if you're taking a bow at the end of a concert.'

Dilys did as Sophie asked. 'Ouch!' she said. 'That's it.'

'Okay, we'll need to look into that. In the meantime let me tell you what we've found.'

'Is it good or bad?'

'It's not as good as I'd hoped, but that doesn't mean it's necessarily bad. Let me explain. One of the tests we do on the bits we removed is to look for what we call receptors. Receptors are just proteins that some cancer cells have and others don't, and they tell us whether your particular cancer is likely to respond to hormone therapy or biological therapy.'

'If you're talking about these different kinds of therapy, does that mean the cancer is still there?'

'I'm sorry to keep saying "not necessarily", but it's the only honest answer at this stage. Obviously what we know about your cancer is based on the tests we've done on the bits we removed, but we know from experience that we have to assume that there is still something there, just in case.'

'I see. Yes, that makes sense.'

'Anyway, we test first of all to see if we can find any oestrogen receptors, or any progesterone receptors.'

'And did you?'

'No, we didn't.'

'Is that good or bad?'

'It's disappointing, because it means that your cancer is less likely to respond to hormone treatment. Then we test for another protein, called HER2. If we find that, it means the cancer is more likely to respond to biological therapy, using a drug like Herceptin...'

'Oh yes, I've heard of that. It's new, isn't it?'

'Yes, we've only been using it for a couple of years. Anyway, that test was negative too.'

'Oh, no! Is that normal?'

'No, it's not, actually. In fact it's quite unusual for someone like you to have what we call triple negative cancer – only about fifteen per cent of cases, in fact, and it tends to be mostly women of African or Hispanic origin. But there are always exceptions...'

'And it looks as if I'm an exception!'

'It looks like it, yes.'

'Where does that leave us?'

'It leaves us with radiation treatment and chemotherapy. Actually I should put those the other way round, because we can't start radiation treatment until your wounds have properly healed, and that will probably take another three weeks or so. But chemotherapy we can start right away.'

'I suppose I should say hooray! But does that mean I'm going to lose my hair?'

'That's what everybody thinks the moment chemotherapy is mentioned, but in fact there are many women who don't – there are some women who have no side-effects at all. There is a possibility of hair-loss, of course, and it's not a particularly nice experience, but the alternative is worse.'

'Yes, I suppose it is.'

'But before we start on that, I want to investigate a little bit further. I think it would be a good idea for us to arrange a CT scan, so we can find out exactly what's going on.'

'Whatever you say. Can you do that today?'

'No, I'd have to book a session for you – probably tomorrow or the next day though...'

Sophie then began to outline to Dilys what her chemotherapy regime would involve, saying that the sooner her first session began, the better; if she were able to begin therapy before the end of that week, she would have finished her first course of treatment before Christmas. In the event, Dilys was able to have her first session on the very next day, and her CT scan the day after that.

At least the first course of chemotherapy was not as bad as Dilys had imagined, and she was at least spared the indignity of both sickness and hair loss, much to her relief. Within ten days of starting her treatment, however, a shadow was cast over Dilys's optimism when Sophie told her that the CT scan had revealed that the cancer had not only failed to be eliminated by the surgery she had undergone, but had spread to her liver – which is what Sophie had feared as soon as Dilys had mentioned the pain she was feeling below her rib-cage.

'What difference will that make to my treatment?' Dilys had asked.

'None whatever at the moment,' Sophie had answered. 'Breast cancer is still breast cancer even if it has spread to other parts of the body, and we still treat it in the same way.'

But at the same time as assuring Dilys that the treatment she was already getting was still the most effective and most appropriate available, even in the light of the new evidence they had gained from the CT scan, Sophie was careful to make it clear that the presence of secondary cancer in the liver meant that the primary cancer had spread via the bloodstream, and therefore other organs were also now at risk of being affected.

Thus, while Dilys was able to participate in that year's Christmas festivities at Jemima's house, surrounded by all her family and by Ted and Valerie too, the celebrations were much more muted than they would otherwise have been, for all present were aware, and none more than Dilys herself, that this could be the last Christmas they were able to enjoy together.

Half-way through January, Dilys began her second course of chemotherapy, but this time she not only began to suffer from some of the most common side-effects of such treatment, but she was also beginning to show signs of the cancer spreading elsewhere, notably, thought Sophie, to her lungs, although she was not in possession of sufficient evidence as yet for her to feel it was the right time to tell her patient.

It was clear to Ted and Valerie, however, that Dilys was not showing any sign of improvement, although they were uncertain as to whether this was the side-effect of her chemotherapy rather than the direct effect of an ever-spreading cancer. Moreover their feeling was shared by Dilys herself, as evidenced by a conversation she initiated with Ted during her third course of chemotherapy, about half-way through February.

'I've been thinking about Jim,' she began. 'Not that I don't think about him an awful lot, but I've been thinking that he died without warning – as far as I know he had no idea that he was going to die, so he didn't have time to prepare himself for it.'

'Except in the sense that he spent all his life preparing for it,' replied Ted.

'Well, yes, I see what you mean. I just hope that all that guilt he used to feel wasn't really necessary...'

'I'm sure it wasn't,' said Ted. 'I mean, what *real* faults did Jim have? What *real* sins did he commit? He wasn't exactly the most wicked of men, was he?'

'No, of course he wasn't. That's exactly what I mean. Surely if God consigns anyone to eternal damnation it can only be for doing something truly dreadful, can't it?'

'That's what I would have thought.'

'And I mean, if Jim went to hell for ever, what chance would I stand?'

'I don't understand what you're saying...'

'Well, Jim used to go to church every week, and I never go at all.'

'What's that got to do with anything? There are plenty of wicked people throughout history who put on a very effective outward show of morality, or even of holiness.'

'Like your Father Kerrigan...'

'I wasn't thinking about him, but I suppose so, yes...'

'Do you actually believe in God, Ted?'

'Yes, I do.'

'Why? It can't be proved that God exists, can it?'

'Maybe not, but that doesn't mean he doesn't. Actually, that's something that used to bother me a lot, but eventually I came to realise that accepting that this world exists without the agency of a creator requires an even greater leap of faith than you need if you believe in God.'

'But you don't know for certain...'

'No, maybe not, but does it matter? It doesn't do any harm to believe in God.'

'Some people think it does – think of all the wars that have been caused by people arguing over religion.'

'But they're not caused by a belief in God. They're caused by self-interest, or by twisted thinking – or just by sheer wickedness.'

During the next two or three weeks Dilys and Ted had a number of similar conversations, and after each one Ted was torn between a sense of relief that Dilys still had an active mind, however weak she was becoming, and an awareness that the exercise of that lively mind was in essence a preparation for death. He tried hard to stop himself thinking that she was getting weaker and weaker, but eventually even he had to admit a reality that was already apparent to everyone else, and eventually, Dilys said to him one day, 'Ted, I'm not going to get better, you know.'

'Of course you are,' he countered, but without a great deal of conviction.

'No, Ted, the treatment's not working, I'm getting more and more pain, and I know I'm not going to last much longer. Sophie virtually said as much too. But don't worry, I'm in good hands, and I know they won't let me suffer too much.'

Only a few days later it was decided that Dilys needed to be moved to a hospice in order for her to receive proper palliative care, because Jemima could not cope any longer with her mother's requirements, even with the invaluable help of a Macmillan nurse. But two days before this move was due to take place, Dilys was suddenly taken really ill, and it was clear that she had had a slight heart attack. As a result, she found herself back in hospital, rather than in the hospice where she had expected to be.

Ted and Valerie visited Dilys every day, sometimes together, sometimes individually, and, at Jemima's suggestion, they had once more moved temporarily into Dilys's apartment, so as to make it easier for them to make regular hospital visits. So it was that one day in the middle of March, Ted found himself visiting Dilys alone in the afternoon, Valerie having been there in the morning, the plan being that Valerie and Ted would keep an eye on Jemima's children when she went to see her mother in the evening.

When Ted arrived, Dilys was asleep. He sat down by her bed and looked at her, saying nothing. After a few minutes she opened her eyes, saw him there, smiled, and whispered, 'Ted... Ted... Hello, Ted...'

'Hello, Dilly,' said Ted. 'Yes, I'm here.'

Dilys closed her eyes once more, and Ted just sat silently by, never taking his eyes off her for an instant. Then, as Ted sat looking down at her, Dilys suddenly opened her eyes, and murmured: 'Ted, do you remember those lines from *A Winter's Tale* that you whispered in my ear when we were dancing cheek to cheek at that Sixth-Form dance? The one about daffodils...'

Ted took Dilys's hand in his, looked into her eyes, and said: 'Daffy-down-dilly, who comes before the swallow dares, and takes the winds of March with beauty...'

Dilys smiled at him, and said: 'That's me – I've always done things too soon, just like the daffodils. I gave myself to you that night before I was ready to love you as fully and as deeply as you deserved...'

'... and before I was ready too, Dilly,' Ted interjected.

'And then all my children were born prematurely, especially the first one,' she continued, only acknowledging Ted's intervention with the merest flicker of an eyebrow. 'I became a mother too early, I became a widow too early, and now I'm going to leave you and Valerie before we've had the chance to make the most of what's already been a wonderful friendship. I know it's March, but I don't know what the wind has to do with it though...'

'But I know where the beauty lies, Dilly,' said Ted gently, bending over and kissing her on the forehead.

'There's something I must tell you before it's too late, Ted. About why I stayed in Scotland and didn't go back to school.'

'You told me, Dilly – it was because your father insisted.'

'No, Ted, there's more. He did insist, and so did my mother. It was because I was pregnant.'

'Oh, Dilly, I wish I'd known. It was something I worried about endlessly, and had so many sleepless nights over. So they insisted on your having an abortion...'

'No, Ted, they didn't. It was even more cruel than that. They let me have the baby and then made me give her away for adoption. I hardly even saw her, Ted, before she was taken away.'

Ted felt his eyes moistening. 'She? It was a little girl then?'

'Yes, it was. So somewhere we have a daughter, Ted. And I have no idea where she is, or what became of her. I don't even know her name. Except …'

'Yes?'

'Except that I gave her a name myself, and never told anyone about it.'

'Oh, Dilly, I wish I'd known! What was her name?' asked Ted through the tears.

'Perdita. I called her Perdita …'

She said no more, but just lay still looking at Ted, the only sounds to be heard being the beep of her heart-monitor and the occasional sign of life from her water-bed.

Then, suddenly, the regular beep gave way to a continuous whistle, nurses came running in, and the ward was immediately a-buzz with activity. But Ted remained oblivious to the commotion. He stayed there staring at his old love, whispering a name over and over again, a name whose relevance was totally lost on all those present: 'Perdita! Perdita!'

Even after a nurse drew the curtains around Dilys's bed Ted still sat there, paralysed with grief. When, ten minutes later, the ward-sister came to tell him they needed him to move to a nearby day-room, he appeared not to hear her at all until she had uttered the message three times, and even then he had to be led there physically by two nurses, being quite incapable of finding the way, or even moving without assistance.

When Ted eventually regained some sort of awareness of his surroundings and of what was happening, he found himself with Valerie, sitting in the drawing-room of Dilys's apartment, although he had no idea whatever as to how he had got there. What had actually happened was that Sophie had seen him in the day-room when she was on the way to see Dilys herself, and, realising the state he was in, asked a porter to arrange a taxi for him, and then phoned Valerie to let her know that Ted was on his way back, and would probably need some assistance getting from the taxi to the apartment.

Naturally Ted was not the only person to be deeply affected by Dilys's death – his son-in-law, Peter, remarked that he had never seen Sophie so distraught after losing one of her patients, whilst Jemima and Michael, faced as they were with having to arrange a funeral for each of their parents in the space of only a few months, also found it hard to cope.

Dilys's funeral, when it did take place, was much less elaborate than Jim's. She had stipulated in her will that she wanted to be cremated, with as little ceremony as possible, and that her funeral should definitely not take place in a Catholic church.

When all was over, and Ted and Valerie were once more back in their own house in

Crowthorne, where they seemed to have spent virtually no time at all since first hearing of Dilys's diagnosis, they sat quietly together for a long time, as if trying to take it all in. Eventually it was Valerie who broke the silence: 'Ted, when Dilys died, one of the nurses told Sophie that you kept saying "Perdita! Perdita!", over and over again. Do you remember why?'

'Oh yes,' Ted replied, 'of course I do.' And he immediately started crying. But after a few minutes he brushed aside the tears, and continued: 'I'm sorry, darling, I'll tell you. "Perdita" means "lost girl", and she's the heroine of *A Winter's Tale...*'

'Oh yes, I know that,' said Valerie, 'but why did you keep on saying it?'

'It goes back a long way. You know I used to call her Dilly – which, as far as I'm aware, no one else ever did...'

'Yes, that often struck me...'

'That goes back a long way too. It goes back to when Dilly and I were still at school, and we were both doing *A Winter's Tale* for A Level. We were dancing together at a Sixth-Form dance, and I whispered in her ear "Daffy-down-dilly, who comes before the swallow dares, and takes the winds of March with beauty..." Then she kissed me, and we left the dance, and we made love on the way home...'

Valerie was on the point of making a comment, but Ted stopped her. 'No, darling,' he said, 'there's more to tell. After I said goodnight to her I never set eyes on her again until last June. But ...'

Ted went on to tell Valerie the whole story: the dismissive letter he received from Dilys, the letters he wrote but which she never received, the pregnancy, the adoption, the secret name Dilys had bestowed on the daughter she was never to see again, everything ...

'Oh Ted,' said Valerie when Ted had finished, her eyes welling with tears, 'I didn't realise you had been as close as that. Poor Dilys ... No wonder she was as sympathetic as she was when I told her about the baby I lost. And poor you ... It explains everything...'

'What do you mean?' asked Ted, puzzled.

'I'm not stupid, Ted. I've been aware for months, even before Dilys was ill, that you were in love with her...'

'And you didn't mind?'

'Not once I got to know her, because I came to love her too. But I realised that it was something that wasn't going to threaten our marriage, or threaten me. The only thing I couldn't work out was how it all started. Now I know that it started over fifty years ago, and I know everything that she kept to herself all those years, and all that you went through too, it all falls into place.'

'I'm sorry, darling.'

'No, don't be! If you did anything wrong – and I don't think either of you did for a minute – you've both been punished for it a million times over already. If anything, it makes me love you even more. You know, Ted, you have many endearing qualities, but one of the most endearing is that you fall in love very easily, and then find it impossible to fall out of love...'

'How does Arlette fit into that thesis?' Ted interrupted.

'You find it impossible to fall out of love unless somebody treats you so appallingly that there's no alternative. It's the same with friends – once you become somebody's friend, you're their friend for ever. I think it's a wonderful quality, and I love you for it.'

'Valerie,' said Ted. 'You are the most amazing woman! You have all these qualities yourself, but you always seem to put other people first. You don't always say a lot, but there's a lot going on in that mind of yours. And I've just come up with a new golden rule for a happy life...'

'Oh yes? And what's that?'

'Never under-estimate a silent woman.'

'I love you, Ted.'

'I love you, Valerie.'

THE END

About the author

Tony Whelpton, like his character Ted Bryant, is a keen choral singer and a former lecturer in French, who was born in Nottingham in 1933; there the resemblance ends.

Before The Swallow Dares is his first novel, but by no means his first book, for he is the author of thirty or so school and college text books, as well as two books on cricket and a history of the Cheltenham Bach Choir. He is also an experienced journalist and broadcaster: he produced and presented the first ever schools programme on UK local radio, a French programme for junior schools called *Écoutez, les enfants!* He has sung at the Proms, come second in the European Final of the World French Spelling Championships, and he appeared on *Mastermind* in 2009.

His views on the English school examinations system are well known, as, drawing on more than twenty-five years' experience as Chief Examiner in French at O and A Levels and also at GCSE, they have often been expressed in columns in the *Yorkshire Post* and the *Times Educational Supplement,* as well as in the correspondence columns of the *Times.*

A second novel, *The Heat of the Kitchen,* which is well on its way, is a racy account of political wheeler-dealing in a small town in the south of France, and detailed plans already exist for the novel which will follow that one.

Tony's attitude to life is that it is there for living and, in particular, getting old is not an excuse for sitting around doing nothing; one of his favourite quotations comes from the French cellist Paul Tortelier: 'Everyone should die young — but as late in life as possible.'

If you would like to know more, check out Tony's website at www.tony-whelpton.co.uk and follow him on Twitter (@SwallowDares).

3446996R00193

Printed in Great Britain
by Amazon.co.uk, Ltd.,
Marston Gate.